CYPHER
BLACK OPS
SECURITY

C ⊕ D E   N A M E :

PHOENIX

LUNA KAYNE

Cover design: The Pretty Little Design Co.

Editor: Caroline Knecht

Photographer: Wander Aguiar

Cover model: Vinicious

ISBN 978-1-989366-44-8 (Paperback)

ISBN 978-1-989366-43-1 (Ebook)

For my dad.

CONTENT WARNING

Code Name: Phoenix contains a recollection of sexual assault of the female main character. It does NOT involve the main love interest and is NOT romanticized. It is written as a past trauma in support of the storyline.

The details of the trauma are contained to the first section of chapter 22 up until the section break. So you can still read, skip that section and just understand that she was caught, tortured and sexually assaulted.

It is not the author's intention to push personal boundaries. If such content is harmful for you, please skip the chapter, or do not read.

Author's note: This was a difficult chapter to write. Heed this warning if you are unsure.

PROLOGUE: JACK
TEN YEARS AGO

"Wake up, Jack. We're moving out. Your assignment is done." My commanding officer barks his orders, jolting me awake.

I sit up and rub the sleep out of my eyes as the dawn barely lights the cold room around me.

On any other day, I would rise and gather my things, but today is different.

"What do you mean, *done*? Last night we were waiting on the search warrants. We had the whole family. It's going down"—I glance at my wristwatch to confirm the early time —"today."

I swing my legs over the side of the bed, and my feet touch the frigid floor as dread sets in at the expression on my leader's face.

The events of the last few days replay in my head. His words don't make sense. I've been on the ground with my unit for months, working special ops undercover with federal law enforcement.

Our orders were simple: collect whatever evidence we could find and round up witnesses who were willing to come

2 CODE NAME: PHOENIX

forward against one of the largest criminal organizations on the West Coast.

Okay, maybe it wasn't that easy.

Matteo Sparr and his organization have been hard to pin down. To innocent eyes, Mr. Sparr and his family are upstanding citizens, hosting charity events for the community and investing in local business. Only those unlucky enough to cross Matteo ever get the chance to see what is under his mask —and once you catch a glimpse, it's already too late for you.

We have a weak case against him for drug trafficking. Then there's the prostitution and some more minor offenses, which is where our current operation comes in.

Word on the street is that these charges are only the tip of their illegal iceberg, that it goes deeper into weapons dealings and more, but after a certain point, everything is locked down. There are no snitches higher up the ladder who are willing to talk about what they are really up to, so all we have to go on are misdemeanors. No one has ever been able to nail him on the charges that matter, on the ones that carry serious jail time. Or worse.

We were called in to work with a group of government agencies. Just say the alphabet—they're all in there somewhere.

With Port Thomas being a smaller city near the Oregon Coast, law enforcement is underfunded. So they called in the feds, who called us. They were thankful for the additional manpower, as long as we didn't step on too many toes.

The red tape has been ridiculous.

First the sheriff phoned in a request for help, but trusting anyone else on the ground was a nightmare. Determining who was and wasn't in the Sparr pocket was the toughest task of all.

Things changed when an officer was found shot, execution style, in a ditch just outside of town. Everyone on the force knew who was behind it. It was an unnecessary hit, meant only to send a message and keep everyone else on the force in line, but it backfired. The officer was one of the good guys, just out doing his job. He was highly respected by his peers and only a year away from retirement, leaving a wife and son behind.

No one said a thing publicly. The conversations behind closed doors were an entirely different beast.

One by one, officers filed into the sheriff's office with what they knew, what they'd heard, and what they saw. It was only a lucky break that the sheriff wasn't in Matteo's pocket.

Once we knew the situation better, working our way into the key players became much easier.

Then everything finally snowballed three days ago.

First, one key witness, who works at Sparr Industries, got nervous and came forward with allegations of money laundering. Then a second witness added another piece to the puzzle, and a third came in with solid proof, including files and damning video they'd managed to scrape together without getting caught.

It turns out the decision not to bring the mayor or his office in on the operation was the right choice. The mayor was in deep with the Sparr family, so a meticulously coordinated and highly secret request for all arrest and seizure warrants was processed through different channels.

We had our mission in place for today. Our ducks were

in their pretty little row, but this wasn't how it was supposed to go.

"It blew up. Shit went down a few hours ago. Apparently, they knew we were coming. They had someone on the inside after all. The Sparr family is gone. All of the evidence against them is now speculative. Four witnesses are dead. Another two are in the wind." Then, as he opens his mouth, hesitation fills his eyes, and his body physically braces for a fight.

"Jack." My commander starts then stops, carefully considering his words with a frustrating pause. "It's Jessa. Both her and her brother's bodies are missing."

"What do you mean *missing*?" Then the weight of his words hits me. "Hold up. What do you mean *bodies*?" Bolting off the bed onto shaky legs, my head spins as my world crumbles piece by piece.

He chose his words carefully.

She isn't missing.

Her body is missing.

"Her family was in a car accident late last night. At the bridge just outside of town. It looks like they went over the steep drop into the ravine. Her parents' bodies were recovered downstream, along with the car. We can't confirm yet that it's related, but three other people from the company are dead as well. It was a quick job." He glances around as panic floods my veins.

"Maybe Jessa and Travis weren't in the car. Did you check their house?" I counter in a desperate attempt to think of something they haven't yet, but I already know I'm behind.

Memories flash before my eyes.

I saw Jessa and Travis yesterday. We were talking about

how fast our high school graduation is coming up in a few months.

For siblings, they are almost inseparable. Twins who look nothing alike but finish each other's sentences at every turn.

When I started this undercover op, six months ago, I never expected to meet someone like Jessa. I was just a kid myself at twenty-three. I was five years older than her and her brother, but I blended into their senior class.

No one knew my secret.

I was sent in to get close to Maxwell, Matteo's son. Because of his family's connections, Maxwell was one of the most popular kids in their high school. He learned how to keep up appearances from his old man, but word had it he was just as deep into all of the family's illegal activities.

The one thing we had in common was Jessa. Maxwell always changed when she was around. He put on a good show for everyone else, but I could tell by the way he stared at her that she could probably write her ticket for life with him if she wanted to.

Everyone around her noticed it too, except her. She always spoke kindly with him, as she did with everyone, but that was where it ended for her.

She only wanted to be his friend.

She was too good for him anyway.

She was too good for the both of us.

I first met Jessa when I was paired with her on a science project. Her laugh was infectious, and I lost myself in her smile. I understood Maxwell's attraction to her instantly.

She and her brother were the most well-rounded kids in that school. They stayed away from the more dramatic groups and kept even farther away from the most undesirable ones. They both had only a couple of friends in their core groups, but they never excluded anyone who wanted to hang out.

Everything about Jessa just fit for me.

And now she and her brother are missing.

"We've been to the house and the hospital. We retrieved the car an hour ago. Preliminary reports say the back passenger window was broken from the inside out. We found her school bag in the back seat. And before you ask, we already have over half the team searching. We've been working with the local guys, and they have all of their information. We're checking the riverbanks as well as the water. Anyone making it out will be found, unless..." His face drops when his brain catches up to his mouth, and he realizes he said too much, but I pick up where he left off.

"Unless they got pulled under and sucked down the rapids." My empty stomach clenches tight.

His eyes stay locked on me as I pause to gather my thoughts. Then, without pretense, I involuntarily spin to get dressed and go after Jessa.

That's when I notice them.

Two men stand still, waiting behind my commanding officer. I can't make out their faces. I'm sure they've been given orders to stand down unless necessary, and the four walls in my room suddenly feel as though they are closing in.

"Look, Jack. We know you and Jessa became close, but you need to let the team handle it. Finding her and Travis is our priority while we're here. Our mission still stands; your orders are to pack up and let them do their job. You'll head out to Fort Stevens in an hour." His attempt at pacifying me speaks to a part of me I don't want to show.

The way he trivializes my feelings for Jessa ignites my fight-or-flight reflexes.

We didn't become close.

She was it.

She became everything.

Days working side by side at school and nights spent talking and growing closer. Everything she said about her past and her future spoke to me. Then the one special night we spent together shifted our relationship, and everything changed.

I know I was out of line. I know I had a job to do here, but I wasn't about to let her go when everything was done.

She was mine, and after the arrests were made, I was coming for her. I was going to come clean about everything. I was going to tell her I was undercover and five years older than she thought. I was going to ask her to forgive my secrets, and I was going to tell her I loved her and start earning every beautiful piece of her back.

Now she's gone.

She's out there somewhere, scared and cold.

Or she's... The thought hits me like a freight train. Without warning, I lunge toward the door, pushing and forcing my way through the guys in front of me, but I don't make it.

Anticipating the move even I didn't know I would make, one of the men standing behind my commander steps into my path and takes me down without effort. In my haze, all my thoughts are of Jessa. Not combat. Not tactical maneuvers. And he takes advantage.

In the next breath, I'm on the floor with both of the new guys on top of me, pinning me in place, and I pivot from flight to fight. But I've already been immobilized.

His tactical experience level is evident by the way I hit

the ground fast without feeling much pain. Or maybe I'm numb from the emotions building inside of me.

"Jack." The sorrow in my commander's voice is unmistakable. It isn't his sadness he's projecting. He's reflecting my own misery, and I shift my gaze to the floor to see the growing pool of tears gathering underneath me. My chances of finding Jessa are slipping away. "We need to get you out of here. You're being sent back to base for eval. You can get up on your own, or you can wake up there." He lets his threat linger as the men shift to take full control of my person. "And, Jack, I am sorry."

He isn't talking about his regret at needing to restrain me.

He's talking about Jessa.

At least a couple of hours have passed since the car went over the edge. The late spring weather has been uncharacteristically cold, and it's made the water deadly.

She either made it out by breaking the window and swimming to shore—but no, she would have been found, cold and close to hypothermia—or she made it out and got pulled under.

Those are the only two scenarios in my head, and as I bounce between them, my commander's voice echoes into my thoughts.

Her backpack was in the car, and the window was broken from the inside.

Their bodies are missing.

There's my line.

I'm not going to be walking out of here today.

My body shakes, and I can't control it. As much as I try to stop the pain from manifesting, I can't. It's too powerful.

I release a guttural cry. A surge of anxious energy flows

through me, filling me with a toxin I can't purge. I need to release this pressure. It's too much to take.

As I struggle to suck in the air I just cried out, one of the guys orders the other to hold me still. It's followed by a pinch in my arm, and my will to fight dulls.

My body relaxes then numbs as my world goes black.

CHAPTER 1
JACK
PRESENT DAY

"Phoenix. What's your ETA? Our pieces are in place, and we're ready to roll the dice. Waiting for your go." Grizz's voice echoes in my earpiece as we turn down the dirt road toward our destination.

His team was the first on site, and they've surrounded our target, effectively caging them in in preparation for our arrival.

"We're approaching target. Five minutes out, speed reduced. Hold tight. Approach on my mark." I direct the rest of our team through my headset then lean forward to speak to Grey in the driver's seat. "Slow it down. Keep the dust low."

"Got it, boss," Grey answers over his shoulder, dropping his speed and keeping his eyes on the road ahead. He's the newest member of our team, barely out of college and still learning the ropes.

I look around the SUV on a status check. The rest of our guys are working on their own parts, checking their weapons and comms and monitoring other channels for any signs of communication coming from the building.

"I don't feel good about this, Phoenix." Logan uses my code name as he aims his disapproving glare in my direction. "I know how badly you want to nail Maxwell to the wall for what happened. We all have our reasons for wanting to put that family down, but I don't think we have enough intel."

I take a moment to let his words sink in.

He's not wrong.

If it were any other mission, I would have held back. We would have waited until we properly confirmed our sources and prepared our teams, but this is different. I've been searching for Maxwell and his operation for almost ten years.

Ten years with leads that go nowhere—or come two weeks too late.

Maxwell's father, Matteo, is the reason Jessa and her family are dead. When she was alive, Matteo Sparr had his hands in everything around town, and most of it was illegal. The only part aboveboard was his cover company, Sparr Industries, where Jessa's father worked. That was until Matteo began using the company to launder money from his illegal activities.

The night before we were preparing to take everyone in, something went wrong. Out of nowhere, the Sparr family packed up. Loose ends at the company were tied up, and they were gone by morning, with nothing but a trail of bodies in their wake. All signs show they had advance notice, but all of the men in our unit were cleared, and post-op review couldn't find any leaks.

The family disappeared into thin air.

Our resources say Matteo retired. He still keeps one hand in his family's dealings, but he's chosen to live out his life with his wife somewhere secluded, somewhere where extradition almost definitely isn't honored.

Matteo and Victoria Sparr also had a daughter, four

Matteo and Victoria Sparr also had a daughter, four years older than her brother Maxwell. She vanished from the family picture about five years before my mission. There was no police report, and Jessa once told me word around town was she went to live abroad with relatives and has never been back. I don't blame her.

So, this leaves Maxwell. That apple didn't fall far from Matteo's poisonous tree. Maxwell is his father's son. To everyone at school, he was the cool rich kid. The mask he wore fooled everyone except those of us who knew the brutal truth.

Matteo groomed his son to walk in his footsteps, and Maxwell did so with enthusiasm, becoming an entirely different person. By the time I came into the op, Maxwell was already overseeing his father's execution orders at seventeen years old.

We had just gotten enough intel to end both father and son and seize all of their assets when they vanished.

They liquidated as much as they could within two days of the family's disappearance. The courts finally froze a lot of their assets, but not before they made off with millions. Strip clubs changed hands fast. Drug operations changed groups or shut down, and Maxwell became almost as elusive as the guy we are looking for today.

Maxwell is deep into digital espionage, fraud, and treason, and his digital team are practically ghosts. After all our digging, we only know the handles of the people at the top of his hacking team. As much as it pains me to admit this out loud, they are geniuses. They've hacked into corporate and government systems with an ease we've never seen before.

And they are always ahead of the curve. Most hackers

have the basic languages down, but usually they use one favorite language to hack. This group seems to jump easily between every computer language out there like they wrote them all, sometimes using processes they make up as they go along. They don't follow hacking rules—they create them, and over the last seven years, most of our clients' system updates have been necessary because of loopholes they've exploited.

Our government has spent massive amounts of money just trying to keep up with their skills, and right now I have two objectives. First, we need to contain his digital team. Their talents are unmatched, and taking them out of play would solve a lot of problems.

My second goal is personal. We need to dismantle Maxwell's empire and eliminate him. His family took away the only person I've ever gotten close to.

I know it won't bring her back. But revenge is all I have left, and I cling to the thought that, in the moment I destroy Maxwell, I will be close to her again.

Even if it's fleeting.

I'll take it.

I would give a lifetime to have one more minute with her. To have her back in my arms. To tell her what I should have told her ten years ago.

While I agree that driving out to this farmhouse in Kentucky on an anonymous tip isn't the smartest thing we've done, we can't afford to let this opportunity slip by.

"It's the best intel we've gotten on this group in nine years. You know we won't get better, and our lookout says there is movement on the premises." I raise my eyebrows at Logan, daring him to challenge me, but he doesn't.

He knows I'm right. Even if this doesn't pan out, we can't let it go.

Logan has been there with me through every failed attempt and close call.

Maxwell and his team are thorns in our sides. They are the longest outstanding contract we've had, and no one has been able to take them down.

I drop my gaze back to the folder on my lap. Thin piece of shit that it is, it holds all of the information we have on this group, which is barely enough to wipe my ass with. Two pathetic sheets of paper. No photos. We don't even have a picture of the guys we're looking for. Just two names: Jay and Zane.

Zane is our main target. He's the one who coordinates the whole team. He's the brains behind everything, but I'll take his second in command and any others I can get my hands on too.

We contract out our services to various companies and work closely with our government, but today's operation isn't on anyone's radar. This is something our company is doing off the record and without documentation. There have been too many failed attempts in the past to waste manpower, but this is a lead our team can't let slide, so we're doing it on our own dime.

"Two minutes out." Grey's update cuts into our silent car, and everyone tenses.

It's almost go-time.

I close the file and drop it to the floor. There's nothing in there that will help me anyway.

I look out through the windshield, and my stomach knots as we approach our target. Our camouflaged vehicle should be visible within the next minute.

"Grizz, Tex, Waldo, I want you around the back and sides of the building. Secure all possible exits. Team one, stay in the tree line out front. Secure the vehicles on site— nothing gets out. Eagle, stay in the woods; stop anything that makes a run for it on my mark. No casualties." Shifting my attention inside the car, I address my team in the front seat but keep my headset active so everyone is on the same page. "Hunter, hang back. We're going in the front door. You're on our six. We need whoever's in that house alive. We aren't a threat until we need to be. If this is only their tech team, there may be no resistance." I pause to listen as everyone confirms my orders, then I return Logan. He nods his approval as he works to adjust his earpiece.

I've known Logan for almost ten years. I met him the morning I lost Jessa. We started out rocky, with him tranquilizing me to get me back to base. Our first days were tense as I went through eval. I was a broken man for a while after the op, and my evaluation turned into mandatory psych sessions.

Being paired with Logan on my first assignment after my all clear was hard to take. But after we talked and got to know each other better, we found common ground. I realized I had been projecting my anger onto him when he was just following orders. He did the right thing.

After that mess, it seemed we were always matched together on projects. As we worked together, Logan helped me to understand my pain, and he helped me focus myself better than those shrinks ever did. It turns out we had a lot more in common than I thought.

Logan knows almost everything about me. The only thing he doesn't know is how wonderful Jessa really was. My descriptions never seemed to do her justice. I think he would have liked her.

A couple of years after we met, we retired from active duty to start our own security and ops company: Cypher Black Ops Security. The goal was simple: we contracted out work, chose the jobs and companies we wanted to work with, and set our own terms. Our company has grown from one small building into many locations around the country, including a few operational bases for tactical training and special assignments.

We provide security and other services to a large number of Fortune 500 companies as well as our own government for far better pay. Putting Maxwell and his team out of business would end a number of our outstanding contracts, and the bonuses alone would set us all up for life, financially.

Professionally, we would be able to secure more business with the news that it was our company who finally put an end to Maxwell Sparr's syndicate.

"Jekyll, you're with me on this. Front door. We go in cool." Logan nods his head once more at his code name.

As the SUV rounds the last corner, leaving the cover of the trees behind, the farmhouse comes into view.

A large two-story house sits in the center of a cleared lot, surrounded by tree line on all four sides. As I look across the yard, I realize our three team members would have had a tough time crossing the large, wide-open space unnoticed.

Intel tells us this property has been owned by an untraceable shell corporation for a long time, so chances are it was set up as a safe house and left vacant until needed. Which is hopefully now.

It's late morning, and the sun is shining brightly against a clear blue sky, not a cloud in sight. I would have preferred to approach under the cover of darkness, but there's a good chance they won't be here much longer. Judging by the supplies loaded into the vehicle our team found out front, I'm pretty sure I'm right. They were preparing to run.

My heart skips a beat over the fact that we are most likely, and finally, ahead of them this time.

Grey pulls the SUV into the driveway and blocks the last road leading off the property. He keeps the car running. Logan and I open our back-seat doors at the same time and step out as Hunter exits the passenger side.

Checking the safety on my gun one last time, I secure it in its strap and move toward the front of the vehicle, meeting Logan and taking in the situation on the property.

Our team is in place, and everything is still. Nothing is moving except for the leaves on the trees, rustling in the breeze.

Logan and I walk together toward the stairs, with Hunter trailing ten feet behind us.

As we step up to the house, a shuffle around the side catches my attention, and Link's voice breaks through my earpiece. "Man down. West side. No visual on the attacker."

Looking up to the drone hovering one hundred feet away, I exhale an exasperated sigh. "Eagle, you there? Who's on the west exit?" I ask our shooter, who's still positioned in the woods.

His response is instant. "Waldo."

I roll my eyes. Of course it's Waldo. "Grizz, Tex, spread out. Find Waldo and make sure he's okay, then cover the back and sides. And if he's down, you know the rules. Grab a photo. I need something for the staff newsletter this month."

"Copy that." There's a huff in Grizz's voice. As long as Waldo is okay, there's no reason we can't have a little fun while we're out here.

Looking at Logan and Hunter, I nod my head to continue, hesitantly, to the front door.

Someone definitely knows we're here.

Logan stands as close to the door as possible so whoever answers doesn't get a good look at our men out front. He rings the doorbell, and we wait in silence for half a minute before he rings it again.

Shaking his head in frustration, he takes a deep breath. I've known him long enough to know that he's about to yell loud enough for those inside to hear.

"We know you're in there. The place is surrounded, and you aren't leaving the property. Why don't you *ladies* open the front door, and we'll have a little chat. Tell you how this is going to go." He looks back to me and nods, a cocky smile stretched across his face. Logan loves taunting his targets.

The delayed response from inside makes me apprehensive about the situation, and I glance around the yard for any signs of manpower behind those front doors. There's only one vehicle parked on the lot, so my assumption is there are no more than four people here.

I take the break to step behind Logan, hiding myself from whoever answers the door. It's a tactical maneuver to give our opponent a false sense of security. Once I'm in place, I shift to examine the house in front of me.

If you weren't in our line of work, the front door wouldn't draw too much attention, but I can tell this house is locked down like Fort Knox. The front windows are reinforced, probably bulletproof. There is an intercom to the side of the door. It's an odd setup for a quaint farmhouse in the middle of nowhere.

Just as I am about to call in a head count, the lock clicks, and the front door swings open, revealing a woman in her late twenties.

Crouching further, I peek over Logan's shoulder, hiding my face behind the hair at the scruff of Logan's neck.

She looks way more confident than we do at this moment, which sets me off even more.

"Good morning, miss. This your place?" Logan drops his voice to a polite tone and waits for her answer.

She takes a half step back, showing me a little more of her. Her blonde hair is pulled back into a ponytail, and her frame is small next to the burliness of my team members.

A familiarity hits me, and I shift further behind Logan as I try to remember if I know her from somewhere, but nothing registers.

My adult life has been a long string of jobs, one after another, most of them undercover. With the number of people I've crossed paths with, remembering her is going to be next to impossible. I hope that, until we have our hands on everyone inside, she can't place me either.

"No, I'm just staying here for a few days. It belongs to a friend." Her answer is careful. Her eyes remain locked on Logan.

She's lying.

She's not looking around.

She's not one bit curious about who is here with him.

The people inside already know.

Logan exhales an annoyed breath. "What's your name, sweetie?" I'm offended for her at his necessary yet condescending tone.

She crosses her arms over her chest, her upper body going rigid in response. "Well, I can tell you it isn't Sweetie." Her expression twists in disdain when she says the last word.

I can't help but roll my eyes.

I know her attitude is amusing Logan as he leans in to taunt her further.

Punctuating each word and speaking as though English isn't her first language, he narrows his eyes on her. "Then why don't you tell me what it is so we don't have any more awkward first impressions—*Sweet Tits.*" He impatiently counters her sass and raises the stakes with his arrogant retort.

Her expression drops momentarily before she gathers her composure. "It's Dee," she seethes through gritted teeth, and I roll my eyes again.

We're already off to a great start.

"Okay, Dee. Is anyone else here?" He reaches out to try the handle on the glass door. Finding it locked, he pulls his hand back as her smile returns.

Now they're both just dancing their little dance, and they know it. Logan is trying to assess the situation, while she is obviously stalling for time.

"Nope. Just little ol' me." She tilts her head, feigning innocence.

I can tell by the way Logan stretches his neck muscles that he's nearing the end of his patience.

She must sense the tension, as she takes two steps back from the door. A moment of doubt shows when her smile slips. Clearly, she's confident that the front door will keep us out.

And there it is again.

There's something about her that triggers a memory. It's the memory of a girl, but it isn't the same one standing in front of us.

I do know her from somewhere, and as I'm diving into

my history to place her, a flash of someone else crosses my mind.

Jessa.

But why her?

What connection could this woman have to Jessa? There's no way she could still be alive.

Could she?

In my haze, I step out from behind Logan to get a better look at Dee. As her eyes shift to me, her expression slips away, along with the color in her face. She gasps, then covers her mouth with her fingers.

Shit, I definitely know her. Or, at the very least, she knows me.

"You're not an accountant." She directs her statement at me before she stiffens.

"Accountant?" Logan repeats incredulously, and we glance at each other in confusion for half a second before turning back to look at her.

"What—"

A female voice from behind Dee halts our conversation.

Our next target comes into view.

"There was one around the side of the house. I think I knocked him—" She chokes on the rest of her sentence when she rounds the corner .

Her eyes meet mine, and my world goes dark.

Standing before me, just out of my reach, is Jessa.

CHAPTER 2

JESSA

Shit.

My skin instantly prickles when my property alarm sounds on my phone.

Someone is within our perimeter.

How were we found so quickly?

This was supposed to be our vacation. I worked for months to set up a solid trail that would lead anyone on a wild goose chase far away from here so we could have a few weeks of downtime. Not the two days we are at now.

Judging by the distance of the dirt kicking up from behind the forest edge, I'd say we only have a couple of minutes to get out of here, and Dana is upstairs. Too far away for me to yell for her without being heard.

Our window for escape has closed.

From my spot in the front room, I can see the whole yard. There's movement in the trees just beyond our car.

If we could have gotten to that car, our backup supplies would have held us over for a few days while we disappeared again.

This has been our life for as long as I remember: jumping

around, covering our tracks, and working under everyone's radar.

Dana and I have had only each other for years.

Outside of Zane, all of our other relationships have been short and impersonal.

We jump around the country constantly. Our only home is wherever we lay our heads down that night.

Being transient has kept us both alive for this long.

I run the operations under Zane. Managing details is what I do.

I hire management companies who deal with other management companies on our behalf. Everything is online now, and that is also where all of the coin and corruption is. So that is where we are. We do the jobs we are hired to do and stay five steps ahead of everyone else.

I can't remember when we last took time off. I've been working job after job lately.

I just wanted to give Dana a break, time to hang out away from our constant work with Zane. A chance to watch movies and eat all the junk food I stocked the place with. A chance to live the lives we barely remember anymore.

I even bought us a little motorboat to take out on the lake behind the property.

The boat.

That's it.

Maybe we can make it to the boat. It's through the trees out back. Maybe they aren't aware of it. It's a chance we'll have to take.

"What's going on?" Dana's voice snaps me out of planning our escape as she appears from upstairs.

"Shh," I hush, and she instantly freezes. "No time to explain. Perimeter is breached. We only have minutes before they're here. I've alerted Zane." I move to the side window, then check the cameras on my phone. I count three men crossing the field toward the back and sides of the house. "Dammit. I'm going to try to take one out. That might open up an escape route."

"Who are they?" Dana asks as she moves away from the windows, panic appearing to set in.

A couple of camouflaged vehicles emerge through the tree cover and pull up the driveway.

"Don't know. But there's no reason for anyone to be here, and they brought backup. So it's not good. Answer the door, but don't unlock the outside one. See what they want. Maybe it's local law enforcement; then you can ask them to leave the property. That will buy us some time. If it isn't, you'll need to get out of here, and I'll take care of the computer. If you can get away, head straight out back and run through the trees. I have a boat down by the lake. Just get in and go. Keys are in a holder beside the wheel." I grab a metal elephant statue off the bookshelf and test its weight in my hands.

"But what about you?" Her eyes are wide now. She's never come this close to being captured before, and I know she's worried.

We've reviewed possible scenarios, and we've practiced our escape plans over and over, but having everything go down like this in real time, with real consequences for failure, is a different game.

I know Dana. Her fear sets in fast, but she'll hit a point where her brain shuts off her heart and she soldiers through.

"You know if I can make it, I'll be there before you. If I'm not, just go. One of us needs to remain free to get the other out. You know what to do when you get into cell range." She nods at my words, and I turn to jog across the living room toward the steps. "Just stay cool and stall them. I'll be right back."

Moving quietly past her, I run up the stairs carrying the extra weight of the statue and turn to move down the hall toward the window overlooking the side entrance.

The farmhouse has an entrance on every side. I was specific when I bought this place. It had to be far from neighboring eyes, and it had to have a lot of exit points—though, judging by the manpower outside, it might not have enough.

As I step quietly to the window, the average frame of a man approaches the side entrance.

Standing quietly behind the curtains, I tighten my hold on the statue as he glances up at the open window. As long as I don't move, I'm sure he can't see me through the sheer fabric.

He returns his attention to the door as he reaches out to test the handle.

Moving quickly between the curtains, I reach through the window, line the statue up, then let the elephant fall toward its intended victim. With a heavy thud, the man grunts and drops to the ground, motionless.

Closing the window, I turn to slowly creep back across the floor. The sound of the doorbell stops me dead in my tracks. My heart pounds in my chest.

I've been caught once before, and it didn't end well for me.

I can't let that happen again.

Memories of those fateful days still creep into my nightmares, and I pray this time it isn't the devil I know knocking at our door.

There is nothing worse than the devil I know.

The doorbell chimes a second time, snapping me back to my reality, and I creep down the hall toward the steps.

"We know you're in there. The place is surrounded, and you aren't leaving the property. Why don't you *ladies* open the front door, and we'll have a little chat. Tell you how this is going to go," a man calls from outside. It isn't the voice I feared hearing today, and I release tension I didn't realize I was holding.

But how do they know there are women in here?

Nearing the top of the stairs, I pause to listen to the conversation. Dana is trying her best to stay calm, but the man at the door is pushing her buttons.

I've known Dana forever. She has the biggest heart out of anyone I've ever met, but she is a force to be reckoned with. Her loyalty is fierce and often overrides her common sense, and I hope she doesn't sink herself into a world of problems trying to stand her ground.

I know the front door will hold until I'm ready to open it.

Before stepping down the stairs, I slip my phone from my pocket and check the cameras on the property once more. Sure enough, the two remaining men have spread out to cover the back corners of the house, leaving the back door unguarded. I just hope it's enough space for us to get past the back porch. Then I can let my trap take care of the men, and we'll be clear to run for the trees.

I open the apps I'm going to need. Then, palming my phone in my hand, I head down the stairs to join Dana.

It's time to assess our escape route and pull her back to help me destroy the computers in the basement.

Turning the corner, I address Dana, knowing they can hear us through the intercom. I go for a taunt to try to throw them off their high horses. They're more likely to make a mistake if they're flustered, and a direct hit to their ego should do the trick.

"There was one around the side of the house. I think I knocked him—" But the rest of my words drain from my thoughts as my gaze settles on Dana's.

Her eyes are wide, and she looks like she's seen a ghost.

I turn my attention to the door in search of what sparked her fear.

The air is sucked out of the room, and everything stops as my gaze lands squarely on him.

As if I've been cast into an alternate reality, memories pummel me from all sides. My heart lurches into my throat, and my stomach immediately knots around itself as my body shuts down on me.

Years slip away, and I'm back in high school with my friend.

The boy who was my first.

The boy who told me he would be my only.

The boy who disappeared without a trace.

"Jack?" The name I've refused to say out loud for years leaves my lips on a whisper.

"Jessa?" His voice is soft, confused, and everyone stands still as the depth of the shit Dana and I are in begins to hit home.

The man standing in front of Jack looks slowly between him and me as a carnal sneer creeps across his face.

"Jay." Dana, using my nickname, snaps my gaze back to hers, and she gawks at me with eyes as big as saucers.

Clearly, we are both out of our element.

"Well, well, well. If this isn't the definition of killing two birds with one stone, I don't know what is. Or should I say *catching* two birds?" The man in front of Jack has an unsettling sense of confidence. Leaning to the side, as if brushing Dana out of the way, he squares himself on me. His gaze turns predatory, and his sneer deepens with each word. "Why don't you open the door, and we can all sit down and have a little chat—Jay." The hair on my arms stands up at his intimate use of my nickname. "Or you could try to run, little blue jay. I like things that run." He ends with a suggestive wink, and I swallow hard as I try to keep my face frozen.

Jack remains still, watching me as my heart pounds into my rib cage.

I have no time to analyze what any of this means. I was never supposed to see him again. He is happily married, with two kids and a white picket fence, and he's an accountant.

But he's not an accountant. My stomach sinks at the lie I was told.

"Jay." Dana's panicked voice pulls me from my trance.

I slipped away for a moment too long, and my lapse is going to cost us. I just hope it doesn't cost us everything.

Quickly looking around the room, I revise our plan.

Steps thud along the porch on the side of the house, alerting me to our new urgency. The rest of their team are getting into position. The two men with Jack grow impatient and move toward the door. All the while, Jack is standing eerily still with his eyes on me, and Dana is yelling at me.

How am I not hearing a word she's saying?

Zeroing in on her lips, I force myself to block out everything else and listen to her as she yells, "THERE'S NO TIME. THEY'RE BLOWING THE DOOR. I'LL DESTROY THE COMPUTERS. YOU CAN'T BE HERE. GO!"

Dana grabs me and attempts to shake me into action.

But I don't feel it.

I don't feel anything.

Why won't my body work? She's right; I can't be here. Of all the people. I can't be near him. I've been warned about this.

Then she leans in and yells one word: "RUN!"

Without another thought, I turn, and I run.

"JESSA!" Everything else is turned off, and my focus is heightened on my escape, but he still breaks through my panic.

Jack.

His voice sounds pained as I clear the living room and bolt through the kitchen toward the back door. I can't afford to stop and analyze anything right now. We've already lost too much ground.

"Zane, open exit four." I yell my command into my phone. As I hit the door, it clicks open, and I'm out of the house and off the porch within seconds as a loud popping sound echoes from the front door.

I hope Dana made it downstairs in time.

Footsteps hammer along the porch around both sides of the house, and voices shout for me to stop, but I won't.

Dana only has enough time to make it into the basement. She won't get out, and I need to escape if I want any chance at negotiating her freedom.

Instead, part two of my plan is set into motion as I speak the next command into my phone. "Zane, drop the porch."

An instant later, wood splinters as the porch breaks away to ground level, taking the men with it.

I glance over my shoulder as I continue my pace to the tree line. I want to confirm neither of them made it off the porch.

Just as I turn back to focus on my escape, a figure catches my attention out of the corner of my eye.

It's him.

Jack rounds the side of the house at a full-on sprint, and for the first time, I'm not sure if I'm going to make it.

"Stand down. Do not shoot. DO. NOT. SHOOT. She's mine," Jack yells, and the determination in his voice sends fear coursing through me.

I steal a second look back. He's closing the distance between us.

His arms pump methodically, his focus remains trained on me. My only chance of escape is maintaining my lead.

"Please, don't," I plead.

Spending my energy on asking the man I haven't seen for ten years to just stop chasing me is futile. I need to focus. I don't want to think of the price I'll pay if he catches me.

I turn my attention back to the tree line in front of me and leave everything else behind.

The countryside slips away, and I fixate on the direct path from me to the trees. Air burns down my throat as I struggle to get enough oxygen into my lungs, and my legs hurt from the pace I'm trying to maintain.

"JESSA. STOP!" His tone is laced with pain, and it devastates me, because I can't offer him the comfort I desperately want to grant us both.

The only way I have a chance is to not look back. To not look at him. My heart breaks apart as I run from the one person I've obsessed about for ten years.

The trees become blurry as tears threaten to burst from my eyes, and I blink rapidly to clear my vision. Get to the boat, get away from the shore.

Get away from him. My heart crumbles at the thought.

"No, don't—" I faintly hear him call out, but I block it out and keep moving, forcing myself to push harder.

My adrenaline blocks out all sound, and everything around me becomes muted. I push him to the back of my mind, telling myself he isn't here.

Get to the boat.

Get to the boat.

Get to the—

A gunshot rings into my mantra and jolts me out of my zone as a patch of grass five feet in front of me explodes.

Thrown off balance, I trip over my own feet and almost go completely down, but I don't. I recover quickly and cry out as I push hard to return to my top speed.

Just as I regain a solid running pace, the weight of a body much stronger than mine slams into me from behind. I grunt as the ground moves up to meet me, but I don't make contact.

Somehow, Jack has managed to tangle himself around me, and we hurtle toward the ground. As we hit, he groans, and I don't feel the impact I think I should. Opening my eyes as we roll, I see he's managed to put himself between me and the grass so he makes contact first.

Our bodies stop, and I cough as I try to clear the air lodged in my throat from the fall. Then I realize he's rolled on top of me, and I freeze in place. The weight of his body pins my soul to the ground.

Then everything hits me.

I've been warned never to look for him. I've been told—shown—what the consequences will be if I disobey that order. And I have no escape. No way out.

I should fight to keep going, but I know I won't win this time. His deadweight alone is too much for me to get out from under. Warring emotions consume my thoughts as I struggle to reconcile my old feelings for him with my desire to survive and save Dana.

Looking up to meet his glare punches me into reality.

His dark eyes are barely holding in his rage. His teeth are clenched tight, and the muscles in his jaw are flexed. He looks like he wants to tear me limb from limb.

In one move, he stands, and his fingers dig hard into my arms to lift me up as his snarky buddy and a few others join us.

They have Dana.

Purposefully, and with intense control, he releases me from his custody and places me into the hands of one of the other men.

I glance at Dana as I evaluate our new reality. The largest of the men holds her firmly in place.

We aren't getting out of this right now.

Dana nods, then looks down at her feet. At least one thing went right with our escape. Her confirmation tells me she was able to destroy the computers I had downstairs, and I exhale a relieved breath.

"Care to share with the rest of us, Dee?" Jack's buddy pipes up, and Dana pinches her lips together, shaking her head.

It's clear that one of these two men are in charge, as everyone else is just standing around, waiting for them.

I have a sudden urge to blurt out everything, to tell Jack about our hell. But ten long years have passed. A decade has been lost, and, as much as I want to, I don't know the man standing in front of me anymore.

I try to derail the conversation. "Just upset we got caught, is all." I shrug. Then, looking at Dana, I continue, "You should have joined me in those online self-defense classes I signed up for."

"Yes, because that worked out so well for you." The guy holding me makes a sad attempt at sarcasm, but I'm not in the mood.

Jerking my elbow up and back, I catch him square in the face, and he crumples behind me as all of the men except Jack and his friend startle and brace for an altercation.

Jack rolls his eyes. There is no joy behind his curled lips, only impatience and disappointment. Pulling out his phone, he leans around me and snaps a photo of the man on the ground at my feet.

Jack's buddy is looking off to the side, as though he is concentrating, probably listening to a voice on the other end of his earpiece. Then he comes back to our group. "Hunter, get Tex off the ground and pull everyone back. The house is secure. These two are the only ones here. You know the drill."

I'm starting to learn some names.

"Grizz, you, Hunter, and Tex will ride back with these two." Jack's partner points to me and Dana as he speaks to the man with his hand wrapped around Dana's arm.

Jack speaks for the first time since I ran. "She stays with us, Jekyll." He stares at his buddy as he jabs a finger in my direction.

And now I know his irritable friend's name too.

"No. They drive back in the van with the team," Jekyll challenges Jack, and, judging by the awkward expressions of the other guys, this doesn't happen often.

Jack and his partner are locked in a standoff. He hasn't looked at me since he lifted me off the ground. The anger radiating off him suffocates me, and I hope they take me away soon. I can't bear to stand here and watch him avoid me.

I've never wanted to be thrown into a solitary cell more in my life. I need to get away from them, and I need to talk to Dana. She's keeping quiet, just like we talked about, but she looks worried, and I need a few minutes to calm her, or Jack's buddy is going to have a field day interrogating her.

"This is the closest we've gotten to Maxwell. She's Jay, and she's one rung under Zane." Jack again points in my direction without looking at me.

I'm absorbing as much information as I can, and my heart skips a beat when it sounds like they aren't working for or with Maxwell. But it's still unclear who their master is. Maxwell has many enemies who would go to great lengths to get their hands on us.

"You and I need to have words, Phoenix," Jekyll retorts through gritted teeth. "We'll follow you in the SUV with Grey and Eagle. They aren't going anywhere." Then, glancing past me at the men standing around us, he breaks up the show. "You heard me. Move out."

The group briefly looks at Jack, who still isn't looking directly at me. A harsh tug on my arm pulls me out of my daze, and Dana and I are turned and moved across the yard toward the waiting vehicles out front. I don't dare look back at him.

There are more vehicles out front than before. Men file out of the farmhouse with our belongings. I steal an impressed glance in Dana's direction at the sight of my computer being hauled out. She did a bang-up job destroying that thing—literally. I couldn't bring it back if I wanted to.

Then I see our bags being carried out, and my heart sinks.

"I'm sorry, Jessa. I couldn't get to it in time. You always told me to destroy the computer first. The bags were upstairs. I only had time to go up or down." Her voice is drenched in regret.

I nod to reassure her. "You did the right thing."

My perception of the world around me has changed in the last twenty minutes.

This is a disaster.

And here I am with the man I thought I would love forever.

The man who now looks like he wants to murder me.

CHAPTER 3
JACK

She ran from me. I stood only feet away from her, and she had two choices.

She chose wrong.

I looked for her for years after her family's car accident. I wouldn't accept that she perished with her parents.

The moment my team lead told me she was gone was the worst moment of my life. Looking at photos from the car wreck and talking about my feelings with a shrink to get cleared so I could be put back out on active duty was brutal. But I went through it all for her. So I could get back out in the field and begin looking for her on my own.

And it was always a dead end. Her body was never found, and she was declared deceased after a couple of years.

No one can stay hidden for that long.

Except her.

There she was standing right in front of me.

Watching her run devastated me. After calling for her and realizing she wasn't slowing down at all, my composure drained out of me.

Hunter moved toward the door to set off the explosive,

and the three of us backed off the porch for the detonation, but I didn't stop there.

Before considering my options, I broke all protocol and bolted around the side of the house as fast as I could. As I rounded the first corner, the front door blew, and I saw Grizz on the porch, nearing the corner toward the back.

Chatter in my earpiece picked up, and I knew she had cleared the house and was running.

The sound of wood breaking caught my attention as the porch collapsed beside me, taking out my team and making me the closest to her in pursuit. I picked up my pace at the thought I could lose her again.

She was halfway across the backyard, but she still had a long way to go before the tree line. Her eyes locked with mine, but she didn't slow down.

Blood pumped fiercely into my head as she continued to run.

I knew then that she would keep running until I caught her.

And I will catch her.

At once, I remember our shooter in the trees. I gave instructions to shoot anything getting away, and the realization snaps me out of my thoughts.

Yelling at Eagle through my earpiece, I keep my pace. "Stand down. Do not shoot. DO. NOT. SHOOT. She's mine." The fierce determination with which I growl my last words startles me.

With an internal force I've never felt until this moment, one thought rages through me and fuels me on:

She is mine.

Then I chastise myself for claiming her out loud. I'll be answering to Logan for that later.

"Please, don't..." It's one of the first things she's said to me in ten years.

Her fear ignites my rage, and I don't back down.

She should fear me right now.

I see it in the whites of her eyes. She knows I won't stop. As she turns to try and keep her pace, I call out her name.

She's more fit than I remember. Even through her clothes and by the way she moves, I can tell her body is toned. Her arms are defined.

Link's voice breaks through my earpiece. "The drone is picking up a boat just past the trees. She's heading straight for it."

My heart tightens. It will only be a matter of time if we both remain on foot. I can't let her get to the boat.

"Female target on foot at the back of the house. Do not let her get to the trees. Eagle, on my mark," Logan commands through our open comms. I quickly glance over my shoulder to see him moving around the side of the house, well behind us.

There's no time to process how I need to handle this now.

All I see is her closing in on the tree line, and my whole body heats up as blood and anger feverishly pulse through me.

"No. Don't. I've got her. Hold your fire." I contradict my fellow team lead with the ferocity of a beast unhinged.

We have one of the best sharpshooters on our team, but the mere thought of a bullet accidentally hitting Jessa makes me want to rip Eagle's head off through his asshole.

"Spook her, Eagle. FIRE!" Logan's tone is detached, and I know the order will be carried out before he finishes speaking.

The crack of the shot echoes against the sleepy countryside as the dirt in front of Jessa kicks up, and her legs physically react as she trips and attempts to recover.

My body relaxes as I take my final few steps toward her.

I've got her now.

She's mine. The thought fills my head once again with a vengeance as I connect with her, and together we crash to the ground. I roll to minimize the damage as my mind starts to work overtime.

My life just got better, but my day just got a metric shit ton worse, and I need to get my shit together before everyone catches up to us.

I need to compose myself.

And Jessa?

Everything is raw and hitting me all at once.

This is Jessa—my Jessa. The life that was ripped away from me. After all of the searching, after accepting her death, after letting her go. She's in my grasp. She's alive, and she's found.

But she's Jay. Or, rather, "J." Somewhere along the line, the letter turned into a name, but it doesn't matter now.

Jessa is Jay, and she's our target. It's her face that matches the code name in that flimsy file lying on the floor of the SUV. She works with Zane, and she works for Maxwell. For the last decade, she's been working for the monster I've been trying to put down.

But why?

She has to know he is most likely responsible for her own family's death.

She's been hiding all this time—from me—and her first instinct was to run.

Pressure builds behind my eyes as my anger swallows my

relief. I don't know which emotion to entertain at the moment.

So it will have to be indifference. For now.

As we shuffle to get up, her eyes lock on mine. She's gone rigid. Her wide eyes refuse to leave mine, and I can tell by her reaction to me that everything I'm feeling is written all over my face.

She's terrified.

She looks like she's seen a ghost. But I'm the one who's looking at a ghost.

Logan and a few members of our team meet us in the field with her friend in tow, and I move to place Jessa in Tex's custody before I change my mind about letting her go.

Both of the women are quietly looking at each other. This is not how I pictured our reunion. I never thought we'd have a reunion.

Now, looking at Dee, I remember her as Dana. Her hair used to be much shorter, and she was heavier back then. She was Jessa's best friend in high school. They were inseparable. Dana's father had been incarcerated for murder before I started my undercover assignment, and it wasn't just any murder.

Gossip was the favorite pastime at the high school, and when word got out that Dana was a cop-killer's kid, she became everyone's favorite subject, and her "friends" dropped like flies.

But not my Jessa. She doubled down. That's who she was. It's why I gravitated to her almost instantly.

I look over at Logan, who seems to be working out his own thoughts.

Things are different between us now.

He's guarded.

I don't blame him.

The only woman I've ever talked to him about is standing mere feet away from us, and she's alive. I've shared everything about her with Logan in an effort to deal with my feelings and move past her loss. I opened up completely because I was finally convinced she was dead. After years of looking for her body, running her prints, checking alerts, and quietly following up on leads, I thought she was gone forever.

But she's not.

She's here.

And he knows everything.

"Care to share with the rest of us, Dee?" Logan levels his gaze on Dana, his patience clearly wearing thin.

Jessa answers for her friend. Always the protector, she attempts to maintain an indifferent tone, but I detect a slight shake in her voice. She's scared.

Standing directly behind her, Tex tries to shut her down with sarcasm, but she's not having any of it. As soon as his words leave his mouth, Jessa jerks her elbow up, hitting Tex square in the nose. Judging by how fast his head snaps back, she made a solid connection, and he buckles to the ground behind her.

A surge of pride bursts through me, but I keep my expression cold as I reach around to snap a photo of him sprawled out on the lawn. Then I shake my head in disbelief. We're going to need to have a group discussion about underestimating our opponents and letting our guard down, or I might lose one of these guys one day.

Distracted by my own thoughts, I catch the end of Logan telling our men to put the women in a different vehicle from ours, and I lose what was left of my composure at the thought of being away from Jessa, even for the four-hour drive back to our compound.

"She stays with us, Jekyll." Pointing my finger in claim at Jessa, I square myself on Logan. I won't entertain the slightest chance I could lose her again.

"No. They drive back in the van with the team." Logan's jaw is clenched. I know he doesn't want to have this discussion here, but I'm not letting her go, so it's going to happen.

Then I notice the guys waiting. This has never happened to us before. He and I have never disagreed on protocol. We've always worked together toward what is best for the mission.

Then I realize I'm not thinking about the mission.

I'm thinking about her, and Logan knows it too. He's trying to give me the chance to fall in line and get my head back in the game in front of our team.

I make one last attempt to have her in the same vehicle with me, but Logan shuts it down. He ends our conversation with, "You heard me. Move out."

As we follow everyone into the front yard, I look over to the farmhouse. Some of our team are still carrying out bags and equipment, but by the looks of the computer and laptop they recovered, we won't be getting any information that way.

Back in the SUV, Grey and Eagle are silent. Grey has his eyes on the road; he knows where we're going. Eagle is packing up his bag in the front seat. We have at least a few hours until we are back on our own turf.

"We're heading back to camp on radio silence. Until we can assess the situation, I don't want any information to get out. Notify the rest of the team, and turn on some music, Grey." Logan's curt command breaks the silence.

"What do you want to hear, boss?" The moment the words are out, Grey's shoulders tense up, and I know he regrets asking.

"I don't give a fuck. Just turn it on. You can even play some of that pop shit you like," Logan barks, and Grey starts pressing buttons as I settle back into my seat and wait.

Taking a deep sigh, Logan adjusts himself in his seat and looks out the window for a long minute.

I take the pause to gather my thoughts. This was an unexpected turn of events, and if Logan loves anything, it's control.

Our two vehicles drive off the property and onto the dirt road, followed by the rest of our team in their own units. I keep my eyes forward, watching the van in front of us, the one that's carrying Jessa back to our base.

Music beats through the speakers, but I'm barely here.

Before I allow myself to drown in thoughts of her, Logan breaks the silence between us.

"Mind telling me where your head is at, Jack?"

Truth be told, my head is in the vehicle in front of us, and we both know it.

I shrug. "Target acquired. Nothing to talk about." My focus stays on the van, which is now kicking up rocks.

He's not buying it. He turns toward me and leans back as though I slapped him. "Who the fuck do you think you're talking to?" The guys in the front seat exchange side glances at his tone. "The only piece of ass you've ever mentioned is in that van. Don't act like it's nothing. I know all about your *nothing*—I know *everything*, Jack." His attempt at asserting dominance is beginning to grate on my nerves, but I know he's right.

This isn't about the mission.

I can't even see the mission anymore.

In our silence, I take a moment to look down before I engage with Logan, and that's when I see it. I'm wringing my hands together, like a junkie waiting for his next fix. I'm on edge, and I'm wired. My tells are all out in the open, and I can't control myself.

The only way out of this conversation is honesty. I owe it to Logan. He's been there for me for ten years. I've told him everything. I'm thinking with every part of my body right now except my brain, and I need to sort this shit out before we get to our destination and I see her again.

"Fine. Yes. It's Jessa. I don't know what the fuck to do. She was supposed to be dead. I got over her. I was—"

His incredulous laugh doesn't let me finish. "You never got over her, Jack. You thought she was dead, but you never got over her. You never stopped talking about her. You mentally compared every woman you've met in the last decade to that feisty little number, and I can see why. She is hot. And that attitude? Jesus, I'd never stop fucking that tight little—"

Now it's my turn to shut the conversation down. "One more word, and I'll rip out your throat." I glare into his eyes in warning. My heart rate picks up, and my face grows hot.

"No need. You made my point for me. Your head isn't where it needs to be. I'm taking the lead on this, Jack." Logan slips back into casual business mode. I hate how he can turn himself on and off. I hate myself even more for falling for it.

Logan is a master at pushing buttons and getting into

people's heads. This was a test, one I failed miserably. In this moment, I envy his emotional restraint.

I know he's right though. He should take the lead on this. My mind and my heart are elsewhere, and until I can sort them out, I am no use to anyone.

"I agree, on one condition." I acquiesce, and Logan's eyes assess my every movement as I finish my thought, "I get access to her. I can question her as well, and I am there whenever you talk to her, either in the room or watching from behind the glass."

Logan sits back and takes a deep breath as he considers everything I've asked for.

"I take the lead. You may be there when I question her, but you do not stop the process or come to her defense in any way. If you do, you know it's protocol to treat you as a hostile." Then, pausing, he takes a deep, frustrated breath. "You've seen me interrogate, Jack. You may want to sit this one out."

I return my gaze to the van in front of us.

Logan puts in a new earpiece and turns his attention away from me. I have no doubt he's asked one of the guys in the van to wire him into any conversations the girls are having, and I've been excluded from this part of his plan.

It's going to be a long, quiet drive.

CHAPTER 4
JESSA

Once I was secured in the van, with Dana seated across from me, the drive felt like it was close to five hours, and I have no idea where we are now.

Judging by the turns, I think we went east after we left the farmhouse, but I can't be sure. With all of the subtle curves in the road, we could be anywhere.

The severity of our situation sank in quickly after the van doors closed. Dana sat quietly for most of the trip, looking down at her feet before she closed her eyes and dozed off for a bit.

I took the time to process everything. In a nutshell, our freedom is gone, at least for the time being, and I don't have my phone anymore, so I can't access Zane.

I don't know who these guys work for, but clearly Jack isn't who I thought he was. I thought he was my friend, the first boyfriend I ever had.

I never saw him again after the night my parents died. I began searching for him once I knew I was far away from everyone and everything that happened, but he and his dad were gone. There were no police reports or traces of their whereabouts; they both just vanished.

Everything about Maxwell and his dad came to light after they skipped town. All of their shady business. My dad couldn't have known he was working for a crime boss, I'm sure of it, but it doesn't matter anyway.

Travis and I grew up with Maxwell. Uncovering the layers of lies Mr. Sparr's family had told was surreal, and I remained in denial over Max's involvement for a few years after I left town. I was so wrong about him.

Was I wrong about Jack too?

His being here is a positive sign. Jack wouldn't work with Maxwell. He even said as much when we were standing in the field behind the farmhouse.

But what is his team's objective?

It's been ten years. I don't even know what side of the law these guys are on, nor who they're working for.

"Hey." Dana's whisper brings me back to the jerking motion of the van as it pulls off onto a bumpier road. Pressure builds in my ears, and I yawn to break the compression. We've slowly been climbing in altitude.

"Hey." I flash a weary smile, hoping to mask my uncertainty.

"So—rough day, huh?" she deadpans, then pauses to gauge my reaction. A genuine smile creeps across my face.

There's my Dana. She's feeling better. As long as we're still together, we're okay.

"Quiet back there." The guy in the front seat attempts to claw back some of the respect he left behind on the field when I clocked him.

"Oh, can it. We're just talking," Dana snaps back, surprising everyone, me included. The other two men chuckle, which sets my nerves at ease, but not by much. Dana's eyes round as she looks back at me, probably realizing our situation, as she mouths, *Sorry.*

For all five and a half feet of her, she is strong, but I know her better than anyone. Her strength is on the outside. On the inside, she's just as anxious as I am. Settling back into her seat, she takes a deep breath.

"You okay?" I ask. Dana is a tough one, but I know she's worried.

"Yeah, you?" she asks back. I'm silent. I don't know what I am. "Jessa? That was Jack. What's going on?"

Our eyes lock in a tempest of confusion.

That was Jack.

"I have no idea." The sheer absurdity of our situation gives me pause.

The van makes a few jerky stops, and I remember that I need to say my piece before we stop for good, because we will most likely be separated. "Look, I need to tell you a couple of things. It's important." Dana straightens in her seat to listen further, and I know the guys around us can hear as well. I don't care. It will be better for Dana if they hear me say this. "First, I don't think these guys work for Maxwell." At my words, Dana releases a relieved sigh, and I continue, "Next, whatever they ask you—anything, no matter what it is —tell the truth. Tell them what you know."

"What?" Dana's eyes go wide. The largest of the men turns to look at me, no doubt checking to see if I'm up to something, but I hold firm.

"No matter what the question is, Dana. Tell them everything you know." The van slows to a definite stop, and I speak quickly before we are separated. "Don't let that Jekyll guy intimidate you. Just answer their questions. Please,

Dana," I plead, hoping to get her to agree before the doors open.

"But why? Won't that be bad for you—and Zane?" The confused look on her face breaks my heart.

As I open my mouth to respond, the door slides open, pouring the day's bright light into our dark space. Squinting in the direction of our exit, my eyes fall on Jekyll. He's blocking the sun from my line of sight with a wolfish grin.

"My, aren't you a smart little bird." Jekyll's gaze travels past Dana and lands on me, and my breath catches in my chest. As uncomfortable as it would be, I almost want Jack to be the one standing here right now.

Then Jekyll shifts his focus to Dana and arrogantly answers her for me. "Haven't you figured it out, *sweetie?* Your friend has been keeping things from you. Probably to protect you. You are on what we like to call a need-to-know basis, and your friend here has decided you don't need to know much. Isn't that right, Blue Jay?"

I wince at his new nickname for me and look to Dana, silently asking for her temporary forgiveness until I get the chance to speak to her again.

"You don't need to interrogate her. She'll tell you everything she knows," I say in her direction. Then I look past Jekyll for a glimpse of Jack, but he is nowhere to be found.

"Grizz, take this one inside. Room two." He leans into the van, unhooks Dana, and guides her out into the open.

Jekyll stands still for a moment. It feels like he is waiting for something. Then, as soon as the shuffle of feet fades away, he looks back to me. I'm still secured in the van, and he ever so slowly leans into my space.

His eyes begin at my chest and slowly roam up to

examine my face. He's so close I can feel the heat of his breath on my cheek.

As if sizing up dessert, he slowly licks his lips as he takes me in completely. The realization that no one else is around sinks in.

"I find you fascinating, Blue Jay." Tension fills his expression and his tone. "I've heard a lot about you." Slowly leaning closer, he inhales, as if he's committing my scent to memory, and my skin prickles under his scrutiny. "Tell me how you go from being dead to sitting here in *my* possession?"

"I—"

"Jekyll," Jack bites out from behind him, and I clamp my lips shut. Jekyll mutters something under his breath, and I get the impression my being alone with him out here was not part of Jack's plan.

Jekyll slowly steps back and straightens. But he keeps his eyes on me, and I will myself to hold his stare and not look over at Jack.

"I was just having a little chat with our *prisoner*." Jekyll emphasizes his last word to remind both Jack and me of the gravity of our situation and my place among them.

I don't need any reminders.

I know what I am.

I'm already planning an escape.

"Where do you want her?" Jack steps closer to the van and looks inside. It isn't lost on me that he isn't making eye contact.

"Lock her in her quarters. I want to talk to the snippy one first."

I temporarily forget my surroundings as my need to protect my only friend boils to the surface, erasing my composure. "I told you, you don't need to interrogate her. She'll cooperate. Just ask her. Or let her go, and I'll tell you anything you want to know."

My words surprise both Jack and his buddy, and they turn to look at me in stunned silence.

Jekyll recovers quickly as he takes a step toward me, his impassive expression morphing into a sneer. "Really? Where's Zane? Better yet, who is Zane?" By the way he fires his questions at me without waiting for an answer, he already knows I'm not going to answer them.

He huffs in confirmation when I break eye contact and lower my gaze away from him. "I thought so."

Leaning around me, Jekyll unfastens the handcuffs that secured me in the vehicle and pulls me out. Then he turns to Jack and nudges me in his direction.

"Lock her in the guest quarters, the small one. I'm going to check in, then start with Dee." Jekyll slams the van door shut, then strides into the closest building. I look around, taking in my first glimpse of my temporary accommodations.

I was right—we did drive east. Judging by the terrain, we are somewhere in the Appalachian Mountains, although I won't be able to pinpoint exactly where without some technology. I can only determine where we are not. We are still under tree cover, and that doesn't narrow it down by much.

The area looks a little like a compound or a military camp. The buildings are solid, mostly cement, with a couple of newer structures added. Boxes of supplies are piled against a wall, and a couple more temporary buildings are off in the distance.

The forest beyond the surrounding fence is dense, and I get the feeling we are many miles from civilization.

I turn my attention to Jack and realize he's been staring at me this whole time, silently taking me in.

My memory of him is nothing compared to the reality standing beside me, and I'm at a loss for words. For years, I would replay what I would say if I ever found him; now I have nothing.

"Jack—"

He jerks me to a stop. "I need to get you to your room. He'll be questioning Dana soon. I want to be there. I trust you won't try to run. I don't need these, do I?" He motions to a pair of handcuffs on his belt, and I shake my head.

He's all business. My heart breaks a little over how much we both lost.

Inside the building, the dim lights are a strong contrast to the bright day outside. I recognize a few men from the farmhouse, but they only briefly glance up at Jack before they return to what they are doing.

Stopping outside an unmarked door, Jack pulls out a key. I'm overwhelmed by an urge to reach out to him, to shatter the appearance that everything is normal.

"Jack."

At the sound of his name a second time, he freezes, but he doesn't look at me. His breathing deepens, and an uncomfortable silence screams into the space between us.

"Ten years, Jessa. It's been ten years." He growls his pain through gritted teeth as he slowly looks up, showing me the hurt in his eyes. "I looked for you for years after. I thought you were dead. What's going on?"

"It's—complicated. I can't explain it right now." And I can't. I need to be alone in that room to sort myself out. There are consequences to every decision I make from here on out, and I need time to decide which decisions are the right ones.

Jack releases an unamused huff at my pathetic answer, then slides the key into the lock. As the door creaks open, he lowers his eyes to the ground, and everything about him becomes cold. "Get in. Someone will come for you when we're ready."

His indifference crushes my heart, and panic takes hold. Jumping forward, I catch him off guard as I grab either side of his jacket and pull him to me. Raising myself onto the tips of my toes to make up for my five-and-a-half-foot height against his few extra inches, I push my upper body into his chest and expect him to immediately pull back in shock.

But he doesn't.

As I wait for an eternity in an embrace only I am actively participating in, my head moves with his breath as he continues to stand still. Slowly, his hands travel up the length of my arms and wrap around my back as he tightens his grip on me.

I don't know who he is now, but I know who he was, and I missed him. My smile pushes my cheeks high, forcing some tears out of my eyes and down my face.

He's frozen in place as his hands move to hold my upper arms. His expression is guarded, marking the distance between us.

I step back to allow him enough space to release me to my cell, but he doesn't let me go. Instead, his grip tightens, and the air is pushed out of my lungs as he pulls me back to him and crushes his lips against mine.

My memories were all I had for all of these years, but now it feels like yesterday.

My footing becomes awkward, and my legs wobble at the

intensity of the kiss as I wrap my arms around him to hold myself up.

I never want to let go.

"I see you found your quarters." Like a piercing alarm, Jekyll's barely composed voice claws through my head, and I jerk back until my back hits the wall.

Jekyll measuredly shifts his eyes between us as Jack straightens and turns to his friend.

No words are offered, but the glares between the two of them suck the air out of the room around us.

Both men are clearly cut from the same cloth, and, from the looks of their silent exchange, neither is about to back down.

The weight of their presence mentally crushes me. I can no longer stand their harsh stares, so I shoot my eyes to my feet, chastising myself for breaking the three-way staring contest I know I just lost, even though no one was staring back at me.

Without a word, Jack nudges me into the room, and I obey, keeping my eyes down until I'm all the way inside and the hinges creak as the door shuts behind me.

Once the lock clicks into place, I lift my head to take in the room that's now mine.

The space is small, but, considering its purpose, that isn't surprising. There is enough room for a cot and a table with one chair. There is a small opening for a window, but it is barred the old-school way, with nuts and bolts. Nothing about the room is computerized, except for the camera in the corner of the ceiling.

Escaping this room will be difficult.

On my own for the first time in hours, I sit down on the

cot and take a deep breath, releasing the tension I've been holding.

I bring my fingers up to my lips where Jack just kissed me, and they feel puffy at my touch. Everything I thought I knew about Jack was a lie. I need to let go of old facts and assumptions and move forward with my new reality.

Does Maxwell know that we've been captured yet? Our working relationship with him, if you can even call it that, is volatile. It's a delicate balance between what Zane holds over him and the leeway he grants us in living.

We are still alive because of two things.

For the most part, we are alive because Maxwell hasn't been able to physically get his hands on Zane. He's more elusive than Dana and I are, and, for the sake of everyone's safety, I can never reveal his identity.

And also, we are alive because we are needed. We have taken on jobs when his own team lacks expertise, which happens fairly often. We do enough work to keep him happy while doing our best to stay away from any jobs that would harm innocent lives.

In short, we've been helping him take down his competition, which creates even more adversaries for us, but it keeps us breathing.

There is a heavy truth in the old saying, *Keep your friends close and your enemies closer.*

Resting my head against the wall, I close my eyes. I need to be ready for things as they come, and right now, that is Dana. I hope she's being cooperative. There is no reason for her to challenge either of them.

Once she tells them what she knows, they'll come for me, and that's what I need to prepare for.

CHAPTER 5
JACK

I kissed her—just like that. When Jessa pulled me close, a fire I hadn't felt in a decade lit me up like napalm, and I wasn't ready to let her go.

And it's just perfect that Logan saw everything, I think to myself as he circles Dana in the interrogation room.

I watch through the one-way mirror. Their eyes are locked on each other, and neither is going to be looking away any time soon.

Judging by Logan's delay in asking his first question, he's not happy that she's challenging his authority. Logan thrives on getting under people's skin and managing the situation around him, but Dana isn't backing down.

She's leaning back in an unforgiving metal chair as though she's resting comfortably in a recliner, and her foot is tapping against the table in a repetitive thud, further agitating him.

Now I remember Dana. Defiant as ever. She's been given the go-ahead to tell us everything she knows, yet her body language tells me she hates giving even one piece of information up to Logan.

"So, Dana, what were you doing at the farmhouse?" Logan starts off easy, extending an olive branch by finally using her actual name.

I'm sure he'd love nothing more than to continue their verbal sparring match, but he needs to approach this with caution. There are so many questions, and this is our chance to fill in some blanks. We can't afford to have her shut down on us.

"We were supposed to be on vacation." She shrugs, appearing to drop her attitude. It's a new approach. "Jessa said she worked it out with Zane so we could take off for a bit."

"And where is Zane?" He attempts nonchalance but comes up short. We really need this information.

"I don't know that." She speaks confidently. When Logan turns to look at her, she sighs. "Look, you said it yourself: I was kept out of the loop. I can tell you what I know, but I don't know who he is, or where he is. I don't know if Jessa really knows either. But I'm not sure I would tell you if I did. We owe our lives to Zane." She cuts her answer short, biting her lip. Logan notices her misstep, but he doesn't push it yet. I know he'll tuck it away and use it to his advantage when the time is right.

"How long have you both known Zane?"

"Jessa has known Zane since high school. I've only known him through Jessa. She and her twin brother were really smart at computers, and they both belonged to groups outside of school. Jessa told me she met Zane in some chat forum. They would work out problems together."

Logan steals a glance in my direction. I know what he's thinking because I'm thinking the same thing: *If Jessa knew Zane in high school, why didn't I know Zane in high school?*

I guess I wasn't the only one with secrets back then.

"How did Zane save your lives?" Logan asks.

"It was Zane who helped Jessa gather the evidence that finally put my dad away." She looks down, and her strong offense disappears as she recounts the past she's probably tried hard to put behind her. "My—*dad* wasn't a good man. He used to hit my mom. I told Jessa about it one day, and she jumped to my rescue. We came up with a plan to stop it, but we weren't fast enough. He got drunk, hit my mom, and I tried to get in his way. Then he turned his anger on me.

"When I showed up for school the next day with a busted lip, Jessa told me she would fix it. She said she knew someone who could help her. A few days later, our home computer was hacked. Jessa said she was trying to access our built-in camera to record the abuse, but she found something else. He—killed a guy. We decided to send it to the cops anonymously. I just wanted it to stop." She lowers her gaze to her hands, unable to look Logan in the eye. I don't blame her. We already know this part of Dana's story. Clearing her throat, she raises her head and straightens her shoulders. "I didn't know at the time that the man he killed was a cop." Pausing again to collect herself, she leans forward and crosses her arms on the table. Then, to make her point, she finishes, "I owe everything to Zane—and Jessa."

I read between the lines. She's telling Logan that she'll do anything for the friend who's done anything for her, and he gets her message loud and clear.

But he doesn't allow her emotions to lead his questioning. He continues in an indifferent tone, "And Jessa? How does she *owe her life* to him?"

Dana glances toward the mirror she doesn't know I'm

standing behind, and my attention sharpens. She thins her lips and wraps her arms around her midsection.

My heart pounds into my chest as Logan follows her gaze to the mirror. Then he shoots his own warning stare in my general direction.

He's telling me to stay put, and Dana picks up on it. She knows I'm here now.

"Her parents' car crash," she starts slowly.

"The accident," Logan clarifies.

"That was no accident," she huffs. "Mr. Sparr had her parents and her brother killed, and they were looking for her. Jessa told me her parents called her that night in a panic. They told her they needed to leave town immediately, and something was wrong at her dad's work. They weren't making any sense, so she asked Zane to hack into the Sparr systems. He found all of their dirty secrets, along with all of the orders to kill, but it was too late to save them. She told me he warned her though. He told her to trust no one, and it looked like even the cops were on Matteo's payroll. He helped her leave town the morning after."

"That seems unlikely. Reports show that people on both sides of the law were looking for her," he challenges.

Dana does a double take at Logan. "What part of 'hacker' do you not understand? Zane is top level, but Jessa is right up there too. If you can manipulate computers, you can do almost anything. Buy a ticket out of town under a different name. Hack into security cameras to show a different day's feed, transfer money that no one will miss into any account. She was on her own for about a year before she sent me a letter asking how I was. My mother was remarried to another loser, but I was old enough to move out. There was nothing left for me, and I asked if I could visit her, wherever she was. When she told me everything, I told her I wanted in. She's my only real family." Dana's loyalty to Jessa is clear, and I'm thankful they had each other all of this time.

Then, as if a thought has just hit him, Logan straightens and asks another question. "How do you know her brother was killed? Only her parents' bodies were found."

"Jessa said Zane told her he was killed in the crash along with them, but maybe he tried to escape and got pulled under. They never found his body."

Still not letting any emotion show, Logan continues, "What do you do for Maxwell?"

Her expression twists into disgust. "We do nothing for that piece of shit."

"Our intel says you are both connected to him through Zane." He stops pacing and leans against the wall to study her response.

This is the information he's most interested in now.

"Zane is not working with Maxwell. Neither is Jessa. It's —hard to explain." She breaks eye contact and looks down at her hands.

Logan picks up on it. "No. It probably isn't. You and Jessa work with Zane out of some crazy misguided loyalty, but you don't really know why Zane works with Maxwell, do you?" He pushes himself off the wall, grabs a chair, slides it across from her, then sits down. She shifts into a defensive position, crossing her arms over her chest and lifting one leg over the other. Logan eases off for now and tries a different question. "What are your roles under Zane?"

"Mine is nothing. I'm there for Jessa. I support her. I'm the only real friend she has." Her gaze wanders back to me, still hidden behind the mirror. "Jessa works a lot of his code for him and handles his operations. She told me once that they work together because the level of necessary code is insane. His whereabouts are unknown to us. He moves around as constantly as we do, and we are never in the same place. Ever. Maxwell would kill to get his hands on Zane. To have his knowledge completely under his control. Could you imagine? It's the only reason Maxwell gave Jessa back to us alive seven years ago." The gasp that leaves her mouth at her last sentence shudders the room into silence as the blood drains out of my limbs.

Now she has all of my attention.

Dana's eyes go wide, pleading with Logan to let it go. But he doesn't listen.

"What do you mean *gave her back alive?*"

Logan is like a wild animal following the scent of blood, and I know he isn't going to drop this. Judging by the look on Dana's face, she knows it too.

"Shit." She resigns herself as she shifts her focus between Logan and the glass I am standing behind. Then she continues, "Jessa was captured. It was all my fault. I got an urgent message from my mom, at an old email address, asking me to contact her right away. It was almost two years after I left home, and I panicked. I thought maybe she was sick, or worse. I went down the block to an internet café to video chat with her, but when I dialed her, she said she never sent the email. I made a mistake and gave up our location with my IP address. I contacted Jessa to tell her what happened, and she took care of it—like always. Except this time, she only had minutes to figure something out." Her eyes drift down to the floor, and when she looks back up, they are filled with tears.

"Two cars pulled up outside the café, and just as quickly as Maxwell's men arrived to take me away, they got back in and were speeding off again toward our apartment. I found out later that Jessa hacked into the café and added a final destination onto the IP string I used to call home. It was down to seconds, so she used the only one she could at the time." She chokes out a cry as she ends her sentence.

"It was hers, wasn't it? She gave herself up in your place?"

Dana silently nods as her eyes turn glassy.

"She didn't have enough time to create a better trail. They would have killed me. I'm no one. I only matter to Jessa. She would have had to either give herself up eventually, or—" She stops on the thought she can't bring herself to put into words.

"Or know that her decision led to the death of her friend." Logan's words meet a silent nod as Dana blinks rapidly, releasing the tears that were pooling in her eyes.

"I only contacted her to tell her to leave. To tell her that it was okay. That I was okay with what was going to happen to me. I didn't think she had time to throw herself under the bus in my place. By the time I got back to the apartment, the computers were destroyed, and she was gone."

"Then what happened?" Logan tries to soften his tone. There's no need for a harsh interrogation when she's cooperating.

"I did what she taught me to do. I packed what was left and went to our next safe house. I set it up, and I waited. We always have our next safe house set up ahead of time for this very reason."

"Did you contact Zane?"

"No. It would have been pointless. Only Jessa has the code to link to him. I have to wait until she checks in with me, then I work to hook her up to him, then she enters the passwords to connect. It was one of the first things she taught me, but it's pretty useless if you aren't Jessa. She's the only one who has the access codes and addresses once I've connected her."

"So, she got in touch?"

"It took four days before I heard anything. I thought she was dead. I was so scared. Then, at the end of the fourth day, there she was. She came through in a chat room, and I made the connection. She was released almost three days later." She looks at her hands as she wrings her fingers together when she adds, "She was pretty beaten up."

"Just like that? Did she say what happened? Why it took so long to contact you?"

Dana is giving us more information than I think Jessa thought she would, and Logan is taking full advantage.

"Not really. She said they tried to get information out of her. She said she didn't want to talk about it, but I could tell something happened. She wouldn't tell me, but she was—different. She said she found out Jack was happily married, that he was an accountant." She pauses, shifting her eyes around the table, no doubt trying to decide if she should trust us with more information.

Hesitantly, she continues, "After her time there, things changed—she changed. She began to put in more coding hours with Zane. I used to know about one safe house at a time, but then it went up to the next three. The security around us increased. She taught herself self-defense and worked out in the little spare time she had. She double- and triple-checked everything, and she became hyperfocused on details and organization. Just ask Jack." She points to the mirror, sure I am standing behind it. "He'll tell you. Jack went to high school with us. Maxwell wasn't right when it came to Jessa. He was infatuated with her. She tried to keep him as a friend, but there was just something off."

Then she looks at the mirror as though it isn't there, and she speaks directly to me. "I think something really bad happened, Jack. But she won't tell me."

My heart softens.

Dana is right about Maxwell. From the instant Jessa showed an interest in me, he was always close by, and it was awkward. Since it was my mission to get close to Maxwell at the time, I wasn't complaining. But now, when I consider his actions from a new perspective, there was something dark about his presence around her.

In our time working together, I've learned to read Logan almost as well as he can read me. He's not sure where to go next with his questions, or if he should even continue due to the limited information that Dana holds.

As he slides his chair back and stands, a knock at the door draws our attention, but Dana stays still, looking down at the table.

Logan opens the door to find Grey. He's standing in the hall holding some books and a bag.

"What's up?"

"Grizz was just going through some of the items we recovered from the house, and he thought you might want to see this right away. For the interrogation."

Logan answers him with a nod and takes the items from Grey before closing the door with his foot. He walks back to the table and drops the bag in front of Dana, but he keeps a notebook for himself. He silently opens it and begins to flip through the pages.

Dana grows rigid, and she doesn't take her eyes off the bag at first. Slowly, as Logan continues to turn the pages, her round eyes creep up, and she looks into the mirrored glass. My muscles tense at what is possibly in those pages.

My palms turn clammy at her guarded glare. The anticipation is driving me insane.

"What is this?" Logan's voice is low, confused.

Dana avoids the question. Her gaze shifts around the room, and it looks like she's trying to figure a way out of answering.

Finally, she stiffens in her seat and tosses her head to the side to get the hair out of her face. I can already tell she's chosen to challenge him. But she's not doing herself any favors by defying Logan on his own turf.

"It's a notebook. Don't they teach you about things like that at secret spy school?" She crosses her arms, taunting him with a sneer, and I sigh.

It's been too long since Logan had something to play with.

For someone who doesn't yet know we are the good guys, she is a little too confident for her own good, and I can only assume it's because she's trying to protect her friend.

"Feisty little thing, aren't you? I'm going to assume this isn't yours. You're trying to deflect for your friend." He holds firm, and my anxiety ticks up a notch at which way this is going to go.

Rolling her eyes to the ceiling, she starts in on him. "What do they call you again? Was it *Jackass*?" She holds her stare, and I chuckle to myself. Logan tries to cover his ire with a strained smile that's pulled so tightly, I almost see his teeth.

Walking over to the table, he purposely drops the notebook beside the bag with a loud thump. Then, leaning into Dana's space, he grips the arms of her chair and jerks it

around to face him. Lowering himself further, he lines his
eyes up with hers and drops his voice into a slow, low
warning.

"They call me Jekyll. As in Jekyll and Hyde. Trust me
when I tell you that what you've seen of me so far is the nice
guy. I can be a very—very—bad man if I don't get what I
want."

Her expression fades along with some of the color in her
face as she attempts to swallow a lump in her throat.

To my surprise, Logan gives her another chance to
answer.

Pushing slowly off her chair, but maintaining eye
contact, he reaches out and grabs the notebook. Then he
towers over her, looking down at her in his typical dominant
stance. Her defensive guard tells me she doesn't like it
one bit.

Opening the notebook, he flips a few pages, then takes a
deep, resigned sigh.

When he breaks his stare with Dana and looks in my
direction, my interest is so piqued, I'm about to explode.

"Why is the name Jack Waters written over and over
again on every page of this notebook?"

At the name Jessa and Dana knew me by in high school,
I'm done. I break my promise to stay out of Logan's way.
Leaving my hiding spot, I take quick steps down the hall,
then push open the door and burst into the interrogation
room.

The look on Logan's face is expectant.

He's not surprised I'm barging in. He knew I would. I
realize too late he's using me as part of his interrogation
process, but I'm not backing down.

I'll play my part.

I want answers now.

Grabbing the notebook out of Logan's hand, I open it to a random page in the middle, then flip a few pages.

There it is. Over and over again. Across every line, filling every page.

Jack Waters Jack Waters

When I glance up, I find Logan evaluating my actions and Dana attempting to mask a regretful sadness. Then I look at the bag. Poking out of the top are more notebooks.

Dropping the one in my hand, I reach into the bag, aware that I am the only one in the room making any noise.

I vigorously open another notebook. This one's a little smaller than the last, but as I quickly flip the pages, I see my name is still there.

The next one I pull out is the same as the last.

My name is everywhere.

Logan has taken two steps back to watch me play the part I just signed up for.

I look up at Dana, and she's just staring now, her eyebrows knitted together.

Shaking the notebook at her, my calm control abandons me. "This is Jessa's handwriting. What is this?"

She stares at me closely for the first time since I saw her at the farmhouse. Slowly, her demeanor changes, and anger replaces her fear.

"You know she looked for you. She never stopped looking for you until Maxwell took her." She stands up and steps away from her chair, placing it in between us to give herself some space. "She loved you Jack, and she left town to protect all of us. She came back looking for you. She searched everywhere, but you vanished. It's like you were a ghost. You and your dad."

I wince.

He wasn't my dad.

He was my commanding officer.

We were playing a part.

I lied to Jessa, and she came back looking for that lie.

"Then, when she came back from wherever Maxwell

had her, she said it was time to move on. She said she saw your pictures. You—married. She said your wife was stunning. Two beautiful boys. Such a happy family." Her anger for her friend's sadness is evident in her sour tone. "Living the glamorous life as a fucking accountant. She said Maxwell warned her to let you go. To never search for you again. He said if he found out she ever looked for you, even once, he would make you watch as he killed your entire family before he put a bullet in your head."

My limbs turn heavy. I drop the notebook on the table and take a step back.

How could I not consider her? I loved her more than anything, and her loss almost killed me.

All expression drops from my face, but that only angers Dana further. Her dedication to her best friend is impressive, and she's not ready to back down just yet.

"So she did what she always does. She protected you and stopped looking. She never spoke your name again, but she never stopped thinking about you. It consumed her. I suggested she write your name down on a piece of paper when you crossed her mind, just to get it out of her head. Then she could burn the paper and try to heal."

She shifts her eyes from mine to the bag, and tears begin to roll down her face again. "Pieces of paper became full sheets; then they became notebooks. When she filled enough of them, she would burn them. She writes your name down every time she thinks about you."

The scope of Jessa's feelings hits me like a bolt of lightning. Day after day, I crossed her mind. I let her memory go a few years ago because I couldn't find her. She couldn't find me either, but she never stopped thinking about me. Even after she was told I had moved on.

She has been left on her own, to fend for herself, to rescue herself, and she survived. She compartmentalized thoughts of me into little notebooks and kept putting one foot in front of the other so she could live another day. She believed I had simply moved on to live a happy life with a family of my own.

Not only that, but she did everything she could to protect what she thought I loved. She stopped looking for me to protect my children—children who don't even exist. Children who should have been hers.

"How long?" My throat is dry.

"What?"

"How long has she been doing this?" I run my finger along the seam of the notebook and ask quietly.

Her tone softens to match mine. "Since about a month after she came back to me, well over six years ago."

The room is silent, and Logan hasn't moved from his spot.

I need to see her now, but I know Logan won't be happy if I leave him standing here empty-handed.

"Why are they working with Maxwell, Dana?" My question sounds more like a plea.

She takes a breath and looks between me and Logan, trying to decide if she should trust either of us.

She knows who really wants her answer, so she looks at Logan when she speaks. "I don't know for sure. I know she was keeping things from me, and I know it was to keep me safe. The safety and anonymity of everyone who works under Zane is top priority—but I have a theory."

A sliver of Logan's kindness returns to him, and he motions for her to take her seat again. Then he sits across from her and lets her speak.

"I think she and Zane are trying to figure out a way to bring Maxwell's organization down from the inside. All of it. Not temporarily disable him. I think they are working to take everything out. We will never be free from him unless he's completely annihilated. I know she is compiling information for Zane—folders, evidence—and she has been running simulations with him on a program they were working on, but it isn't one they've ever used for Maxwell or any other job."

"What program?" In spite of his eagerness to obtain any information he can, Logan maintains a calm, curious tone.

"I understand more than she thinks I do, but I still don't know many details. She's been running test code on a new program that will hack backward but will temporarily make it appear as though it's working as intended. So, like, if a hacker used a server to hack into a system, they could initiate the program to make it look like it's functioning, but in reality they are actually taking control of their own servers. I think they are planning on sneaking the program into Maxwell's servers if they ever get the chance. I read her notes. A lot of it doesn't make sense to me. I think it only works for a short time before it's discovered. But that's just a theory. I don't even know if something like that would work. I asked her what it was once, and she said it was part of our exit plan."

Link has been listening in on the conversation from our head office. He's our tech lead, and he's one of the best there is—behind our mysterious Zane.

If anyone knows the feasibility of her claims, it will be him. He's probably already started barking orders at his team to get him a report on the likelihood of Dana's theory.

I'm agitated now.

I need to get out of this room.

When I meet Logan's eyes, he nods once to indicate his satisfaction with the interview, and I turn to push open the door.

I need to make up for the ten years I've lost, and that starts now.

I don't do well in enclosed spaces. As much as I tried to stretch out on the cot with my eyes closed, breathing deeply and trying to imagine myself on a quiet beach, it just didn't work.

Twenty minutes in, and I was already talking into the camera, asking to be let out, using the excuse that I'd like to take a shower. It was the only thing I could come up with.

A few minutes after, the one they called Hunter was at the door, negotiating the terms under which I could leave.

I was given a large towel, and I had to leave my clothes in the room, so if I wanted to run, I'd be doing it wet and naked.

The shower room was larger than my holding cell, so I took my time under the warm water. Hunter covered the only exit. It was another stipulation, that he be able to see the top of my head over the stall, and I agreed.

Hunter wasn't as talkative as Jack or his domineering friend, so I gave up on the small talk after the one-sided conversation on our walk to the shower.

Now that I'm standing under the spray, breathing is a little easier. As the hot water washes over my body, my mind wanders to Jack. Ten years is a long time, and he looks just as I remember him. Maybe a little rougher around the edges, but he's matured.

His presence feels the same as it did a decade earlier. He was my protector, and I was safe when I was with him. I had forgotten how blissful that ignorance was.

"Five minutes." Hunter's voice echoes off the tiled walls.

I reach for the soap to finish up. As I rinse my body and hair, I think about Dana. I only hope that Jack is there with her, and she is cooperating.

Jack's partner is intense. I'm not looking forward to my time with him, but I'll get through his questions, then I'll figure a way out for me and Dana both.

I'm confident Maxwell doesn't know we've been captured yet. Jack would have heard from him by now, and I'll need to come up with a plan for that later.

Twisting the shower handle, I step back to dry myself and wrap the towel around my body to make the walk back to my room and my clothes.

Hunter is quiet once again, so I use the silence to listen for anything I can use to help in our escape later.

As we turn down the last hall before my room, my heart jumps at Jack's gruff voice as we reach the door to my cell. "I've got it from here."

Hunter startles and takes a cautious step back, relinquishing possession. "Jekyll is wrapping up in interrogation; he could use your help on a couple of things."

Nodding, Hunter walks down the hall, almost a little too happy to be away from us, and Jack turns to open the door. He steps aside to let me in. As I pass him, I expect to hear the hinges creak shut. Instead, there's the warmth of his chest on my back as he follows me into the small space and closes the door behind us.

My heart thuds erratically against my ribs as I take a nervous step away and turn to look at him. The lights aren't on, so seeing small details is difficult, but I don't miss the white in his eyes. They're lit by the faint light coming in from the window. The sun is no doubt setting behind the mountain range.

Maybe it's the dim room, but his eyes look different; he looks sad and angry, and there's something else, but he doesn't say a word. He just stares at me. I still only have my towel on, and I shiver from the cold.

"Is Dana okay?" I ask in an attempt to break the growing tension.

"She's fine." He offers no more and continues to stare in silence.

I'm suddenly curious what information they got out of her, but I decide not to ask.

"Is it my turn now?" I break his gaze and walk over to pick up my clothes from the cot, gesturing that I could get dressed and be ready.

He matches my steps and covers my hand holding the clothes with his. He pushes them back onto the cot, leaving me shivering in my towel.

"Not yet, Jessa." His solemn tone makes me sad.

He almost sounds regretful, and I want to be back in the moment when he kissed me earlier.

"I don't like to be cold." A chill sinks into my skin, slowly stealing away the warm comfort I had in the shower.

His close proximity confuses me. Feelings I thought I had pushed down long ago surface, and somehow I feel a little smaller standing in front of him. The silence is paralyzing.

As if lost in his own world, he looks from me to my towel, then shifts his eyes to take in as much of the room as he can without turning his head. Then, breaking out of his frozen stance, he pulls his phone from his pocket. "Link, black out the room I'm in. No audio or video." He pauses to listen to the response, and when he speaks again, he sounds irritated. "It's a direct order from me. I'll deal with him later."

As he puts his phone down on the table, his eyes slowly move to the video camera in the corner of the ceiling. I turn to look in the same direction. The light on the camera is still on. Then, a moment later, it blinks off.

Our eyes meet again as we return to our original positions, and I stand still, frozen in uncertainty.

Taking two steps toward me, Jack stands flush with my damp body, and I take a step back to center myself. I can't afford to let my guard down.

He doesn't allow the space. He matches my step, and I take another, then another. We only stop when I collide with the cold wall, and even then he takes a final step, pinning me in place.

I lift my hand to his chest, trying to create space between us, but he doesn't allow it. As I brace my hand against his shirt, he lifts his arm, and he continues until his palm is on my throat. His fingers slowly wrap around my neck.

"I looked for you, Jessa. For a long time before I finally accepted you were dead. You need to know I did look. But I stopped. I accepted you were gone. But I never—not one day —stopped loving you." Then, leaning into my face, his lips just beyond my own, his voice is a murmur. "You were mine, and I was yours."

Chills prickle across my skin as goosebumps form over my entire body, and I clutch the thin towel wrapped around me.

This isn't the Jack I remember. It is him, but he's grown into this man standing in front of me.

"Jack, I—"

His actions steal the rest of my sentence as the warm fingers of his free hand graze the inside of my thigh.

Keeping his hand firmly around my neck, he's lost in his own thoughts as he looks over my face. As his eyes drop lower, his fingers trail higher. He stops just as he reaches the spot where my thighs touch, and he waits.

My eyes are locked tight onto his. Keeping his head in place, his eyes slowly move back to meet my stare.

"This is mine, Jessa." His voice is soft but demanding.

He refuses to look away. Drawing his fingers in small circles, he continues his path. I lose my composure and whimper as I capitulate to him.

My legs buckle, but I shift to strengthen my stance. Jack presses his body against mine, pinning me to the wall as his fingers find a sensitive spot, and I brace my hands on his arms, clutching at his shirt.

That simple move makes me vulnerable, and he takes advantage of my position. His weight against my body lifts briefly as a wave of cold air hits me. My eyes shoot open in time to see him dropping my towel to the floor.

I'm still pinned in place by his hand around my neck. In one move, his body is back against mine as he picks up where he left off.

I'm unable to restrain myself when he slips his finger inside of me. I moan loudly as his lips crash against mine, muffling my pleasure and physically laying claim over what we both know has always been his.

I abandon all rational thought as I lift my leg to wrap myself around him. He removes his hand from my throat to slide it under my ass, lifting me against him. Then he turns and moves across the room, kicking a chair to the side and placing me down on the table.

My heart pounds into my throat as I release my grip and lie back. The surface of the metal table is cold, but I no longer care.

There is only one thing I want right now.

CHAPTER 7

JACK

When Dana told me why my name was written over and over again in Jessa's notebooks, I dared to hope everything we had was still here.

The moment Jessa's back pressed up against the wall and I pinned her body in place, I knew she was still mine.

Her body trembled under my weight, no doubt partly from the cool air hitting her wet flesh after her shower. The goosebumps that swelled along her skin betrayed the calm composure she failed to project.

Her eyes flit around wildly, as I'm sure the man here with her now is nothing like she remembers.

She's a survivor and a fighter, doing what's necessary to stay alive. She created her own controlled atmosphere, but it's time to relieve her of that. She needs to know that the responsibility of keeping her safe can be shared. She doesn't need to walk alone any longer.

I never thought I would get the chance to tell her I never stopped loving her. I stopped looking. I stopped thinking, but I always loved her, and I open my old wounds as I tell her just that. "You were mine, and I was yours."

I've never wanted anything as fiercely as I want her right now, and this isn't up for discussion. *She belongs to me.* The thought is as natural as breathing, and a fervent urge to show her just what that means settles in.

"Jack, I—"

This conversation isn't hers to lead. I've suffered years without her, and this is my time.

Dropping my free hand under her towel, I gently touch her inner thigh, reining in her attention and bringing all of her focus to me.

Her eyes snap to mine, and I don't give her a chance to process her thoughts. "This is mine, Jessa."

It's not a request. It's not a question. This is me telling her we aren't done.

My need to know every inch of her pushes me dangerously close to insanity as I reach the apex of her thighs, which are firmly pressed together.

She watches me with rapt attention, waiting for me to lead. I'm seconds away from completely unraveling my barely contained calm and embracing the chaos.

"Jessa. You. Are. Mine."

Her mouth parts with a soft gasp; her lower lip trembles before she bites it. She exhales a shaky breath as she listens to my words. Closing her mouth, she swallows and steps her feet apart to allow me to continue—and I do.

Her eyes close as her head falls back, and I intensify my touch. In response, she lifts both hands to hold on to my shirt, leaving herself open to me. A heady need to see her bare consumes me, and I grab the towel from between us and remove it.

There are protocols to follow. There are rules that ensure we operate at peak performance—but none of them matter in this moment. As I return to touch the wetness between her thighs, she gives herself to me in a beautiful moan that I devour in a punishing kiss.

Her weight shifts. She lifts her leg to circle my waist when I step into her, and I pull her up and against me, carrying her across the room to the table.

The rest of the room fades into the background. There's only her.

My heart could explode, and I would be okay with that. I have the only thing I've ever wanted lying in front of me, giving herself to me.

Her curves are firm, and her breasts bounce softly as she adjusts herself for me on the table.

Then, not wasting another moment away from her, I move my hand to the waist of my pants and tear open the button, taking the zipper down with it. In one swift move, my pants are halfway down.

There's a place in the back of my mind where I wish we could go slow. I wish I had the control to be gentle and the time to show her how much I hurt when I lost her, but those are luxuries I no longer possess.

In one move, I end our anticipation.

I want the rest of the world to slip away—one ornery business partner included—but we can't be here together forever. These walls aren't soundproof, and I'd be surprised if no one was listening outside the door.

I should be the strong one who puts an end to this, who listens to reason, but the discord consumes my rationality. My need for her outweighs the castigation that awaits me.

Thick shadows fill the room around us, and only her silhouette against the small amount of light entering through the window is visible.

I want to turn the light on, to see all of her clear as day, but I can't risk the possibility that the camera might come back on at any minute.

A nagging thought in the back of my mind builds, and I glance at the camera up in the corner.

There it is. The little light shines into the room, telling me it's on.

Only one person could get that damn thing turned back on.

Logan.

I don't have time to think on this though. Not when I finally have Jessa back in my arms, and I'm not willing to cut my time with her any shorter than I have to. But at that angle, he can see everything.

She's not his to see.

Shifting her body down toward the edge of the table, I flip her over onto her stomach and step behind her, ready to take up where we left off.

Arching her back, she lifts herself off the table, and I reach into her hair to grab a fistful. I pull her head back, touching my lips to her ear so she can hear how she affects me.

Her body turns rigid. She attempts to move up the table and away from me, and I don't relent. I need her to understand this in all of its intensity.

I need her to feel what I feel.

I tighten my fingers around her hip. I know I'm going to leave a bruise, but I don't care. I want to see myself on her as proof that *we* still exist.

Her body shakes at the start of her release, and my growl answers her cry as we reduce ourselves to our base needs. We convulse together before a silence breaks me out of my hedonistic trance.

The room is now cloaked in darkness. The sound of her exhausted breath matches my own. I ease off and turn her to face me, running my hand down the full length of her body, imagining what she looks like by touch.

Out of the corner of my eye, the light on the camera catches my attention again, reminding me we are not alone, and the cameras have night vision.

Lifting her quickly, I move us to the cot, shoving her clothes to the floor. I pull back the sheet and slide her underneath, then slip in with her and cover us.

As we settle, I realize my mistake. Being caught up in the moment is no excuse. "I'm sorry. I didn't use—anything."

She pauses for a long moment, and I wonder briefly if she knows what I'm talking about.

"It's okay. I've been told I probably can't have kids," she says awkwardly, and my heart sinks.

She used to want kids—before.

Sensing my hesitation, she fills in the silence. "It's fine. I've accepted it." Then she pauses and shifts. Although I can't see her, I sense the moment she turns her face away from mine. "I was—in an accident a while ago. The doctor told me there was too much internal damage, and the chances of—that—are slim."

I open my mouth to tell her I'm sorry, but a loud knock at the door shatters our moment. "Playtime is over. My office in five minutes, Jack."

Logan's tone tells me this isn't going to be an easy conversation. I roll off the bed, pulling my pants up from my thighs.

A pang of guilt flashes through me that I can't spend more time with her. Our first time together after all of these years consisted of me not even getting my pants all the way off, and I silently vow to make up for it as I step to the light switch and turn it on.

I'm desperate to see her face again as I cross the small room and lean in to kiss her forehead.

A tentative smile graces her lips as I pull away.

I pick her clothes up from the floor and place them gently beside her. "Get dressed. The camera is back on, and it's getting late. Logan will want to question you in a bit."

"Who's Logan?"

I grit my teeth and wince. I'm already letting my guard down around her.

"He's the person behind Jekyll's code name. Look, I've promised not to interfere in your questioning. I can't be a part of it." At my words, she nods in understanding.

I'm too close to her to properly question her, and she knows it.

Where this leaves us, I'm not sure, but there is one thing I am certain of.

Now that I have her, I will never let her go.

CHAPTER 8

JESSA

As Jack opens the door to leave, one of the men who rode back with us enters the room, and Jack introduces him to me as "Grizz." I'm going to assume this is his code name, and it's fitting. He appears to be the most muscular of the group, and he stands a fraction taller than everyone else I've seen.

Grizz nods when he's introduced, then he addresses Jack. "I'm moving her in with her friend. Jekyll's orders. He'll question her in the morning." Then he glances at my state of undress. I pull the covers up to my neck, and he snaps his eyes back in awkward silence.

"Give her two minutes to get dressed." The Jack from moments ago is tucked away. His guard is firmly back in place.

What did we just do?

I forgot myself and our situation, and now I'm sitting here naked on a cot, watching him turn and leave the room with no further glance in my direction.

Once Grizz follows him out, shutting the door behind him to allow me some privacy, I slide out from under the warmth and safety of the covers to gather my things.

Then it catches my eye.

Like a moth to a digital flame, my attention instantly homes in on the table.

Jack forgot his phone.

I'm in the room alone, with a phone that no doubt has access to the internet, maybe more, and if I dig, I can probably access their servers from that one little device.

This is our ticket out.

Our freedom is lying on the table next to me, and my palms twitch at the thought of what I'm about to do.

I need to be smart about this.

I have two options.

I can give the phone back as a sign of good faith. That might go a long way in my interrogation with Logan.

Or I can keep it and use it to secure our freedom. But what kind of freedom is it if Dana and I are still trapped with Zane under Maxwell's demands?

Before I decide to run, I need to know if staying here is better for our final plan. If Jack and Logan want the same things, it might be better to hang around.

The bolt to my cell door clicks then slides unlocked, and I make the quick decision to keep the phone for now. I can give it back later, but I need more time to think about this.

Moving swiftly across the room, I grab the towel off the floor and toss it onto the table, concealing the phone as the door swings open and Grizz reenters the room.

Sliding my hand under the towel, I palm the phone and turn to the burly man standing in the entrance.

"I had a shower earlier. Where should I put the towel?" I pick up the towel and hold it out to him.

"Just leave it. Follow me." Then he turns his back to me and leaves the room.

I follow him out, dropping the towel onto the floor and sliding the phone into my back pocket.

Less than a minute later, another door groans on its hinges. As I enter, Dana stands from her chair and rushes to me.

As soon as Grizz closes the door, I'm met with a big hug. She hasn't hugged me like this in a while. We haven't been apart in a long time, and she's never been interrogated.

"Hey. I was wondering where they put you. You okay?" Her eyes are light with relief.

I break away and glance around the room. It's more comfortable than my last room, but the opportunity for escape is just as nonexistent. The beds look like real beds, and there are even a couple of comfortable chairs in the room, along with a small table to eat at.

"I'm okay. Don't get too comfortable. They probably put us together in the hopes that we'll talk and give them something they can use," I say.

Dana pinches her eyebrows together and straightens her spine.

The look on her face tells me she really didn't think they had an ulterior motive.

I walk to the two chairs and sit in one, curling my legs underneath me as Dana takes the other seat.

"How was your interrogation? Are you okay?" I keep the conversation simple.

I'm not ready to talk about Jack, and I don't want to make it easy for anyone listening in on our conversation.

"Yeah, I'm good. It was fine. That Jekyll guy is a little intense. He could use a tall, cold glass of chill the fuck out," she deadpans, forcing a chuckle through my lips. I haven't really laughed in a few days.

When we arrived at the farmhouse, I spent the first day checking the perimeter and making sure everything was set and working right.

Dana and I would be laughing and drinking margaritas under the stars on that little boat right now if it wasn't for them. Then I realize how much time has passed since they took us. Coming off of the adrenaline from my time with Jack, my body is sluggish, exhausted.

"Can we talk more about the interrogation in the morning? I'm tired. I think I need to sleep." I look over, and Dana's eyes are practically shut.

"Sure. It can wait. I'll tell you all about it in the morning. I call the bed furthest from the door." She stands and moves quickly, pulling the sheets back and sliding under the covers.

I walk to the entrance and hit the switch beside the door, then turn and make my way to my bed, careful to avoid the chairs in my path.

I close my eyes, quickly succumbing to exhaustion. We are running on fumes. My brain has been working on overdrive for the last few days. I need to recharge, or my emotions will begin to kick in, and I'll lose my focus.

CHAPTER 9

JACK

Logan doesn't bother to look up as I enter his office. His features are tight with disappointment as he writes something on a piece of paper. "I'm pretty sure I've said this a few times in the last twelve hours," he says, "but what the fu—"

"Save it. You knew this would happen the second you found out who she was. You said it yourself. I told you everything about her."

He leans back in his chair with an arrogant smirk inching across his face.

I look over his desk to his computer screen. The feed from the room Jessa was in with me is still open. He makes no attempt to hide that he saw us.

He's trying to push me into feeling shame, but I don't. Not one bit, and I never will where Jessa is concerned. Given the chance, I'd march into her room right now and pick up where we left off.

"Still." Leaning forward, he clicks the keyboard to change the view. Now it's Jessa and Dana in their new room, and she's turning out the lights. "You need to keep a level head, Jack. We don't have their whole story. We don't know where Zane is, or even who he is. We don't know what they do for Maxwell. That girl only told us what she thinks, and Jessa has kept her out of the loop for good reason. She only gave us hunches. I'll be interrogating your *girlfriend* in the morning, Jack. Your little fuck changes nothing."

Having Logan as a partner is a blessing and a curse. There is no one I trust my life with more, but at the same time, our personalities are so much alike that he constantly reminds me how insufferable I can be.

If the roles were reversed, I would be doing the exact same thing to him.

"I told you, I understand."

The phone rings, and Logan reaches over to pick it up, keeping his eyes on me, as if to tell me our discussion isn't over.

"Yes." As he listens, his expression sours, and his eyes stay locked on mine. "Give me a second." His lips curl into a snarl as he stands, then jabs the face of his phone and sets it on his desk. Placing his hands on either side of it, he speaks to the person on the other end, but he keeps his eyes trained on me. "Link, you're on speaker. Jack is here. Say that again."

"Our systems have been breached. We're working to see where it's coming from, but someone is in our servers who shouldn't be." I don't often hear Link in a panic. "We've shut down access on our sensitive areas and are working to secure everything else. There may be some disruptions in service on base."

Logan digs his fingers into the desk until his knuckles turn white. "Can you tell where it's coming from?"

"We have an initial report that it started on the compound. I don't understand it. Someone on base made an unauthorized connection with an external server. I'll know more by morning."

Not wasting any time, Logan ends the call. Then he looks back at me, steeling his expression, but I already know what he's thinking. The only change here is Jessa and Dana, and my stomach sours at the thought that I might be wrong about them.

"Jack." I cringe inwardly at my name. It's not so much my name as the way Logan is saying it. He's trying to prepare me for the worst-case scenario. "I'm willing to give them the benefit of the doubt—for you—but you need to understand we have a mission, and we need to know who is currently infiltrating us." He's talking to me like I'm a rookie, and I'm near the end of my patience.

I reach into my pocket to grab my phone. I need to get Hunter in here to help us figure out what is going on.

That's when I notice it—or the lack of it.

I check two more pockets, and my heart sinks into my stomach. Logan notices the change and aims a silent, questioning look in my direction.

"My phone. I don't have my phone."

Judging by Logan's clenched jaw, he's trying really hard to maintain his composure. "Where did you last have it?"

I don't want to answer him, but I need him to run this show. I won't stand in his way if his hunch is correct.

"With Jessa, in her room. Before we—"

Logan doesn't wait for the sordid details, and I'm thankful I'm not spelling it out.

He clicks away at his keyboard and pulls up the security footage to the moment I told Link to block access to Jessa's room. I dropped the phone on the table just before the screen went dark.

Less than a minute later, the feed comes back to life to show me removing Jessa's towel.

As he types away, the images on the screen fast-forward. When Grizz enters the room to speak to me, Logan slows it back down.

My phone is still on the table when Grizz and I exit to give Jessa time to dress.

Just as I think that I'll go and retrieve it from the room myself, I watch the expression on her face change.

She's noticed the phone.

A voice in the back of my head silently pleads with her to leave it be, but as I hear the sound of the door opening through the speakers, my world comes crashing in on me.

In an instant, she's hidden then pocketed the phone, making the choice to hide it from Grizz.

She could have left it on the table.

She could have handed it to Grizz.

She could have asked to see me.

She could have done so many things.

But she didn't.

Logan kills the feed with a scowl on his face.

Any kindness he may have reserved for Jessa is gone.

"Logan—"

I don't even know what I'm going to say next, but he isn't interested.

"Enough, Jack. She has your phone. A known hacker has your phone, and our systems are being breached by an outside server as we speak." He picks up his phone and barks his orders. "Grizz, meet me at the girls' holding cell, and tell Hunter to prep interrogation room one immediately."

Stepping out from behind his desk, he walks past me. As he reaches the door, he turns to me with a grim expression.

"I highly encourage you to sit this particular interrogation out, Jack. You are not to interfere. Remember that." Without another word, he turns to leave, and I follow him quietly down the hall.

I saw her betrayal with my own eyes.

I need to know what's going on, and I'm too close.

I'll let him question her.

I won't get in his way this time, no matter what happens.

I swear I've just closed my eyes when the door swings open and collides with the wall. Bright light from the hall streams into the room, disorienting me.

My whole body is exhausted, and even though I just fell asleep, my mind works to remember where I am.

One set of hands reaches out from the blinding light, picking me up out of my bed as Dana argues in the background.

"What's going on? Leave her alone." The panic in her tone jolts me conscious, and when I look past the burly man holding me up, I see Logan enter the room with Jack trailing quietly behind—and he looks rough.

"We're here for Jay. It's time to talk. You stay out of this." Logan's voice is cold, and a sudden fear grips me as I scramble to work out what has caused this change in our situation.

"Like hell you are. We've been cooperating. She needs to sleep. Look at her." There is fear in Dana's voice as she argues, and I realize I must be more out of it than I think I am.

Logan steps to me as he nods to the guy holding me, and the grip on me loosens.

"Sleep is for those who deserve it." Logan gets in my face. "Tell me, Blue Jay, do you feel you *deserve* to sleep?"

Something is definitely off, but my tired brain won't focus enough to sort it out. Jekyll is angry, and Jack is keeping out of it.

I open my mouth to speak, and Logan answers my unasked question for me.

Reaching around my waist and into my back pocket, he pulls something out. I try to focus on the item in his hand.

Then everything floods back to me.

I remember the choice I made—the wrong choice.

Dread grips me.

"I can explain..." I look over to Jack, who is still standing in the same place. He's detached from me and from the connection we just forged together. "Jack, I—"

"Jack isn't the one you are going to explain everything to." Logan steps between us, breaking our connection and demanding my attention. "And trust me, you are going to tell me everything I want to know." The threat in his voice tells me he keeps his word, and for the first time since the farmhouse, fear truly sets in. Straightening up, Logan takes a step back and looks to the man holding me. "Grizz, take her to room one."

A jerk on my arm sets me in motion, but my feet move in more of a shuffle as I struggle to follow. My body and mind are wholly exhausted. I'm not prepared to talk.

Grizz grabs my free arm with his other hand and almost lifts me to move me out of the room.

As I'm pulled down the hall, the men file out after me.

Dana yells something back in the room, but I can't make it out.

Above everything, the one thing that breaks through my exhaustion and sticks with me, the only thing I see right now, is the pain on Jack's face over my betrayal.

The walk was painfully long, and I tried to keep up so I didn't have to be carried.

When we enter the last room, Hunter, the one who walked me to the shower earlier, stops what he's working on and moves out of the way to allow Grizz some space to force me to sit.

The light in the room is bright—painfully bright—and I blink, struggling to adapt.

Grizz steps back, joining Hunter against the wall.

A third person enters the room. I know it's not Jack. He's told me he can't interfere, and after what he thinks I've done, I don't think he would, even if he could.

As Logan walks into my line of sight, I know all formalities are gone.

I'm being treated as a traitor.

My mind slowly catches up to the situation, but something doesn't fit.

I screwed myself when I took the phone, but they have to know I didn't do anything with it. An easy scan from a low-level computer team can see that. So why the hostility? This is excessive.

"Your friend almost had me convinced your intentions with your boyfriend, Zane, might be in line with ours." My breath hitches at Logan's insinuation as he turns to look me in the eye.

His demeanor has changed.

He isn't just asking questions. He's painting his own

picture of me. I've become his prey, and he's going to tear me apart if I don't diffuse the situation.

"I wasn't going to use it. I panicked when I saw it, then I forgot I had it. I would have returned it in the morning. I was just so tired."

My answer doesn't placate him. "You expect me to believe that after you fucked my business partner and stole his phone, you were just going to give it back? All while our servers are currently being hacked?" He makes no effort to mask his disdain as he bites out the accusation.

The other men in the room stay silent.

I'm catching up to his words when I realize what he's implying.

"What?"

I didn't use the phone.

I didn't access anything.

Then it hits me.

"Maxwell." It was just a whisper, and before I register that I've said his name out loud, Logan sees red and goes straight for my bared jugular like any predator would.

"Now, Jay, you're going to tell me exactly how you got into the servers so we can shut this down, and then I'll deal with you later."

"It wasn't me." My mind races with possibilities, and I speak as I process. A strong hunch bursts to the surface. "I think..."

I stop myself.

This isn't the time or place for my accusations.

If it wasn't me—and I know for absolute fact it wasn't Zane—then there is someone else here who opened access for Maxwell's pathetic little hacking team.

Someone here, and probably someone close to Logan and Jack.

They have a traitor among them.

Judging by the look in Logan's eyes, he isn't going to believe me, and neither will Jack right now.

In their eyes, I've done nothing but lie and keep secrets from them since they found us.

"You think what?" He challenges me to speak, to answer his question, but I don't, so he continues, "You know what I think? I think we aren't going to get anywhere treating you as...*nicely* as we have. I think you're going to start talking, and you are going to tell me everything. And I think you are going to do it on your own, or I'm going to tie you to this fucking table and beat it out of you." His anger flares.

There is no leniency in his tone. This is going to happen.

I see the two-way mirror on the wall. I know Jack is watching everything.

In my exhaustion, a flicker of a memory floats into my thoughts. I try to push it back, but it's too much. A hot tear falls down my cheek, and I take a deep breath.

I won't live through another interrogation.

Technically, I didn't live through the last one.

As sound and light seep from the room, memories of a belt and chains move to the forefront. A cold, wet floor in a dark room, my own eyes burning raw with tears until I had no more left to cry, an unbearable pain, and my throat sore from begging. Then a sneer dripping in pure evil decimates my clarity, and I only have one option left.

This time, I need to fight.

CHAPTER 11
JACK

When Logan threatens to tie Jessa to the table, the color drains from her face.

I lean closer to the two-way glass as a tear runs down her cheek.

A tense silence fills the interrogation room. Hunter and Grizz are frozen in their spots, watching Logan.

And Logan is watching Jessa.

If I can see her change in body language from here, Logan is definitely tuned in to her. He stands motionless, with his back to me and across the room from her, waiting for her to respond to his threat.

Taking a deep breath, she calmly moves her hands to the table. Then, as if in slow motion, she slides her chair back.

Something isn't right.

She doesn't seem aware of her surroundings any longer.

With her eyes on Logan, she slowly stands up. I remain frozen in place, wondering what on earth she thinks she's doing.

Stepping carefully to the side of the metal chair, she

raises a shaky hand and places it on the back of the seat she just occupied.

Logan nods to Hunter as he moves forward to sit her back down so he can continue. But as Hunter peels himself casually off the wall and takes a step toward her, all hell breaks loose.

In a flash of a second, Jessa lifts the chair and hurls it in Hunter's direction, catching him off guard and hitting him square in the head. He falls back toward the wall with a grunt.

In reaction, Grizz and Logan lurch toward Jessa.

Grizz is closer.

She's too small to win any fair fight with the guy, and she knows it.

Spinning quickly, she crouches and puts all of her weight behind her punch, hitting Grizz square in the groin, and he buckles.

Jessa isn't holding anything back. She truly believes she's fighting for her life. Her face is void of any expression, and Logan is too consumed to notice how caged she is as he continues to move in on her.

She spins back around, and her fist flails at anything, hoping to connect. Her prayers are answered as she hits Logan square in the jaw.

His head snaps to the side, and he takes a step back, raising his hand to the spot where she hit him.

I take a half step to the door, but then I stop. I want to diffuse the situation, but my presence won't help anyone. She deceived us, and my heart isn't in the right place. Now she's chosen to fight, and she needs to learn that her actions carry consequences.

Jessa quickly scans the room. I wonder where she

learned her moves. She's not trained in anything in particular, but she is holding her own, though I know it won't be long before the situation is back under control, and Logan is going to make her pay for her outburst.

As my team fights to regain their composure, Jessa reaches out as she lunges for Logan's belt. Before he can grab her hands, she flips the heavy metal clasp, and, lifting her foot to his stomach, she kicks him back as she pulls it out of the loops. Stepping back from the three men in the room, she folds the belt and holds it up as a weapon, with the buckle ready to maim.

"Now, now, Jay. We're just talking." Logan raises his hands to show he's unarmed, and he stays still as Grizz and Hunter flank the sides of the room in an attempt to cage her in.

"STAY WHERE YOU ARE. DON'T MOVE. JUST STOP." Her voice is raised to a high pitch, and both men freeze.

Logan steps cautiously toward Jessa, and she nervously shifts in place. Her poker face is gone, and her eyes dart around the room. All signs point to extreme anxiety, and I'm beginning to worry about her.

Logan isn't backing down.

He's locked into her fear, and he keeps pushing.

Why wouldn't he? This is where he reigns. Dealing with disobedience and doling out pain and punishment is his specialty.

Jessa is cornered.

Her fear has gripped her, and this is where Logan has her. He won't let her escape behind her guarded façade.

"Sit down now, and we'll pretend like this never happened." He gives her an out she is too far gone to use.

She will defy him, and he will show her what he's capable of. Then we'll know everything. Her fight is futile. She just doesn't know it yet.

From her left, Hunter makes a motion to move on her, but he pulls back just as she draws her arm back to strike. Grizz jumps in from behind, grabbing her wrist and holding her in place.

"NO! DON'T!" she cries as Logan moves directly in front of her, cupping his fingers under her chin and lifting her head up to force her to meet his eyes.

He looks at her for a few long seconds.

"You're hiding something from me, and I'm going to find out what it is." Then he speaks to our men without looking away. "Tie her to the table."

At his quick escalation, everyone in the room freezes.

Everyone except Jessa.

She's struggling in Grizz's arms. Her crazed eyes flit around the room, but she isn't focusing on anything. My heart breaks over the tough road she chose to walk.

Instead of fighting, she tries to pull away and sink into herself.

"Please. Don't do this." She is in a state of panic, and a bad feeling creeps into my bones.

Jessa is tired. More than tired. Her body and mind are exhausted, and I realize neither of the women have eaten since we took them. All of this will work in Logan's favor, but not Jessa's.

Logan towers over Jessa's trembling form. Grabbing her wrist tight over Grizz's grip, he takes his belt back from her and doubles it over before holding it in front of her face. "You're very good with my belt. Now it's my turn." He bites out his words, then motions to Grizz to move her to the table.

She jerks back as the front of her thighs hit the cold metal surface.

"Please, don't do this. Help me. No." She's pleading now, and I reach for the door handle, but her next words sober me in place. "No, Max. Don't do this."

Her body visibly trembles, and Logan shoots a warning glare to the mirror.

Stay put. That's the message I get loud and clear, and it takes everything I have not to go to her.

Something is wrong.

Jessa's fighting something that none of us see, and for all five and a half feet of her, she is extremely strong in her duress. It takes all three men to subdue her.

"Get the restraints," Logan barks to Hunter, who breaks away from the group and moves quickly to the box in the corner as Jessa struggles to break away.

Hunter secures each ankle to a leg of the table. Then he moves to hand Logan the last two zip ties before taking over Logan's spot holding Jessa down.

Grizz watches as he holds Jessa in place. He's unsure of Logan's approach since we've never done anything like this before. I stay still, certain that this interrogation won't go much further.

This isn't who we are.

As he moves around the table, Logan's eyes don't leave Jessa. Her use of Max's name isn't lost on either of us. He's carefully trying to determine the best way forward with her in the headspace she's in.

He grabs one of her wrists and secures it quickly so she feels the jerk of being tied down. She fights to keep her other arm, her last bit of freedom, away from his grasp.

He effortlessly reaches under her and pulls her arm out with ease.

Her body has exhausted itself.

Now it's just her mind.

He drops his voice down low, forcing her to focus on his words. "We could have done this the easy way. Now we're going to do it my way. Just remember, you brought this on yourself. It's time to sing, my little blue jay."

He roughly secures her wrist into its final position, and she no longer has the freedom to move. Her body tenses as all three men step back.

Grizz and Hunter resume their spots on the wall, while Logan remains close. He towers over her in a show of dominance, and she lifts her head to look at her hands in their restraints.

Tentatively, she attempts to pull her arms back to her, then she jerks her body.

As Logan starts with his interrogation, my phone, which Logan retrieved from Jessa earlier, rings in my pocket. Link's information flashes on the caller ID, and I hope he has something we can use to question her with.

"Sorry, Jack. Logan isn't answering. We're working to secure everything. I wanted to tell him the hack didn't come from your phone."

The room tilts as I pause before diverting my full attention from Jessa to Link. "What? But then how did she—"

Link jumps in. "That's the thing, Jack. The initial breach came from near the file room."

"I don't understand." Neither Jessa nor Dana have been on that side of the base yet. Not even close.

"Jesus, Jack. I don't know how to say this." Link's tone is

strained. "The malware that initiated the breach tonight was uploaded to a file on our servers shortly after we established operations here—five years ago. It sat dormant, waiting for access, and last night it was granted."

"Could she have granted access?" I ask, not sure I want to know the answer.

"I'm confident it wasn't her. I reviewed the tapes; she only grabbed your phone. She had no access to anything else, and I ran your records. From the time she had it until you and Logan retrieved it and turned it on, she didn't use it. She didn't even attempt to power it up. She's telling the truth. I need to get back to this. I'll update when I know more." The click in my ear signals the end of our conversation, but the shock of his findings stuns me, and I stare stupidly at my phone.

I'm suddenly jolted back to our present situation with a gut-wrenching scream.

When I look back into the interrogation room, I find Logan fighting to hold Jessa down as she screeches out another wail, and this time it registers.

She's yelling my name.

"Jack, I need to sedate her." Logan is looking into the glass.

I move quickly to the cabinet on the wall in the observation room. Grabbing a small medical bag, I run to the interrogation room to find all three men holding her to the table as she fights hard to escape.

Anger surges through my veins. "What the hell," I growl, but Logan stops me.

"No time. She's going to hurt herself on the ties if she keeps struggling. I need it now," he yells at me above her screams.

I unzip the bag, pull out a syringe, and search for the vial I need.

"No, get the midazolam. She's struggling too much for a needle," Logan shouts as he continues to use most of his weight to keep her down. He holds her arms in place so she can't slice her wrists against her binds.

Dropping the syringe, I pull out a small bottle and twist off the cap as I slide toward Jessa. Handing the bottle to Logan, I take his place pinning her down, and he tilts her head up and slides the tip into one of her nostrils to shoot the mist into her nasal cavity.

As soon as it's in, he drops the bottle and covers her mouth so her only option is to breathe in through her nose.

"She's already exhausted. This should only take a couple of minutes." Logan's voice is all business, but confusion mars his features.

What triggered this level of anxiety in her?

Minutes feel like hours as her body slowly loses the last of its strength. She's no longer articulate, and her eyes are vacant.

As she relaxes, the three of us move away from her, leaving Logan to monitor her. Hunter and Grizz both look pale as Logan leans over her and brushes the sweat-soaked hair out of her face.

Her cries turn to murmurs, and my heart breaks as I fail to imagine what hell she's locked herself in.

"Shh, Jessa. Go to sleep. It's okay. Just relax." Logan is concerningly gentle.

Never in the time I've known him has he ever shown a kindness like this. He's almost brotherly toward her.

As she relaxes against her binds, Logan gestures for

Hunter and Grizz to quietly leave the room, and they are all too happy to obey.

Jessa's eyes flutter shut, and I move back to the table to wrap my arms around her.

Logan frees her arms and legs, and I roll her into my arms, hooking one hand under her knees while the other hugs her upper body to my chest. Her wrists are raw and wrapped in angry red lines where her skin almost broke open.

"Take her to the room across the hall from Dana. I'm not in the mood to deal with that spitfire tonight. I need to process a few things before we talk. I'm going to sleep." Logan turns to leave, but I can't let him go yet.

Not after what just played out in front of me.

"Logan, what happened? I took a call from Link, and when I looked back up, you guys were piled on top of her, and she was screaming for her life." I stop, and a hard silence fills the room as Logan's eyes roam over Jessa in my arms.

He looks regretful, which is another first for him.

"I pushed her too hard. She's keeping something from us. Whatever it is, she's pushed it far down. I thought I had her ready to tell us what we need to know about the hack, but she kept sinking. She said Maxwell's name again, but I don't sense they are accomplices. I think she's terrified of him. Then I grabbed her hair to focus her on our conversation, and she snapped and screamed your name. That's just before I called you in." He glances at Jessa, and I follow his line of sight. She's out cold against my chest.

"It wasn't her." I don't want a repeat of this in the morning. "Link called. We've had some kind of vulnerability in our server for years. It was activated last night, from near the file room."

Not taking his eyes off Jessa, Logan knits his brows in thought. "Jack." He's drained. "Put her to bed. Get some sleep. We'll revisit this in the morning. I'll have Grizz talk to Dana so she gives her some time."

Walking out ahead of us, he turns left. I turn right, toward her new room.

Her soft murmurs tug at my heart as I lay her down on the bed. She's both helpless and strong, and I will find out what she's keeping from us. But first I need to wrap my arms around her and comfort her.

Stepping out of my shoes, I kneel on the bed beside her and gently remove her sneakers. I smile to myself at my tender handling of her feet. She's so sedated that we could be under aerial attack and she would sleep through it, and I'm worried I'm going to wake her with something so mild.

Reaching to the foot of the bed, I pull the covers over us as I instinctively slide in beside her and wrap myself around her slumbering form.

I may not be able to protect her from the monsters in her head yet, but I sure as hell will protect her from everything else.

CHAPTER 12

JESSA

When I closed my eyes last night, sleep hit me harder than I thought it would.

I roll over, then pause, holding my breath as the scent of cinnamon and sex registers.

Jack.

We had sex.

I had sex with Jack.

But something is off.

I fell asleep alone last night.

"You can open your eyes, Jessa. I know you're awake." Jack chuckles deeply as he kisses the top of my head.

"I didn't hear you come in last night." Then I look over to the other bed—that isn't there. "Where's Dana?"

Inching his body back and dropping his head, he takes a long look at me. "Dana's in her own room. Logan thought you might want some privacy after last night."

Confusion swirls around me, and I think out loud. "Why would I want privacy? Did someone move me? Or did someone move Dana?"

His hesitation sets off warning bells, and I struggle to

remember what happened after I was brought into Dana's room.

I attempt to sit up, and a throb at the back of my skull makes me wince. I lift my hand to my face to hold the pain back, and that's when I see them.

Thin red lines circle my wrists. Some more prominent than others.

"What the..." I pull my other hand out from under the sheet to examine it. The marks are there too. "What happened?"

Jack doesn't answer.

His body has gone tense around me.

Something obviously happened last night, and I don't remember any of it.

Before I ask my next question, the door swings open, and Logan walks into the room carrying two mugs.

The smell of chocolate fills my nose, and I push myself up and swing my legs over the side of the bed.

"Jack told me once that you used to love his morning coffee, and his secret was adding cocoa powder and a little caramel. I had to improvise and use Grey's caramel ice cream topping." He rolls his eyes and continues, "You'll have to tell me how this measures up."

I reach for the mug but pull my hand back.

Logan's different.

Something happened since I last saw him.

We stare at each other for a long minute. The smell calls to me again, and I reach for the coffee. Then I remember.

I have Jack's phone.

"Wait. Jack, I just remembered. I'm sorry. I was so tired last night. I took your phone. I swear I didn't use it." I hope he believes me as I reach around to my pocket to pull out something that isn't there. "Um, just a minute. I must have dropped it in my sleep." I pat down the sheets.

Both men exchange a glance, and I hope I haven't lost what little trust they had in me.

"It's okay, Jessa." Jack's smile has always calmed me. My confused look must have been an invitation to continue, and he does. "It was returned to me last night."

I feel like I'm missing something. Like I'm the only one not in on the whole story. My confidence slips as I slouch back, but Logan pulls me back to his conversation.

"Here." He hands the coffee over, and I lift it to my nose to smell it before taking a sip. Jack's coffee was always my favorite. "Just wait a bit. It's hot."

"Is that mine?" Jack asks as he swings his legs over the side of the bed and into his shoes.

"No. Go get your own," Logan answers incredulously, not taking his eyes off me. "I thought Jessa and I could have a little talk." He raises the second mug, claiming it as his own.

"I'm not sure that's a good idea." Jack sets his palm on my lap.

"Jessa's okay with me. We'll sit over there." Logan tilts his head in the direction of a sofa. When I look back to Jack, he isn't quick enough to hide the uncertainty in his eyes. "I'll leave the door open, and I've granted your phone access to the security feed. You can keep an eye on us and send in that delightful friend of hers if you're not happy."

I snort into my cup at the absurd thought of Dana being *delightful* to anyone here.

I still don't know what's going on, but I have a feeling that Logan, in all his abrasiveness, is going to tell me.

Jack has made it his priority to protect me, and I need to know what happened so I can figure out how to deal with it.

As Jack leans forward to speak for me, I grab his arm to get his attention, and he immediately stills and turns to me.

"It's okay," I say. "I'll be fine. Why don't you grab a cup of coffee and come back and join us? Is that okay?" I offer as an option.

Logan shrugs, and Jack considers it. Their mutual stare is intense, but Jack's lips remain sealed, keeping all the things he wants to say locked away in his head.

Leaning in, he places a soft kiss on my forehead before walking toward the door. When he glares at his partner, Logan doesn't flinch.

"Shall we?" His cordial tone is such a contrast to yesterday, and I wonder if anyone really knows the real Logan.

Exchanging the bed for the couch, I tuck one leg under me and sit down, blowing on my coffee and enjoying the smell. Logan sits on the other side of the couch, placing distance between us.

Stealing a glance at Jack's friend while he makes himself comfortable, I see a lot of similarities between them. They carry themselves in almost the same way. Logan's every move is methodical, yet, if I hadn't met him before, I would say he is extremely personable right now.

Logan unzips his jacket and leans back against the couch to get comfortable. Matching him, I attempt to relax into the cushions. The ridges in his shirt show an athletic build. My eyes travel up until I meet his gaze and realize he's been doing the same to me.

The silence is right at the border between natural and awkward when he breaks it.

"What's the last thing you remember from last night, Jessa?" He's using my name. Not my nickname, not the name he gave me, but my name, and his voice is full of concern.

Something tells me whatever answer I give isn't going to be the right one, so I look into my coffee for a quiet minute as I try to remember.

The last thing I remember is being in the room with Dana. I remember being tired, and we went to sleep.

But I know that can't be all of it.

Dana didn't wake up in our room this morning.

Looking down at the couch, I realize it's me who isn't in the same room. Our room didn't have a couch.

"I'm in a different room." I say it as a statement, but I mean it as a question.

"Yes. But you don't remember how you got here. What is the last thing you remember?" He repeats his question.

"Falling asleep with Dana in a different room."

Now I'm worried, and I know it's written all over my face. Jack has his phone back. I have marks all over my wrists, and I'm in a different room.

His eyes don't leave me, and his face is unreadable. "It's okay, Jessa. I want to help you. I think, in the end, we both want the same thing." The hairs on the back of my neck stand on end. As I remember they have their own agenda, and I'm merely a pawn, my guard slowly returns, and I wonder if he notices.

"And what is that?" I ask slowly as my eyes leave his and move to my coffee. I was never good at staring contests.

He answers without hesitation. "We both want Maxwell and every part of his operation completely gone and your freedom to do as you wish."

This guy is good.

"Really? Are you honestly telling me you're interested in

my freedom? There is no such thing as amnesty for people like me." I pause, looking for a sign that he disagrees, but he doesn't offer one. "My skills have reduced me to nothing more than a tool to be used. Zane works hard to keep us hidden. When Maxwell is gone, another will come looking for us in his place. Don't tell me you wouldn't do everything in your power to keep me even if you knew where Zane was."

I'm proud of my calm composure. There is no anger in my tone.

His eyes land on me as he considers my words. He knows I'm right. I'm currently his prisoner, and even if there was no reason to keep me any longer, he wouldn't let me go.

"I get it. I've accepted it. No one else made the choices that led me to Zane, thereby making me a priceless commodity. You didn't come here to talk about my freedom."

A devious smile creeps across his lips. "You are very perceptive. I see why Jack cares for you."

"Did I hear my name?" Jack calls from the doorway, pulling our attention away from each other.

"Ah, good. I was waiting for you before we continued. I thought you'd want to be here for the next part," Logan answers, then turns back to me. Pulling his phone out of his jacket, he continues, his voice still comforting, "Jessa, something did happen last night. But before I show you, I have one last question. What happened when Maxwell had you for those seven days Dana told us about?"

As my grip around my mug tightens, my body turns heavy, and I force my expression to stay in place.

He couldn't have asked a worse question.

CHAPTER 13
JACK

My composure is long gone as I speed walk down the hall, trying not to spill my coffee. I shouldn't have filled it to the top.

After casually exiting the room where Logan had Jessa to himself, I all but ran to the dining area to grab my coffee.

Dana was seated off to the side with Grizz while they ate breakfast. I moved quickly and quietly to avoid speaking with her. It didn't seem to matter much. They were deep into a conversation, and she didn't notice me until I was almost done.

I settled for black coffee, deciding against making it the way I usually like so I could leave as stealthily as I entered. I managed to make it to the door before Dana called my name.

Weighing my options, I chose to pretend I didn't hear her, and I hustled back to Jessa's room just in time to hear my name.

Attempting a casual entrance, I lean against the doorframe to catch my breath and steady myself when both sets of eyes turn toward me.

My first instinct is to go to Jessa, but I push it down and stay in my spot, giving Logan some time with her.

Logan asks her point blank what happened with Maxwell, and her face fall for a fraction of a second before she clears her throat and recovers. "Why do you want to know about that?"

It's not lost on either of us that she's stalling by answering a question with a question. My guess is she's attempting to buy herself time.

"Jessa, I'm going to show you some of our security feed from last night, and this may be shocking for you. I need you to talk to us after you've seen it." Logan's concern for Jessa is comforting, but only to me.

Jessa's gaze slowly shifts between Logan and the phone sitting in his hand. "Let me see it—please."

She leans forward, placing her mug on the floor in front of her. She reaches for the phone as Logan slides a little closer to her to watch the screen and her reaction to it.

Jessa startles as the sound of her own screams erupts from the phone. He's showing her the end of her night, just before I rushed in with the tranquilizer.

She sits as still as a statue as she watches herself, restrained to the table, screaming my name. I lean to the side to get a better look at her, and I notice Logan is doing the same thing.

Jessa's eyes are wide. She hasn't blinked since the video started. She flinches at the sound of her screeching my name one last time, then quickly taps the face of the phone to pause it.

Her eyes remain locked on the screen as she sits frozen in silence. Logan carefully takes his phone back, turns it off, and slips it into his jacket.

He makes no move to say anything further, allowing her space to process the time from last night she doesn't remember.

She drops her hands lifelessly into her lap and traces one marked wrist with her index finger. Then slowly, raising her eyes, she glances in my direction. I offer a soft nod to let her know I'm here for her, and she moves her gaze back to Logan.

"I don't remember that." If the room weren't silent, I would never have heard her.

"I know, Jessa."

"Wh-why was—I—" An awkward tension floods the room as Jessa tries to make sense of what she just watched.

She doesn't need to find the rest of her words. I know exactly what she wants to know.

She wants to know what the hell she was doing bound to a table with three men around her. Logan knows it too, so he answers her.

"We had a misunderstanding last night—with Jack's phone. You were treated as an uncooperative interrogation because, at the same time we discovered you had Jack's phone, we also learned our servers were breached."

Jessa's arms go up in defense. "But I didn't—"

"We know you didn't use the phone. That's not what I want to talk about. During the questioning, you said Maxwell's name a couple of times. We're concerned for you. Jack is worried. We can't help you if you don't tell us what he's done."

Logan attempts to include me in the conversation, to get her to open up, but I'm not sure it's going to work. Jessa has always protected those around her. If she thinks this information will hurt me in any way, she'll shut down.

"He—he asked me questions about Zane. Where he was, stuff like that." Her answer is short.

She's trying to protect herself—or me.

"Dana said you were gone for over six days. What did he do?" His question is direct, and she shifts uncomfortably in her seat.

"He and his men. They interrogated me. Just like you are. They wanted to know where Zane was. I wouldn't tell them. I couldn't. We don't share our location with each other, ever—this is why. They cut my food and water and stuck me in a cage outside for a night." She shrugs to deflect the severity. "Stuff like that."

When she crosses her arms defensively, I sense there is more. Logan must feel it too.

"Jessa, it's just us. Tell us what he did." There is no animosity or challenge in his tone. Logan's expression is blank.

"There isn't anything else to tell." She shifts her glance away from him, over to me, but she won't make direct eye contact.

She's lying.

"You know that's not true, Jessa." Logan eases in. "I've been doing what I do for a long time, and people don't react this intensely to low-level interrogations. You weren't just questioned, were you?"

Jessa shakes her head. She's not denying his words. There's a level of urgency in the way she jerks her head from side to side. She's silently pleading for him to stop, but he doesn't.

"You were tortured."

All color drains from her face, and her lips pinch

together. She looks like she's barely keeping her composure, and the cracks are beginning to show.

I slump hard into the doorframe as the blood drains from my head.

Tortured.

I didn't see it, but it fits, and my heart shatters for Jessa sitting quietly on the couch, lost and unsure of herself.

Now I won't stop until I know everything.

I'll kill Maxwell myself.

Shifting off the doorframe, I take a step toward Jessa, determined to get an answer for every question.

Two steps into the room, and I'm suddenly pushed aside as Dana enters and barrels toward Jessa, shifting the tension around us. Grizz hangs back by the door.

"There you are. I woke up and you were still gone. I was worried something happened when they took you last night. They told me to let you sleep."

The moment Jessa hears Dana's voice, her whole demeanor changes.

A smile so big and relaxed hides her pain as she recovers to keep her secret from her friend.

"Oh, they asked me some questions and didn't want to wake you when it was over, so they gave me my own room. Everything's okay." She makes eye contact with both Logan and me. Before either of us can say a thing, she leans over and grabs her coffee off the floor, taking one big gulp as she stands. Then, turning to Logan, she hands him her empty mug. "Thanks for the coffee, and the chat."

Logan blinks a couple of times before recovering. "I have some more questions. But they can wait. I have a couple of things to do. Jack, join me in my office for a few?" He nods at the women as he passes by me and exits the room.

"Dana, Jessa." I acknowledge both before I continue, "Jessa, I'd like to talk to you later—alone." I don't wait for her response. She'll be talking to me later whether she wants to or not.

I won't let this go until I know everything she's hiding. I can't protect her if I don't know what she's up against.

From the corner of my eye, I see Dana smirk at my request. I know where her mind is going, but the sobered look on Jessa's face tells me she knows exactly what I want.

Good.

I leave the women with Grizz and make a beeline for Logan. I want answers now, and I know he has some.

As I enter his office, I catch the end of his conversation with Link, who's on speaker.

"So you can confirm no one was in the comms room when I was talking to Jessa just now? No one heard the conversation we just had?" Logan looks up from his phone and motions for me to take a seat.

"Confirmed. I called in a room clear just before you walked in. Tex and Waldo were in there running reports and writing up their evals like you asked them to. Hunter was assisting them, and Eagle was listening in and providing intel. No security feeds were being monitored, and all four men cleared the room when I called it in." Link's voice echoes over the phone.

"Send the recording of my talk with Jessa to my computer, then remove it from the feed in the comms room and store it off-site. I also want a list of everyone on base who was on their phone or logged on to any of our computers from the time we arrived at base yesterday until midnight. Keep this between us." Logan is deep in thought and watching my reaction as he leans over and hangs up without saying goodbye.

He's not one for pleasantries when he has the scent of something.

"So, where do you want me to start?" Logan asks with a look that tells me he already knows my answer.

"Torture? You could have warned me before you dropped that bomb."

"I wasn't sure until I saw her reaction to the footage. I'm sorry, Jack. Until we know what happened, I can't help her. You know that." Then, leaning back in his seat, he reaches for a bottle of water on the desk, twisting off the cap and taking a long drink before continuing, "We need to talk about something else. Last night. You're right. The hack wasn't Jessa."

There it is. The elephant in the room. I know what this means, and so does Logan. Leaning across the table to grab my own bottle of water, I take a big gulp before saying the last thing any of us wants to hear. "It's one of us."

Logan sits silently for a minute, disappointment etched onto his face.

This means it is one of our own trusted team members. One of our own over a known hacker. This was something neither of us saw coming, and it's a tough pill to swallow.

Logan takes a deep breath, then hangs his head in acceptance. "Process of elimination leads me to believe it isn't either of us, or Link. I can't be one hundred percent sure about anyone else until we rule them out. Link's on it."

I mutter a profanity under my breath.

Until everyone else is cleared, we can't trust anyone. When Link was hired, his own paranoia about accountability led him to set up a cross monitor on himself.

His own team would have reported him for anything out of the ordinary. On top of that, he started with us about three years ago, which is two years after the initial malware was uploaded.

"So, for now, we keep this information between us. Look, Jack, I know I'm an asshole for saying this, but we need Jessa to get in touch with Zane. We need both of them on our side if we have any chance of taking Maxwell down. You know if that happens, his old man might be forced out of retirement, and we can end it all."

He looks at me for understanding. I know he's right. It's going to take all of us, working together, to eviscerate their empire. But I also know asking Jessa for this right now will backfire. She has her back up against the wall, and she already doesn't feel safe here.

She figured out we had a mole during the interrogation, and she almost tried to warn us, but she stopped herself. She knew we wouldn't have believed her, not then.

"I know we do, but you need to give Jessa a little time to bounce back. Just let her breathe for a bit, okay? Tonight is downtime. The guys will be hanging out in the common area. I'll ask the women to join us. Play some cards, watch a movie, sing karaoke...whatever. Everyone should be there. We can monitor the guys too. See if anything is off," I offer, hoping to buy Jessa some time to find her way back to a clear head and a safe space.

Logan considers my request. I can tell he agrees with me. He just hates that I'm the voice of reason.

"I'll allow that." Taking one last gulp of water before ending our meeting, he slides his chair back and looks me straight in the eyes. "But I'm not singing karaoke. No matter what."

CHAPTER 14

JESSA

Watching yourself experience something you don't remember is surreal. Less than twenty-four hours ago, I needed to be restrained and drugged, and I don't remember any of it.

Logan only played that small part of the video, and I can't stop obsessing over everything he didn't show me.

What did I say? I couldn't have given them much to go on, or things would be in motion today, and Dana and I would most likely be locked away, for our protection—and theirs.

Still, my curiosity is getting the better of me, and I wish I had a distraction. I wish I could sit down at a computer and lose myself in some code.

I haven't gone this long without putting my hands on a keyboard in years. If Dana knew how much time I really put in, how late I'd work after she turned in at night, she'd have me committed.

I have an endgame with Zane, and I am so close to crossing the finish line and cutting all of us free.

Being captured, especially by Jack, wasn't part of the

plan though, and I still need to work out how to execute everything and take down Maxwell with these new obstacles.

Having a computer would solve so many issues right now.

Instead, I'm banned from anything that needs power, and I'm currently under strict supervision. I got up to turn on a light earlier, and the young one they call Grey looked like he was going to tackle me.

A quick glance at the door tells me Eagle is the poor sucker charged with babysitting us today. It could be worse. At least he responds when we speak to him.

What I wouldn't give to touch a keyboard right now.

"Penny for your thoughts?"

I jump out of my scheming to see Dana bouncing where she sits on my cot.

"Just wondering what happens to us now, you know?" Which isn't a complete lie.

"Hmm. I thought maybe you were thinking about a certain someone from your past. You know, a certain *hunky* someone, maybe?" She waggles her eyebrows at me as she attempts to pry.

The look on her face takes me back to high school. To the night I told her I had a crush on the new kid in school, and his name was Jack.

I remember it like it was yesterday, yet it also feels like it was someone else's lifetime ago.

Jack was nothing like the other boys in school.

He never cared to prove himself to anyone around him. He never went out of his way to be the popular kid, but he was liked by everyone.

Well, almost everyone.

He and Maxwell never got along, but they tolerated each other around me. I always thought Max was a good friend. It wasn't until Jack showed up that I clearly saw the jealousy he somehow hid from me.

I remember Dana slept over at my place one night. It was close to Halloween. We decided we would watch a horror movie together, then we were going to fall asleep with the lights on and one flashlight each. We had it all planned out—until I told her how I felt about Jack. Then we spent the rest of the night talking about boys and what we thought our first time would be like.

"Maybe I was thinking about him. This is all so..."

"Crazy? I mean, what are the odds? Like, if I was reading it in a book, I'd be all like, *That's one hell of a coincidence right there*," she jokes, and I smile. She always knows how to make me laugh. "He hasn't changed, really," she continues. "Except he's kind of bossy, and he smells like cookies. I can't quite put my finger on it."

"Cinnamon. He smells a little like cinnamon." I chuckle, and Dana's face lights up in agreement.

A throat is cleared near our open door, and I look over to see Grizz standing in the entryway.

Dana jolts to her feet and smooths out her pants. Her tone flips on a dime. "Oh, hey," she sings out as I watch her tilt her head to the side.

"Hello, Dana." The burly man at my door nods his head at her, and my senses tingle.

These two have obviously spent some time together, and I'm not the only one keeping secrets.

"Tonight is downtime. Most of us usually end up in the common room, to play games or watch movies, and Jack

mentioned you both would probably be joining us tonight."
He takes a minute to shuffle in place. "I was wondering if
you ladies would like to walk down with me later. I'll show
you where it is. If we get there early, you could pick the
movie, and I have a bottle of wine I picked up the last time I
was in California that I've been saving."

I may as well be invisible.

Neither has looked my way since he started speaking.
When I glance at Dana, I'm met with something I'm not sure
I've seen before. She's close to being a puddle on the floor. I
don't think she realizes he's stopped talking and it's her
turn now.

I almost can't keep myself from bursting at their mutual
interest as I answer for the both of us. "We would love that.
Thank you."

"Great. I'll be back in a few hours. How about just after
dinner?"

Dana nods, and he leaves us to our conversation.

Except I'm no longer interested in the conversation we
were having.

"Care to share, Dana Bear?" I stand, then tuck my legs
under myself as I sit back down on the sofa to get
comfortable.

"What?" I can tell by the way she shrugs her shoulders
that she already knows I don't believe her for one minute.
"Fine. We were talking earlier this morning, over breakfast,
and he was really easy to talk to. We have some things in
common. His real name is Michael. He's actually a great guy.
Well—for someone who is holding us against our will, I
guess." Then half a worry creeps into her smile. "Wait. Do
you think I have that Swedish disease?"

"Stockholm syndrome?" I laugh. "No, I think you're okay. I'm starting to get the feeling we've been captured by the good guys after all."

"Phew." She smiles, feigning a wipe of her brow in relief. "Because he is hella cute. It'd be a shame to hurt him during our escape." As she opens her mouth to continue, I cut her off.

"You know they are listening to us, right?" I point to the camera, and her hand shoots up to her mouth. I knew she forgot. "I am in need of some fun tonight. Don't ruin this for me. Your jokes about escape are just going to get us locked up."

Looking toward the camera, Dana flashes an innocent smile and waves. Then she stands. "Let's check out the kitchen. You didn't eat breakfast, and we've been talking so long we missed lunch. Maybe we can grab a snack, then hit the showers." She heads toward the door. "Hey, are you the one they call Easy?" She flashes a wink in my direction. She gets off on taunting people almost as much as Logan seems to.

"Eagle." The lean man propped up against the wall does not share our appreciation of a good jab.

"Oh, right. Well, you missed lunch too. We'd like to go to the kitchen and grab a snack."

I stand and follow her out in agreement. A rumble in my stomach tells me she's right about food. I am hungry.

I also need her to show me around here a little more, so I can get a better idea of what I'm up against. I know Logan and Jack say they're on our team, but my final play differs from theirs, and I need to keep working toward my original goal in case things go sideways.

If I am successful with Zane, when Maxwell goes down, everyone will have their freedom. Not just from him, but from anyone who might take his place.

I just need a few more things to fall into place before I set everything in motion.

CHAPTER 15

JACK

My downtime is usually spent in the gym or in my office, and from the looks the guys are shooting me as I walk into the common room carrying my beer, my previous absences were noticed.

Our core team is fairly small, and most of the other guys who work with us are local, so they travel the couple of hours home to their families when they aren't required on base. We have a training mission in a couple of days, but other than that, it's good timing that our staff count is low. Having Jessa and Dana here is easier without the extra eyes on them.

Grey and Waldo are already seated around a table, playing cards. I'm followed into the room by Hunter and Eagle, who break off to join them. Grabbing a chair on his way, Hunter drops a case of poker chips on the table and turns toward the beer fridge.

"You want in on this, boss?" Waldo calls over to me, and I'm sure he already knows the answer.

"Naw, I'm good. Just going to watch for a bit." I tip my beer bottle in their direction and sit down on the couch as Dana appears and hesitates by the door.

Taking a quick scan of the room, she jolts to life when she sees my team setting up their card game.

"Can I play?" She's already at the table before anyone answers, and Grizz enters the room behind her and grabs a chair for her to sit on.

I shift my focus back to the door. Jessa is paused at the entrance. She's looking around the room, no doubt for the best place to sit, and I cringe inwardly as I silently hope it's beside me.

It's like I'm back in high school all over again.

Well, at least *her* high school. She has no idea I'm five years older than her. I haven't told her I was undercover when we first met, and I vow to come clean about everything as soon as I can.

Masking my deception with a smile, I nod when her eyes meet mine, and she saunters toward me. "This seat taken?"

"No, sit down. I got you a beer. It's from a brewery a couple of hours away." I point to the unopened bottle beside her, and she reaches over to pick it up and twist off the top.

"Thanks." She takes a couple of sips and continues her examination of the room.

I notice she looks away when any members of my team glance over, and she's nervously picking at the label on the bottle.

"I'm glad you could make it tonight." My weak attempt at an icebreaker makes me wince.

There is so much wrong with my sentence, I don't even know where to start.

Luckily, she saves me with a smirk. "Well, I was really busy tonight, you know. I had plans—big plans—to lie on my bed and stare at the ceiling until I fell asleep."

I want to reply, but I don't. In my mind it would be

something witty, but in reality it would probably land just as hard as my previous line did.

Beneath her sass are layers of walls and guards. She's been hurt, and she's struggling. She just doesn't realize how much yet.

My need to comfort and protect her is crushing my chest, but this isn't about me. I vow I'll make it about her. I won't lose sight of her in our mission, and this time, when it's over, I will be coming for her.

"Well, I'm glad you made the choice to be here. As exciting as that other option sounds." Apparently, I'm attempting to lighten the mood with another flimsy response, but it must be working, because her expression is bright.

It's the same look I couldn't wait to see every single morning when I saw her at school ten years ago. It's the look that told me I was the only one she saw, the only one who mattered. It's the look I should have woken up to every morning since then. But I didn't, because it's the look that was taken away from me.

"I've missed you." My voice is a whisper, and as I realize I've said my thoughts out loud, her face falls. The smile she hides behind drops, giving me a glimpse of her suffering.

"I've missed you too." Her words are only meant for me.

She swallows her truth hard, and I want to pull her into me. I want to wrap my arms around her and physically show her I won't let anything get to her.

But I can't.

I shift in my seat to get more comfortable in our conversation just as a squeal takes Jessa's eyes away from me.

Dana's triumphant voice rings out into the room. As she reaches across the table and pulls a heap of chips away from my team and toward a mountain in front of her, Jessa chuckles.

"Do you want to play?" I offer. So many years have passed now, and I don't know what Jessa likes to do anymore.

"No way. You couldn't pay me to play against her." She laughs, catching Dana's attention as she reaches across the table for more chips.

"What?" Dana grins from ear to ear. "I have no idea what you're talking about." She winks at Jessa.

"Are you sure about that?" From the door, Logan cuts through their friendly banter, catching everyone's attention. "Because from where I'm standing, it looks like my team is unknowingly playing blackjack with a card counter."

Four sets of eyes silently turn back to Dana, and she feigns doe-eyed innocence as Jessa snorts into her beer bottle, confirming Logan's accusation.

"Fine. You're no fun, Joker." She sits back in her chair and crosses her arms with a taunting smile on her face, and Logan walks right into it.

"Again—it's Jekyll, but I'll tell you what. Since, miraculously, not one of my guys realized you were counting cards"—he motions around the table, unimpressed by the ease at which his own team got played—"you've earned yourself the use of my real name. Mostly because I can't stand you butchering my code name. Please, call me Logan," he requests patiently.

"Wow. Really? But I had so many other names ready to go! Let's see, there was Jolly, Jinkies, Jerk Face, and Uptight Motherfucker. Except I think that last one was kind of a stretch as far as plays on words go, don't you agree?"

Jessa's eyes round into saucers, and all of the men at the table are frozen in place as they look between Dana and

Logan, unsure of whether to laugh or hide. In truth, I'm not even sure which way this is going to go.

We've agreed to a cease-fire, but Logan has his limits.

"If you'll agree to give my men back their poker chips, I'll agree that 'Uptight Motherfucker' is a bit of a stretch. Anyone want a beer while I'm up?" Unfazed, Logan walks to the fridge as everyone around the table relaxes and resumes their game—with Dana now demoted to spectator.

"Hello, Jessa. Jack. Where's Tex?" Logan asks as he takes a seat across from us.

"He said he was going to go for a run, and that he'd be by later for a drink." Grizz's voice comes up from behind the couch. As Dana slides a chair over to sit beside Jessa, I realize my alone time with her is now over.

"So what kind of movies do you guys have?" Dana asks. Grizz hands her a glass of wine, and it isn't lost on me that he isn't offering anyone else some of his private stash.

Then I notice her smile when she takes the glass from him. No one else gets that smile either, and I worry this will cloud his judgment.

Who am I kidding? I'm the last person to have an opinion about these things. I glance at Jessa while Hunter leans back in his chair to offer his two cents. "TV is down again, but I'm sure I can fix it after this hand. I'm losing my shirt over here anyway." He motions to his three chips and slides them all in as something else catches Dana's eye.

"Is that what I think it is?" She points to the contraption sitting beside the TV. "Is that a karaoke machine?" Her grin stretches across her entire face. Grey perks up as Logan groans, and Dana looks like she's about to vibrate out of her skin. "Jessa, do you remember Des Moines?" She's practically squealing.

"How could I forget?" Jessa laughs and tries to calm her friend down. Then she looks toward Logan and me to explain. "We had a couple of quiet days while we were running code. We wanted to unwind, but rules are rules, and we couldn't go out, so we brought the fun home and—"

Jessa doesn't get the chance to finish as Dana jumps in, and I notice Logan listening and observing.

I was right.

Their guards are coming down, and they're starting to relax.

"And I saw a beat-up old karaoke machine on sale in the window of a pawn shop when I was out grabbing supplies. We had so much fun singing at the top of our lungs in that big old house. Remember, Jessa?" I follow Dana's gaze to Jessa, and a pang of sadness stabs my heart.

They've had to seclude themselves for almost a decade, hiding away from life, creating their own world within the world that went on without them.

"I remember. It was fun. Except for the part where we can't sing." Now they are both smiling, and everyone around the room has stopped what they were doing and joined the conversation.

Even Logan smiles as they reminisce.

"Does it work? Can we sing?" Dana looks hopeful, and Grizz answers by stepping toward the machine to plug it in. "Oh, goodie! Jessa, let's sing a song. Just one. While he fixes the TV." She points in Hunter's direction as she jumps out of her seat.

"Okay, but just one." Jessa is a little slower to rise than her friend is. Her hesitance is adorable. Judging by her apprehension, I'd say she's only doing this for Dana.

Dana walks over to Grizz, picks up the song list, and

scans the titles. Then, looking up and smiling at Jessa, she leans to the side and points one out for Grizz to play, and he smiles and nods.

"If it's only going to be one, it's going to be a good one." She picks up two microphones and waves one excitedly at Jessa. "Do you want to know which one it is?" Dana bounces in place.

Jessa takes the mic. "No. Let it be a surprise. It's going to end the same way: with both of us off-key."

Logan leans back in his seat, watching the two women interact. I won't mention it to him, but I think he's enjoying the brief truce.

Grizz pulls up the song, and music pumps from the speakers. An old pop tune roars to life, causing Grey to bounce along with the beat. All of the men at the table turn to watch. Only Hunter is distracted as he continues to fix the TV for a movie later.

A knowing smile crosses Jessa's face, and her hips move in rhythm. Dana does a little twirl in place, catching Grizz's attention.

Both girls raise their mic at the same time. As they sing, they continue to look at each other, and when the first verse rolls to an end, they dance along to the tune as the beat picks up for the chorus.

Jessa's hips sway more prominently as the song goes on, slowly pulling me into the music with her. Watching her body move makes me want things I shouldn't be thinking about right now, and for a moment I'm thankful Logan took the lead on this mission.

I quickly glance out of the corner of my eye, and I see him watching both her and my reaction to her. I try to slow my roll, but she sucks me back in as she spins in place, and I catch the smile on her face. She isn't hiding anything with that smile right now. She is truly enjoying herself.

As the music slows, indicating the end of the song, a need to be with her bursts inside me. Without looking around and without thought, I stand, walk to the karaoke machine, and glance at the song list.

I've learned the hard way that time is fleeting. I don't want to add another thing to the long list of things I regret where Jessa is concerned.

There is one song I want to play.

For her.

I saw it when we first got this machine, and I could never bring myself to listen to it.

Dana sets her mic down and moves toward the couch as though she's about to watch me sing. Jessa hands me her mic and turns to move to a seat, but then she freezes when the first chord plays.

She swirls in place with a surprised look on her face. "Is that—"

I set the mic down. I'm not fucking singing.

But there is something I do want to do right now.

"The first song we ever danced to." I finish her sentence for her, then hold out my hand.

Jessa's eyes are almost as wide as her mouth as she gapes at me, then at my hand, and she snaps her mouth shut when she realizes I'm asking her to dance.

Lifting her slender fingers to mine, I no longer notice if anyone is still in the room with us the moment we touch. Then, in one move, I pull her into me and wrap my free arm around her as she keeps her eyes on mine.

We're dancing closer than we ever have before, mostly

because old Ms. Straub in high school insisted on the arm's-length rule at our dances.

But we're not in high school anymore.

She's not a girl anymore either.

Her body is warm against mine, and her chest pushes against my own with each deep breath she takes.

Her face flushes a soft shade of pink, and I can't help but run my thumb along her rosy cheeks. She feels hot to my touch.

As the song ends, the clearing of a throat reminds me we are not alone. I glance around.

Hunter has fixed the TV, and the guys are wrapping up their game. Grizz and Dana are sitting on the couch, discussing movies, but she's watching us out of the corner of her eye. Logan has already left.

The door opens, and Tex walks in.

"Hey, man," Grizz calls to him from the couch. "We're just about to watch a movie. I think you're going to get along with Dana here. She wants to watch—and I quote—anything with lots of action and violence."

"Nice." Tex sits down as the opening credits start up.

Without goodbyes, I wrap my fingers tightly around Jessa's little hand and pull her toward the door.

I'm no longer in the mood to share her, and I need to clear up a few things.

CHAPTER 16

JACK

Most of the guys who work with us on this base are local to the Pittsburgh area and travel home for the weekends. We maintain a satellite office just outside of the city, so they don't need to sit around the base with us unless we're preparing for an op.

The halls of the compound will be quiet for the next couple of days. Our *guests* are secured, and we need to organize our away teams for a short mission that will have most of the men off this base for a few days.

In our line of work, we take advantage of our breaks. Some months, our teams will go weeks before they get back to their own lives. If the job requires undercover work, it could be longer.

It's quiet nights like these that amplify the echoes of our footsteps down the vacant halls. As I walk through the dark corridors with Jessa, her hand fidgets in mine, and she hastens her pace every few steps as she tries to keep up.

But she isn't saying anything.

Good.

That means she's waiting for me to lead, and as soon as we get to our destination, I'll be more than happy to.

As we exit the main building, she takes a deep breath, gasping as the night air hits us.

Our compound is at a slight elevation, and the evenings get cool, but the view up here is worth it.

With the nearest city lights almost two hours away, the stars light up like diamonds in the sky. Her gasp isn't because of the blast of cool night air, but the view above us.

As we near my personal quarters, a soft tug of my hand draws my attention. I stop to look back at Jessa, who is enjoying the display above us.

She shivers against the chill, but her hand remains limp in my own. "It's beautiful."

I'm taken back to only days ago, to when I thought I would never know her again. "It is beautiful."

I can't see her cheeks flush in the darkness. I wish I could. She drops her head down and to the side, just like she used to when I would compliment her.

When she reacts to the cold again, I wrap my arm around her and continue toward my room.

As we enter my private quarters and shut out the world breaking apart around us, the weight of our situation weighs on my shoulders.

There are no more distractions.

Barring the apocalypse, no one will bother us for the rest of the night.

"Can I get you some water?"

The tension pulls taut between us. I want her full attention now, and judging by the look on her face, I have it.

Jessa opens her mouth to respond, but her words catch in her throat, and she clears it while she nods instead.

When I return from the kitchenette and hand her a bottle, I'm met with a kind thanks and an awkward silence.

She's trying hard not to look around the room as she shifts on her feet.

Our rooms are simple.

We aren't here on vacation.

My quarters consist of one main room, which is also my bedroom. There's a small kitchen to one side and a bathroom. The space is large, but I only have my bed and a table to eat on that doubles as a desk and a dresser.

It isn't lost on me that Jessa is still near the front door. When she finally does take in the room around her, her eyes linger on my bed for a moment before she returns her attention to me.

"Have a seat, Jessa. We need to talk." At my last word, her shoulders sag.

I think I know what she was hoping for. There's nothing I'd like more than a repeat of last night, but we need to take a couple of steps back and begin again by creating a foundation, and that will be done with words, trust, and respect.

Her steps to the bed are rigid. Her guard is going up, and I need to tread lightly. There are a whole host of issues I could talk to her about right now, but most of them will probably get me nowhere, and I can't risk her shutting down on me.

As I search her cues for a good place to start, it dawns on me that I need to start with myself.

How can I ask for her trust when everything outside of my feelings for her was a lie? How can I expect her to tell me the truth without granting her the same courtesy?

I grab a chair from the corner of the room and seat myself

directly in front of her. Then I lean forward until our eyes are at the same level. "What do you want to ask me?"

She pulls back a few inches in surprise. "What?"

I know she heard me.

She just wasn't ready for my question to be in her favor.

"Ten years is a long time, Jessa. I think it's clear there are still feelings between us." At my insinuation, her cheeks flush red. "A lot has happened, and I know you have questions, so I'll make you a deal. I will grant you complete honesty wherever I can, and I ask the same of you. We—"

Before I get my next sentence out, her body stiffens. She's preparing herself to fight me on the subject, so I switch gears.

Raising my hand to request her silence, I continue, "The deal is, we will be honest with each other. I think you'll find I want to be open with you. When you don't want to answer, I only ask that you tell me, so we are still being honest with each other."

She takes a long minute to consider. In that time, her eyes never leave my face. Shifting between looking into my eyes and scanning the rest of my features, she observes me in excruciating silence.

Tilting her head down and moving her eyes to her lap, she nods silently, indicating that she is willing to try. My chest swells with hope that she's chosen to trust me knowing what is at stake.

Wasting no time with her newfound sense of freedom, she asks her question.

"What happened to you, Jack? How are you here?"

It's the question I knew she'd ask first. It's the question I want to ask of her. When I meet her watery eyes, sadness sets in. I never had the chance to come clean before now.

"I risked a lot to look for you," she continues. "Your family was gone. I couldn't find you or your dad anywhere. I thought maybe Maxwell got you. I checked every hospital in the area; I hacked into all of the police precincts within three counties. There were no reports. No files. It was like you didn't exist."

"I didn't."

She furrows her brow in confusion, and I decide to tell it as straight as Logan probably would. Reaching out to cradle her hands, I begin. "Jessa, when you knew me back then, I wasn't a high school student. I was in the military. I was working on a federal investigation. At the time, I was working special ops within a classified arm. I wasn't a main player; those guys had been working undercover within the Sparr organization for almost a year when I came on board. I was recruited to report on other sides of the Sparr family. The man you knew as my dad, he was my commanding officer. That's when I met you."

Her grip tightens in my palm. "But how could you do that? We were only eighteen. Didn't your parents have a problem with you putting yourself in danger?" Now I see my Jessa in her eyes. The girl from high school who trusted me unconditionally, and I almost don't want to tell her.

But admitting to my deception in order to rebuild her trust is the only way through this, and I gently loosen her grip on my fingers and cover her hands with my own. "I wasn't eighteen, Jessa. I was twenty-three when I met you. They sent me in because I was the youngest-looking guy on the team at the time."

She jerks her hands out of mine as my deception sinks in, and I decide to keep talking in an effort to counter the voices that are probably working things out inside her head.

"Jessa, total honesty. Those guys tried for months to get close to Matteo Sparr. He trusted no outsiders. I was sent in to try something different. It was my job to watch his son, Maxwell. It wasn't my job to fall in love with you. I did that all on my own. The time we spent together, that was real. That was me. As much as I denied it to the guys around me, I wanted you from the minute I saw you. We were ready to take the whole family down the day you disappeared. I was going to come and find you, to tell you everything after all of the arrests were made." I keep my hands on her knees in an attempt to maintain a connection with her. I'm thankful she's allowed me to stay, but her questions keep coming.

"Why couldn't I find you?" She would know the answer to this question if she were thinking rationally, and I wonder for a moment if this is a good headspace for her to be in.

"Because you were looking for Jack Waters. My real name was Jack McCaskill, but even that is probably wiped out of searchable records by now. My parents died in a boating accident when I was a kid, and I went through foster care until I was old enough to join the military. With no family and no traceable past, I was the perfect candidate for some of the more...secretive missions. That's how I met you."

She scans my face, attempting to reconcile the boy she knew with the man sitting in front of her.

"How are you planning to bring down Maxwell?" She fires her next question at me quickly, probably hoping to deter me from asking some of my own, and I tense at his name.

I wasn't prepared for the shift in topic, and I'm not ready to end the conversation about us.

"We don't have a plan yet. Jess, we need you and Zane. I think the only way we can end all of this is by working together. But I don't want to talk about that tonight. I would like to ask you some questions."

The truth is, I do want to talk about her and Zane, but I know she's not ready to open up about any of that yet, and I don't want her to stop talking.

I give her a few seconds to let my last sentence sink in. It's my turn to ask some questions, and I'm not asking for her permission.

"What happened to you the night your parents died?"

Her nervous smile stays plastered on her face, but the emotion behind it falls away. Sadness fills her eyes as she shifts her focus down to our hands.

"I remember you said your *dad* was mad about something, and you had to stay home." She reminds me of the lie I had to tell her as we prepared to end our operation. "I decided to do some studying at the library. We had a chem exam the next day. Anyway, I got a call from Travis. He said Dad got a call from a guy at his work, and they were panicking. Something about the Sparr family being corrupt and Dad accessing something he shouldn't have. He told me that Mom and Dad were running around the house grabbing things and throwing stuff in the car. Travis said Dad wanted to know where I was, and I told him I was in town at the library. Then he told me to stay where I was, that they were coming to get me. I've never heard him sound like that." She mutters, "He was so scared," to herself as the memory comes to her before she returns to her story.

"I told them to leave. I told them to just take the road straight out of town and I would meet up with them and we would figure everything out. They wouldn't listen. I waited, and they never came. After forty-five minutes, I got in my car and drove back to our place. We were only fifteen minutes from the library. I was coming around the bend at the bottom of the ravine when headlights at the top caught my eye. I saw their car go over the side at the top, by the bridge."

Listening to my Jessa replay the worst night of her life leaves me paralyzed.

"I shut off the car and ran down the bank to the bottom, right alongside the river. There were people up at the top with flashlights, but I was far enough down that they wouldn't have seen me in the dark, and the sound of the water was so loud. The car went under pretty fast. It looked like some windows broke open on impact. I drove downriver to try to find a place to get to them, but the rapids were too strong, and the car was gone. Jack, I couldn't save them." Her guilt stitches itself across her face.

She's lived with a lifetime of what-ifs. What if she left earlier? What if she tried to brave the cold, rushing river? What if she refused to tell her parents where she was? What if she stayed home that night?

Instinctively, I move to her side to pull her out of her trauma. She needs me to help her through this, to shoulder some of her pain, and I won't let her down.

"Jessa, there wasn't anything you could have done. No one saw this coming until it was too late. On our end, everything seemed by the book. I was ordered to stay in. We were going in first thing in the morning as backup. When I woke up, all hell had already broken loose. The team knew about your family within the hour. My commanding officer decided not to wake me because he knew how I felt for you. I found out early the next morning. Jess, I thought you were gone. Your backpack was found in the car."

"I know. I read the police report."

I take a moment to let everything sink in. Catching up

like this and hearing what really happened feels like waking up from one long, drawn-out, hellish nightmare.

"Then you know they never found your brother?" I lean in to console her.

I expect her to lean against me for support, to allow me the chance to finally comfort her in mourning the loss of Travis, but she doesn't move, setting off all of my alarm bells.

I'm missing something.

I steal a glance down at Jessa, and she won't meet my eyes.

She's treading carefully now.

My guard goes up at her apprehension, and suddenly I realize I've made some assumptions I need to revisit.

"Do you know what happened to your brother?" Again my question is met with a long pause, and I decide to finish my thought. "Jessa, is Travis alive?" The thought is so far-fetched that I hadn't considered it before.

She inhales deeply. When she finally returns my stare, there's a hint of confirmation on her face.

She does know something I don't.

Her voice is low, and I'm both happy and frustrated when she adheres to our deal with her next words:

"I won't answer that question."

The ball is back with me.

Do I push this now? Go against what I promised and try to learn more about what she knows?

If I poke the bear on this, our night will most definitely end abruptly, and I'm not ready to let her go.

Taking a deep breath, I rein in my emotions and push back the chaos building inside. The only way she will continue to relinquish control this evening is if I can control myself—and I can do that for her.

Disappointment creeps into me at this turn of events. This is the first of many questions I won't be able to answer for him.

I want to feel him close to me again. I know this won't last forever. Everything over the last ten years has been too temporary for me to get my hopes up.

I ready myself for a confrontation, so I'm surprised when he reaches for my upper arms and pulls me into a partial hug, nestling my head under his chin.

The heat from his chest against my cheek and the rhythm of his breathing dance along to the beating of his heart as he sits in silence, no doubt trying to find a loophole in the deal he made with me.

His deep sigh tells me he's settled on a decision. "I can't promise I won't bring this up again later, but I thank you for your honesty." He lifts his hand to my hair and combs his fingers through my strands.

This isn't what I expected.

To be honest, nothing has been what I expected since I first noticed the breach in our perimeter at the farmhouse a few days ago. Since then, I've just been rolling with the punches, waiting until I can find something to grab on to and run with.

But this? I expected him to push this.

How could he not? He just point-blank asked me a question I know the answer to, and now he knows I know the answer.

My story and Travis's story will come out in good time, but it's too soon to share everything. My final move depends on keeping my secrets locked away for the time being.

The longer we stay on this subject, the more difficult it will be to stick with my plan. "I don't want to talk about that anymore."

Jack stills around me, tightening his grip before relaxing. "We don't have to talk about that. What would you like to talk about?"

Throwing the ball back in my court, he waits for me to ask my next question.

I don't have the luxury of time to beat around the bush. I need to know their game so I can decide what part, if any, I will be playing in it.

"What's your plan to take down Maxwell?" I examine his features as he decides how to answer.

"We've been trying for a decade to take down Matteo, and Maxwell is now a big part of his father's business. After that night, Matteo vanished, making him untouchable, but we can still nail Maxwell and his associates. We hope if we can remove the son, then the father will have no choice but to come out of hiding. We have a few different tactics we've been entertaining. Link seems to think if we get enough on Maxwell and capture him, he'll turn against his father to save himself."

"Link?" I clarify.

"Sorry. Lincoln. He's our head tech and comms guy."

I nod for him to continue. "Logan and I don't think Max will really flip on his father, so we've been trying to get as much as we can on him to put him away, then we can refocus our resources on finding his father. Logan seems to think, and I agree, that once Max is out of the picture, Matteo will have to come out of hiding. It's been tough though. Those who know enough to put both of them away are extremely loyal to the Sparr family, or they're dead."

Jack is right about one thing: Maxwell will never turn his father in.

Where Jack is wrong is focusing his attention on finding dirt on the family itself. I've learned the loyalty shown to the Sparr family comes from the leverage Matteo and Maxwell hold over their friends and enemies.

Blackmail is a favored tactic, and they dangle many carrots over those around them.

Simply taking them down won't be enough. Their tracks will always be buried, and their crimes will go unpunished. Their claws stretch far into the criminal underbelly of the world, and even further into our everyday law and order. Politicians, lawyers, and everyone else up the ladder have something to lose should a member of the Sparr family be caught.

The only way to take them out is to find everything they have on everyone.

From what I've seen, they can only stretch themselves so far, and there are just as many good citizens ready to stand up and fight as those who have chosen to be bought. I've worked alongside many of those groups over the years.

I get the impression that I have a better handle on Maxwell's situation than they do, and Jack is right: they do need Zane and me, but I'm not ready to share everything I know yet, because this will be ending my way.

"Is there anything else about your plan?"

"We have a couple of other ideas that I am not able to discuss at this time." His trust in me only goes so far.

I'm keeping just as much from him as he is from me, and this is a good reminder that I need to keep my cards close to my chest, so I go with a question that will lead the conversation elsewhere.

"How did you know we were at the farmhouse?" Now this is an answer I'm curious about. I was confident we were completely off-grid and untraceable.

"Complete honesty here; it was an anonymous tip. Called in through back channels, directly to Link's team. It's a number no one has. I mean, it's a number no one *should* have. The voice was distorted, nothing traceable. But the caller had too much credible information to ignore."

Jack's answer opens up a lot of new questions. I'm not sure if the informant gave us up to benefit my goal or not, so this is another piece of information I'll need to table for now.

"And what happens to Zane, Dana, and me? If I help you, can you guarantee we go free when this is over?" I already know the answer to this one. What I want to know is how Jack will respond.

He takes a long minute to look at me, then he drops his eyes to his lap and tangles his fingers in mine.

"I don't know. I can't tell you you'll be released. I can tell you I don't want to lose you again, but I don't know what will happen." A heavy silence follows his words.

"Thank you for your honesty." I let the conversation linger around us before I change the topic. "Last night. I, um

—" Suddenly, my cheeks warm in embarrassment. How have I become the person who doesn't know what to say?

"It's okay, Jessa. I can't put into words what last night was either. It was something I never thought I would have again. You, here. I've been playing it over in my head." He cocoons my hands in his own. "The moment I found out you were missing was the single worst moment of my life. I should have been there to protect you, but I wasn't. Instead, I broke down in front of my commanding officer and had to be sedated then transported back to our home base. I should have been out there looking for you. Having you back here like this is—there are no words."

I crane my neck and reach my lips up to his. I want to taste him again. His mouth, the softness of his lips, the strength behind his kiss, but he pauses, his features tight with restraint.

"I want you, Jessa. More than you know."

The rest is unspoken.

We can't entertain this. Not now, when there is so much at stake.

He hooks two fingers under my chin, then tilts my head up and pushes his lips against my forehead before settling his eyes firmly on me.

"I want you to sleep here with me tonight."

The extent of my exhaustion becomes evident when he says "sleep." Jack relaxes when I nod my agreement, and we slip into a comfortable conversation, returning to our high school days.

He focuses on his memories of Dana and things that happened with other kids and teachers. He stays away from Maxwell, and after another thirty minutes of talking, pieces of me are living in the past with him.

I remember how at ease I was around him. Everything came naturally. With Jack, I never needed to wonder where we were going, I never assessed or read into anything. We just were.

So when he offers me a T-shirt to sleep in, I accept it without hesitation. Then, when he stands to get his own sleepwear from the dresser, I turn away from him, remove my sweater, and lift the fabric over my head to slip his shirt on.

It's only when a strangled gasp registers from behind me that my reality comes crashing down.

"What the fuck are those?" His low timbre is laced with rage, and I don't need to see him to know his whole body has gone completely stiff.

I forgot about my scars.

CHAPTER 18
JACK

This night couldn't have ended any better.

The more we shared our memories, the stronger our connection grew. I noticed Jessa scratch her forearms a couple of times. No doubt her sweater must be getting itchy, so I offer her one of my shirts to sleep in.

I'm not going to lie, seeing her in my tee is going to be the highlight of my day, right beside dancing with her earlier.

She turns away from me, tugging her sweater off, and I grab a shirt of my own, then spin around to put it on.

I'm ripped out of the moment when I see it.

Not it—them. Many of them.

Thin pale lines cover Jessa's back like they were painted on with a dull brush.

These aren't recent. She's lived with these scars for a long time now, and they will forever be a permanent part of her.

"What the fuck are those?" The words are out before I can stifle my fury.

Someone did this to her.

Her expression drops instantly as she spins around to

face me. My shirt is tangled in her arms as she rushes to cover herself, but I won't let her hide.

I want to know who harmed her so I can kill them.

I close the distance between us before she can get the shirt over her head. Her wrists are tangled in the fabric and held against her upper body. I turn her to face the wall behind her and walk her into it, placing one hand on the back of her neck to hold her in place and another on her hip so she can't turn around.

Her panic sets in. There's a distant voice in my head telling me to stand down, but I'm not ready to release her.

Like a moth to a flame, my hand leaves her hip, and I reach out to touch the angry, pale lines across her back. When I trace along the worst one, I feel the ridges of the scar tissue under my fingertips.

"No, please, don't look at them. Let me go." She struggles, trying to push off from the wall as she pleads, but the ringing in my ears commands my attention.

As I trace each line one by one, the rage inside me continues to climb. Some scars are so faint I can barely see them. A few are so deep I wonder if they still hurt her.

"Who did this to you?" I'm clawing at every ounce of sanity I have left to maintain control over myself.

"Stop, Jack. STOP! I need you to let me go right now."

That sinks in.

My heavy limbs go limp, and I step back, allowing her the space she is desperate for.

Tears flow freely down her flushed face, and she tries to take a step away from the wall but falls short. Tripping over her feet, she drops to the floor and fumbles with my shirt in a desperate attempt to hide herself away.

She looks lost, ashamed.

I watch in a daze as a scared little girl emerges from my strong Jessa. Then I spin on my heels to grab a blanket off the bed and wrap it around her shaking body.

Her pain crushes me, but I can't let her hide from me. I know our deal is still in effect, but this is one thing I need to push.

"Was this Maxwell? Did he do this to you?" Deep down, I think I already know the answer.

"Yes."

She offers nothing else.

I've made her feel unsafe.

Without another thought, I crouch down, wrap my arms around her, and help her up to sit beside me on the edge of my bed.

I need to be here for her now. I remind myself she isn't in immediate danger. I leash my need to protect her and rein in my tone. "What happened, Jess?"

The space between us becomes thick as she takes a short breath.

"I can't answer that question."

What? Incensed by her sudden defiance, I stand up and move a few inches away from her.

My Jessa was hurt badly enough that she will have these scars for the rest of her life, and she's refusing to let me in?

How can I help her if she won't trust me?

There's my line.

I won't allow her to keep this from me.

My anger boils dangerously close to the surface. I'm pissed right off at Maxwell. He will pay for this. But I'm also angry at Jessa, and I never wanted to be.

"This? You're choosing not to answer this? Why not?" There's no hiding my anger and disappointment.

"I didn't say *won't*, Jack. I said *can't*. I can't answer it because I don't remember!"

I pause to let her words register, and as my body deflates, the severity of her situation sinks in.

Her interrogation with Logan went horribly wrong, and she didn't remember it the next morning. She blocked out her time with Maxwell for a reason. If the scars on her back are any indication, she suffered a horrible experience at his hands.

But to forget it?

"What do you mean you don't remember?" I lift my hand to gently touch her, and she doesn't flinch away.

That's a good sign.

I take up the space beside her while trying not to crowd her.

She folds her body into me, tightening the blanket around her. She's held on to this for so long. I'd be surprised if she's ever allowed Dana to see her scars.

"It's just that, Jack. I don't remember. Years ago, when Maxwell had me...I don't remember a lot of it." As she starts to open up, I realize she doesn't want to keep this from me.

She doesn't want to hide, and I'm comforted by the realization that she trusts me.

"What do you remember?" I lower my voice. I don't want to lead her too much. I want her to feel her strength. I have a feeling she's going to need it.

"I remember being taken. The look on Maxwell's face scared me. It wasn't the Max we knew. It was like he wasn't even there. I remember the first part of my interrogation. There were a few people in the room with us. He was asking me questions about Zane. I wouldn't answer most of them. I couldn't. But it almost felt like he didn't care about the answers. He just kept looking at me with such a disgusted look on his face—like I did something horrible to him. At some point, he ordered his men to put me outside, in a cage next to the one that held his dogs. It was cold, and they wouldn't stop barking and snarling at me every time I moved. I couldn't lie down; there was dog feces everywhere, so I stood. I tried to stand still so the dogs would stop barking. I remember up until the first night. He came outside with a big plate of steak. I hadn't eaten since lunch the day before. It was over twenty-four hours, and I was starving. It smelled delicious. He fed it to the dogs, then he left a bowl of dog food in my cage." She pauses, then looks away from me before finishing her story. "I don't remember anything after the first night. Just bits and pieces that don't make sense."

When she looks back at me, her eyes are wide. It's taking everything inside me to keep a passive, comforting look plastered on my face.

All I want to do right now is tear something apart.

"Maybe it's better that I don't remember." The tremor in her soft voice breaks me out of my rage.

"I'm so sorry, Jessa." Hesitantly pulling her close, I shift my body to lay her down on the bed, and I join her. She doesn't realize it yet, but she's about to crash hard, and it's best I let her rest.

"What's the next thing you remember?" I ask my question with my lips pressed to the top of her head.

"I remember waking up in a room to a man in a doctor's coat checking my pulse. I wasn't in a hospital; it was just a room. He worked for Maxwell, but I didn't see Max again after I woke up. The doctor bandaged me up and took care of me for almost two days until I could leave. It was he who told me it looked like I had some internal damage, and there was a chance I wouldn't be able to have kids. I confirmed that later at a clinic. I don't think he was supposed to say anything.

"Then some men came on the second day. They didn't say anything to me. Just packed me up and drove me into Seattle, to a drop-off point I had apparently arranged with Zane. I don't remember any of it. Then Dana was there, and we vanished after that."

I have no words.

It's too much to process, and my raw anger won't do Jessa any good.

Combing my fingers through her hair, I coax her to close her eyes. Her arm slides across my chest, and she squeezes her body against mine. Her warmth is the only thing centering my sanity.

Staring at the ceiling, I make a promise I should have made and kept a decade ago. "You're safe with me, Jessa. I won't let anyone harm you again."

Eventually, her embrace relaxes as her strength leaves her in search of sleep. She sighs deeply, and I barely make out her words before she drifts off: "I know."

Lying beside her, my entire being is a contradiction to hers. Her softness is wrapped in my fury. Her strength is urging my chaos, my own weakness, to calm, and I've never felt more challenged in my entire life.

Not knowing what happened during those days is taunting my sanity.

How can I help Jessa if neither of us know what demons are lurking in her head? Her scars have faded, but their stories are locked away somewhere in the recesses of her mind.

Logan is right. I need his help. My heart hurts, and I'm

not thinking rationally. I can't fail Jessa this time, and I'll need his guidance if I'm going to break through and help her heal.

Jessa murmurs something unintelligible as her head digs deeper into my arm. Then she's out cold, and she'll most likely sleep right through the night after everything she's just shared.

I shift just enough to get comfortable beside her and close my eyes.

A gentle movement beside me stirs me awake.

I stay still but shift my eyes to look at the man wrapped around me, and I take him in with a deep breath.

I've dreamt about this for years. What it would feel like to be in his arms again.

His chest rises and falls steadily. He's still asleep.

The room is bathed in a soft glow as the light from the full moon shines in and stretches itself across the bed. It almost reaches us. If I shift down a bit, I'd be able to see how bright it shines, but I don't want to wake him.

Sharing what I remember of my time with Maxwell lifted a weight off me. For the longest time, I wanted to tell Dana, but I couldn't bring myself to. I know she feels responsible for me being taken. Knowing about this would crush her.

But there is something about sharing it with Jack that feels right.

He is a deep part of me. He always has been.

Me not remembering my time with Maxwell must kill him.

It bothers me too, but for different reasons.

I don't remember some vital parts of my time in captivity. Something took over and threw me into autopilot, and I don't know how I was ever able to make contact with Dana and Zane. Did I give anything away? I had access to their servers to make the connection. Did I see anything while I was there that could help end his whole ordeal? Did he say anything to me that could be useful?

For all my remaining days, I'll never forget the look on Max's face when he stood in front of me for the first time since my parents died.

It was like he wasn't there anymore.

It wasn't a lack of emotion; it was more like a furious overload. It was barely contained insanity.

When I look back at that time, I think my connection to Zane is the only thing that kept me alive. Actually, it didn't even do that. I left out one part the doctor shared with me because I honestly don't think Jack would be able to function with that information.

Just before the men came to transport me back, the doctor told me to do everything I could to make sure I never ended up in Maxwell's clutches again. He was scared for me, and for a stranger on the Sparr payroll to be that terrified for someone he didn't even know sent chills through my body. He wouldn't give me any further details beyond the fact that my heart had stopped. I had essentially died at Maxwell's hands at some point.

I can never let myself be captured again. And I can't allow Dana to be caught up in this.

Without the weak level of protection Zane gives us, we only have each other.

I became determined to be everything Dana and I

needed. I increased our security after that happened and practiced self-defense online whenever I could.

I'm terrified, and I don't even know what I'm scared of because I don't remember most of it.

The bed bows as Jack rolls onto his side, wrapping his arm across my body and tucking his leg over mine. The warmth of his breath on my forehead comforts me.

As scary as everything else was, and as uncertain as our future is right now, I know I am safe with him. But he doesn't see the same things I see.

He doesn't know what I have to do to release everyone who works under Zane without consequence. He doesn't know about all the pieces I've put in place over the years. He won't accept my final move, the last thing I will need to do in order to free everyone.

And he doesn't know I'm only one piece away from making it all happen. It's a piece that's hidden among my lost memories from my time in Maxwell's captivity.

If I was functioning well enough to contact Zane without giving up his location, I think there's a chance I tagged Maxwell's servers. It's what I would have done if I was thinking clearly.

Remembering all of the codes I needed just to make the connection to Dana was a huge feat. I must have been on my game and driven to get free.

I want to be able to give everything to Jack. I want to be his entirely, but I can't go along with their mission. My actions will protect him too, and the only clear end I see is the one I have planned out.

Jack, Logan, and Maxwell have some similarities. They are tactical, operational. They will go to war, fight, and there will be a lot of damage on both sides. The possibility of a happy ending is slim. Then they will fight again another day. All while Dana and I remain trapped and more lives are ruined or lost.

Over the last ten years, I have obtained a mountain of documents, evidence, video, bank accounts, and verifiable lists of people who are in Maxwell's pockets. I have almost everything I need. Well, everything digital, anyway. But it's enough.

Almost.

If I can confirm I planted the code, I will be able to sever Maxwell's connection to everyone from Zane down. Then I'll cut off his head and let him bleed out while his allies tear him apart to save themselves. There will be minimal casualties on Jack's side, and Dana will have the freedom we always daydreamed about.

"You okay? You're shivering." Jack breaks me out of my thoughts, and I wonder how long he's been awake beside me.

"I'm good. Can I get a little bit of that blanket?" I smile up at him as he reaches behind him to grab the soft cover that fell off during the night.

"Anything for you." His words are comforting, but I know they're not entirely true.

In the end, I know he won't be able to give me everything I'm going to need.

I know he won't be able to let me go.

Tears well in my eyes, and I bury my face in his shoulder before my regret becomes obvious. Those thoughts are better pushed far below the surface.

I have a plan, and success requires I stick to every step and keep my emotions out of it.

And that is what I will do.

Even if it kills me—again.

CHAPTER 20
JACK

"What do you mean she doesn't remember?" Logan is frozen in his seat behind his desk.

He's been still as a statue since I started speaking five minutes ago.

"You were right. She was tortured. She has scars all over her back to prove it, but she doesn't remember any of it. Whatever he did to her, it was bad enough that she's blocked it out. She doesn't even remember how she was able to contact Dana and Zane to get her out of there."

Logan swears under his breath, then leans back in his chair, dragging his hand down his face in disbelief. "Do you think you can help her remember?"

I expected his question but not his reaction. Any piece of information that will get us close to Maxwell is top priority, but etched across Logan's face is something else.

"I'm not sure. I don't know what her triggers are, how to open a path to her memories. We might need to work around it. Logan, I know our priority is the mission, but—"

"Save it, Jack. I know where your head is at. I get it. Look, between you and me, I hope it works out for you."

Then, leaning in, he continues, "For both of you. I really do, but you need to respect that my priority is taking down Maxwell. Just know that I will try to do everything in my power to protect and save what is important to you. Can you do that?"

His question is fair. Shoes on the other foot and all—I would do the same.

"Yes. I can."

Logan stands, stretching his legs. "So where does that leave us? Jessa doesn't remember her time in captivity, but I'm not convinced any of it will help our operation. I'm willing to assist you with her later, but right now we need to focus on Maxwell. Tactically speaking, we have one of his top two hackers. Hackers who, for all intents and purposes, have ulterior motives. Do you have any further information on that front?" After a few steps, he takes his seat again.

"We spoke briefly about her brother last night. You know his body was never found. She mentioned to me that she knows what happened to him, but she wouldn't elaborate."

He slumps into his chair, and his frustration boils to the surface. "And you didn't push? What the hell, Jack?"

"No. I told her I just wanted honesty, and she could pass on any question she wished. I wouldn't have gotten any further if I pushed it. I think it's best we keep this to ourselves for now and operate under both pretenses, that he's alive and he's dead. In the end, it doesn't matter who Zane is. It matters where he is, and how we can convince Jessa to get him to work with us."

I can tell it pains him, but Logan nods in agreement.

I change the subject. "Are we any closer to finding out who our mole is?"

"I only know who it's not. Outside of me, you, and Link,

I can only clear Grey right now. He started with us last year. As for internet access and phone use, everyone was online during that time frame. We're in the boonies; there's nothing else to do out here once work is done, Jack. Social networks, games, movies, email. Everyone was online that evening, and since the public computers are only located in the library, near the file room, everyone except Hunter and Grizz was in there, but they were next door, in the common room at different times, which is probably close enough. If they were on their phones or tablets, it would still show as coming from the router in the file room. I have Link working on the exact time frames and confirming all web addresses accessed from the laptops and the phones. But that'll take a while."

Clearing our most inexperienced team member doesn't build a lot of confidence in me. There is still a lot of training Grey needs to go through and protocols that need to be taught, so we can't bring him into our circle for the time being.

People slip up, they make mistakes, and I'm not willing to risk his life unless it is absolutely necessary.

Logan's phone vibrates on his desk. He checks the display, then taps the screen, and Link's voice fills the room.

"We have a breach right now. Someone is attempting to access our communications. They're trying to force a connection and speak with us."

My chest tightens as I stand up and move behind Logan while he responds.

"Allow it, but monitor the connection. Shut down anything else they're trying to do. Take all vital information offline. Open nonessential communication lines only, and shut down all access to the comms room. Send them to me. Can you do that?"

"On it. Sending now."

Link stays online, and I listen to the tapping of his fingers against the keyboard as he furiously works to open the connection to Logan's computer.

Then, all at once, the camera light on Logan's laptop flashes on, and we still. Whoever is on the other end can see us as we wait for the confirmation that I feel in the pit of my stomach is coming.

A window opens. It's a wheel working to complete the connection. Then we come face-to-face with the one person both of us have been dying to put away for the past ten years.

Logan's voice holds no surprise and no welcome. "Maxwell."

The breaches, our prisoners. It wasn't a matter of if he would make contact; it was a matter of when.

Looking back at us through the screen are the eyes of my nemesis. He's a lot older, his face hardened from years under his father's guidance, but I'd still recognize him anywhere.

He was the kid I competed against for Jessa's attention, though it wasn't much of a challenge.

From the first time we spoke, I felt like I'd known her forever. It was just meant to be. But Maxwell wouldn't accept it. He inserted himself between us every chance he could, which was good for me since it was my job to stay close to him.

And now here he sits across from us, sizing up me and Logan in his monitor. He looks around the little bit of room he can see behind us before he answers.

"I'll get to the point. You have something that belongs to me, and I want it back."

Anger slices up my spine. Jessa is not his; she never was,

and I want to reach through the screen and strangle him until he's dead for what he did to her.

"Jessa is not an 'it,' and she's not yours." I fist my hands and growl the warning.

Logan reaches his hand over to steady mine. I've lost control already.

"She's exactly that. Or did she not tell you she owes her life to me?" His ego is too big for the room he occupies. Leaning into the camera, he continues, "Her literal life, Jack. Did she really not tell you how I so graciously gave her her life back after I took it away?"

A calm I'm not expecting washes over me.

Maxwell doesn't know that Jessa doesn't remember most of her time with him, and he takes my pause as surprise. His satisfied sneer deepens. He shifts his gaze off to the side. It appears as though he's working on something as he speaks with us.

"Ah, here you are, my dear. I've been waiting for you." Maxwell sits up straight in his seat, and I notice too late that our screen isn't the only one on the compound he's accessed.

Rising from his seat, Logan pulls over his secondary laptop and taps a few keys, opening up security for the base.

Jumping from screen to screen, it isn't long before he finds Jessa. She's standing in front of the TV in the common room along with Hunter, Grizz, and Dana.

She's frozen in place, staring at the monster who gave her her scars.

CHAPTER 21
JESSA

I'm telling you now, you haven't lived until you've done the walk of shame with a friend like Dana around to witness your pitiful entrance.

"Well, well, well. Would you look at yourself, you little hussy! Where were you last night?" She sits up from her sprawled position on the couch and smirks as I nonchalantly cross the room like I didn't sleep somewhere else last night.

"I, um...I was with Jack last night."

Her smile tells me she is loving every second of this.

"Really? I wouldn't have guessed. What did you do? I'm assuming, due to our location, that dancing at the local club is out of the question." She taps her finger against her chin as her eyes go up to the ceiling as though my answer is hiding there. She feigns confusion. "Hmm. I wonder what on earth the two of you could have done all of the way out here—all alone?"

I don't want to go into the more difficult parts of the evening, and I attempt to shut it down. "We talked—that's all. Then we fell asleep together. It was nice."

She opens her mouth to rib me further, but then she quickly closes it and smiles.

She's cutting me some slack.

"Well, I'm happy for you." She sets her palm on her chest. "What did I do, you ask?" I chuckle because I didn't, and she answers anyway. "We all watched a movie. Then Grizz walked me back to my room to go to sleep."

"Oh, is that all?" I attempt to deflect the attention away from me.

"Yes. That was all, you little tart. It was fun. Those guys are nice, but that Tex guy sure can talk all the way through a movie." She rolls her eyes. That is one of Dana's pet peeves, and it's the very reason she won't watch mysteries with me, because I always try to figure them out before the end "You missed breakfast. Want to grab lunch?"

The rumble in my stomach answers for me.

I am hungry. Starved, actually.

We collectively turn our attention to the door when someone knocks. The door is ajar, but Dana crosses the room to answer anyway.

"I thought Tex was watching us." Dana glances down the hall, exposing Hunter when she leans out of the way.

"He's got some work. I'm taking over. He tells me you haven't gone for lunch yet."

Dana takes three steps to a chair and grabs an oversized sweatshirt I haven't seen before. It's close to three sizes too large for her, and I wonder if she got it from her new *friend*.

"We were just talking about that."

"Can we stop by the common room real quick? I left my poker chips in there last night." Hunter takes a step backward into the hall to allow us enough space to pass. Then he turns and heads toward their canteen.

"Sure." Dana answers as we follow close behind.

As we walk down the corridor, Dana has me laughing about the guys' attempts to shut Tex up during the movie. When we round the corner and enter the common room, Grizz is standing in front of us, blocking part of the room from my view. Dana steps around Hunter to say hello to Grizz, and she freezes in place as a voice I wasn't ready to hear fills the room.

"Ah, there you are, my dear. I've been waiting for you."

My stomach erupts into my throat as a cold sweat breaks out over my skin. He sounds close by, like he's standing inside the room, which is currently spinning.

I will my feet to shuffle to the side of Grizz. A very small part of me is thankful he isn't here. But he is still on the television.

Monster.

Frozen in place, I silently hope he can't see me, but he immediately proves me wrong.

"Don't be shy, Jessa. I was just telling everyone about our...rather unique relationship."

"There is no relationship." Bolstered by the security of the compound, my own courage shines.

My time with Jack has strengthened me, but I know instantly I shouldn't have said anything.

"Oh, isn't there? Maybe I should remind you who you work for. Maybe I should remind you of the consequences you will suffer should you disobey me."

All of my instincts scream at me to cower, to run away and hide. I shouldn't be so brave, even if I'm only standing up to a television screen.

Then the thought hits me.

This is my chance.

Maxwell's eyes are wild; he's livid. His type A personality won't let sleeping dogs lie. He won't hesitate to show me my place. And when he does, maybe then I'll remember everything I need to know, far away from him and from the safety of this base.

I know I have an audience, but I need this. I never let on that I couldn't remember my time with him. He thinks I remember everything.

If I force his hand, I'll know for sure what happened to me. I might be able to remember and finish this.

This is the single riskiest thing I've ever done, but the payoff would be worth the sacrifice.

Mustering everything I have, I push him to the brink I know he will push back from.

"Go ahead. I'm not afraid of you anymore." My voice is shaky, but I think the uncertainty will work to my advantage. Maybe it's good he thinks there is a part of me that is scared of whatever he did to me.

"Jessa, maybe you shouldn't..."

Dana's voice trails off when I glare at her, our laughter from just minutes ago long forgotten.

I need this.

I need to know, and I'll never get a chance like this again.

Silence fills the room as the four of us stand still in front of the TV. Maxwell is staring into the screen, analyzing me, probably trying to decide what to do.

I know that look.

He's trying to remain in control, removed, and I know I can push him. All he needs is that one little nudge, and his need to put me in my place will consume him.

Then I remember something he said to me on my first day with him.

I take a deep breath, and I push. "Who's the little bitch now?"

I fire my insult straight at him in front of everyone, and in a fraction of a second, with the slip of his smirk, I know I have him.

His eyes flare as his cold expression drops into a sneer of pure hatred, and I know there is no turning back.

"What the hell is she doing?" Logan is captivated as he watches everything unfold right in front of us, and it's completely out of our control.

I want to go to her, but I'll miss too much running down the halls.

Dana is with her, and I know she'll do everything she can to protect her friend.

"She's trying to take back her memories," I whisper to Logan so no one else can pick it up. It doesn't matter; no one is paying attention to the two of us anyway. Jessa has tapped into Maxwell's anger, and he isn't going to let her get away with it. "She's pushing him to reveal everything she doesn't remember."

"I hope this doesn't backfire, Jack." Logan adjusts his screen directly in front of him so he can take everything in.

Then, through the security feed, I hear Jessa. She sounds stronger than I've ever heard her, and it rattles me to my core. "Who's the little bitch now?"

As soon as her words are out, I know Maxwell's ego will give her exactly what she's asking for.

"You'll regret this, Jessa. You and your little buddy, Zane, belong to me. I'm here to generously coordinate your release, and this is how you speak to me? Very well. If you want a reminder, who am I to deny such a lovely request?" Then, with an evil sneer, he continues his tirade. "You brought this on yourself."

Reaching forward to his own laptop, Maxwell jabs at a couple of keys, and a video abruptly fills the screen. It's clear this was part of his plan all along; he was always going to play this video.

She's here with me, and it's eating him alive. Of course he's going to show me what he did to her, and my stomach drops as a younger Jessa comes into focus.

She's sitting in a room with two men standing on either side of her. Maxwell is seated across from her as he asks questions about Zane, and Jessa was right. There is no fire, curiosity, or intensity. He doesn't have the same interest that Logan did when he questioned her.

He's consumed by something else. It's almost as though her answers are irrelevant.

Jessa's posture is passive. She's trying her best not to challenge him with her answers, and he is growing more frustrated with each question. Then the video jumps ahead to Maxwell ordering his men to take her outside.

My heart lurches at the sight of Jessa's fallen face. She doesn't understand what's going on, but she cooperates.

The video fades to black for a moment, then comes back on. They are outside now, and feet shuffle along the ground. They stop, and as the camera is raised, I see where Jessa spent almost two days.

Iron bars surround her, and the ground inside the cage is damp and muddy, while the dirt outside is dry. They put all of the dogs in one cage and placed her in another, and she stood in piss and shit, barefoot, unable to kneel or sit on the ground.

"Tell me you belong to me." Maxwell's tone is manic.

Jessa is confused. "What?"

"You heard me. Tell me you are mine, Jessa."

I'm sickened by his words. I knew how he felt about her, but I never thought he would be capable of this, not with someone he claimed to care about.

"N-no."

"You'll feel differently after a night out here." Maxwell lifts his hand to the lens to stop the footage.

When the video cuts in, it's the same scene, but, judging by the darker surroundings, it's later in the evening.

"Please can I have something to eat? Some water?" Jessa's pale fingers clutch the bars, and she speaks into the camera as her teeth chatter together.

"Tell me you belong to me." The words are the same, but his tone is different now. It's as though her answer no longer matters to him. He's already decided that she is his. He's just waiting for her to tire herself out to the point of surrender. "Kneel down and tell me you are mine."

Jessa lowers her gaze to the damp ground. Her fingers are still wrapped around the bars, holding her to the side of the cage. When she raises her head back up, her brows are furrowed. She has no idea what he's asking. He's already decided her fate. Her educated consent is inconsequential to him.

As if finding a hidden reserve of fight, Jessa stands up to Maxwell. She hasn't noticed that she's no longer speaking with the boy she knew in school.

"I will never kneel down for you."

"Have it your way, Jessa. Just remember I gave you a chance. I offered you a different life than this."

Backing up a couple of steps, Maxwell motions to two of his men. They step toward the side of the cage and, without warning, unzip their pants and urinate on her before she is able to jump out of the way.

The camera focuses on her body as wet stains cover her jeans and her dirty, torn top, and I suddenly realize this was before her first night in the cage.

She remembers this.

I glance at the security feed in the common room. It appears she hasn't moved a muscle. She's waiting for him to get to the part she doesn't remember.

Maxwell's voice snaps my attention back to the video. "You will kneel for me, Jessa. You can't stand forever, and as soon as your knees hit that fucking ground, you will belong to me, and I will take what's mine. Until then, I've decided you are standing in my men's new toilet. You will know what it means to be nothing, and you will keep learning that lesson until you drop down in front of me. Good luck sleeping. It's going to be a cold night. Until then, here's some water." He tosses an unopened bottle of water onto the damp ground and steps back. The camera focuses on a dinner plate with a nicely grilled steak topped with potatoes and carrots, and my own mouth waters at the sight. "As for this, you will come to learn that you earn your rewards, and you did not earn this."

The camera jerks as he tosses the food at the cage with the dogs in it. The plate shatters on impact, and the dogs fight each other as they claw at the gourmet dinner through the bars.

The camera shifts to the ground, and Maxwell's disgusted voice ends this part of the video. "Put the dog food in her cage. If she wants to act like a little bitch, I'll treat her like one."

The next clip is bright. No doubt the next morning. There is no sound, and Logan reaches across the laptop to make sure his volume is turned up. Then she comes into view.

Jessa has entwined her arms around the bars, and she's holding herself in place as she takes what little sleep she probably got in a standing position.

A yell jolts her awake, and the camera is close enough on her face that I see it. It's small, almost unnoticeable. Her eyes are unfocused, and she's a little slow to respond.

This is her on autopilot.

This is her protecting herself, and I steal a glance at the security feed on our second laptop to watch as Jessa takes a step closer to the TV in the common room.

Her head is tilted, and she is examining herself closely.

This is the point from which she doesn't remember.

"Boss said you could have one bottle of water for the day. Make it last." As a bottle is tossed into the cage, she turns to reach down for it.

Before she stands all the way up, there's the sound of a zipper, followed by a relieved sigh from the guy outside the cage as he pisses on her, and she scrambles to move away. Her reflexes are dull, and her feet almost give out as the man holding the camera speaks. "Careful now, princess. Boss told us to tell him when you were ready to kneel. You're taking away all of our fun if you give up too soon."

His laughter cuts into my head as she scurries to the far side of the cage, and the video quickly cuts out, then back in.

Jessa is standing in the middle of the cage.

More time must have passed.

Her body looks like it's ready to give up. She's swaying in place as her eyes, void of life, drift around the ground. She looks lost in her thoughts, and I know what's coming.

Her body is about to collapse, and Maxwell is there to witness it.

He says her name.

He knows she is no longer a challenge.

He's coaxing her to give up.

Her body is showing no signs of awareness now, but he speaks anyway.

"Forty hours, Jessa. You've been standing in this little cage for forty hours with only two bottles of water." The camera shifts down to the ground, and I see the two empty bottles lying beside the bowl of dog food. My stomach heaves when I notice the bowl is empty as well.

She must have been so hungry.

"I'm not here to convince you to give up, Jessa. I'm here to witness it." The video zooms in on vacant eyes. Her head moves slowly from side to side, and her lips move as she mutters to herself. No doubt she's lost to the voices inside her head now.

She never could have imagined this level of cruelty, the depth of his depravity, and he's only getting started. Her surrender is just the tip of his hellish iceberg.

A silent minute passes. Then, as if in slow motion, her knee buckles. She catches herself and attempts to stand up straight, but I see it in her eyes.

She knows she's done.

She knows she's at her limit, and a tear rolls down her cheek as she looks slowly up to the sky.

The sun shines bright across her face, and she closes her

eyes for a moment, as if to feel its warmth as her entire body sways, held up only by the position of her stance now.

She opens her eyes, and her disillusions are gone as tears openly pour down her cheeks.

She knows what's about to happen.

She knows she fought her fight, and she's done.

And, most importantly, she knows I'm not coming for her.

There is no rescue, no safe haven for her now.

Her eyes close, and I know this is it.

She's out cold before her fragile body buckles into itself.

She feels nothing as she drops to her knees and falls forward.

She's gone before her face hits the piss-covered ground, and her body bounces limp in place as her fight leaves her. She takes my will to live with her.

The door to the cage creaks open. Then two men pick up her lifeless body and drag her out of her prison and toward her hell. Her bare feet trail limply behind her.

The video focuses on Maxwell's body. His head is out of the frame, and he's holding a tree branch in his hands as he uses a pocketknife to remove some leaves.

"Wash her, then let her sleep for a couple hours. I want her exhausted but aware. Don't allow her any clothes. Then feed her. She'll be starving. Have the cook make three meals, then feed them all to her and let her fill herself up. I want her on a full stomach when I start with her. I want to watch her vomit everything I allowed her to eat back up when I beat her."

"Jesus," Logan mutters with a shudder under his breath beside me as the video cuts out again.

Then, without mercy, it cuts back in with a change of scenery.

The room is partially lit, and I can make out my Jessa clearly. Her naked body is tied stomach-down on what looks like a bench. Straps around her legs hold her lower body open and in place. Rusted chains attach to cuffs on her wrists, and her arms are clipped to the bench, allowing only her head to move.

The camera is stationary and propped to allow a full view of the room, and it isn't lost on me they are alone. I have a feeling Maxwell didn't want an audience for this part.

Then he approaches her, his voice low and calculating. "I remember the first day I saw you in fourth grade, Jessa. You were like an angel in your pretty sundress. I knew, even then, you would be mine."

Jessa's eyes are open, but she is making no effort to move. She flexes her hands in their binds.

She's too scared to challenge him now.

He touches the soft skin on her back, and I bare my teeth in silence as she flinches.

"I decided to bide my time and wait for you. You just needed time to figure it out. So, until you did, I protected you." Brushing her hair back from her neck, he leans in, and his expression comes into focus.

There's no kindness in his eyes.

"By high school, I knew what my father did. I knew he wasn't a good man. He took, he bullied, but he always got what he wanted. I learned how to take, how to force obedience, and how to punish those who didn't do what they were told. But still, I wanted you to come to me. You would be the one good thing in my life. My solace. Then *he* showed up, and you fell for his lies."

She knows he's talking about me, and, without hesitation, Jessa slips up to protect me. "He didn't lie to me."

I see it in her face that she instantly regrets her outburst. Dropping her head back down, she waits, terrified for his response.

"Oh, didn't he? Did he come looking for you when you disappeared? Do you know where he is now? Because I do." At the suggestion that I'm alive, her body stills. "Jack, the love of your life, moved on. He married the next girl he met. I've got to admit, he moves fast for a guy in love like you say he was. Don't take my word for it though. Look." Fisting her hair, he yanks her focus up to the wall, where an image flashes onto a television screen.

It's me.

But it's not me.

I'm smiling. I'm much younger than I am now, and I'm the groom in a wedding photo. Except I've never been married. And just as I open my mouth to say that, a slideshow starts, filled with photos of me with a woman I've never met.

Retouched photo after retouched photo paint a picture of a perfect life. Smiling, vacations, work functions, birthdays, then a baby. A son. Then a second. The slideshow ends with a family photo that remains on the screen.

A happily married man who moved on without her.

A man who had a family and forgot about her while she fought to stay alive.

A man who didn't care where she was or what happened to her.

Except it was all a lie.

A lie she believed. Tears roll down her face in the video.

"He got what he wanted, and he moved on." Disgust

laces his words as he releases her hair, and she drops her head back onto the bench as he continues, "And now I'm going to show you how much you've disappointed me, because since that day, I stopped waiting for you to come to me, and I decided my father was right. If you want anything in this world, you just take it."

The threat in his words lands, and Jessa jerks to life.

"What? Maxwell, please! You wouldn't do that. You're better than your father." She tries to look at him, but he's directly behind her.

The Max we knew in school was never real, and Jessa somehow doesn't realize it yet.

Maxwell picks up a belt and doubles it over in his fist. Then, without warning or further conversation, he steps to Jessa and brings the belt down across her back with such force that it makes her whole body go rigid for a moment. As the shock of impact sinks in, she chokes out a low scream.

"You knew I wanted you, Jessa." Unhinged, he spits his words, and he wastes no time in pulling his arm back for another strike as the beginning of an angry red welt forms along her upper back.

"NO! WAIT! DON'T!"

The crack of the second hit causes Logan to shift uncomfortably in his seat, but neither of us will look away as her screams echo through the laptop.

Logan nervously taps his fingers on the desk near the volume button. This is affecting him as well. He has always taught me the importance of self-control above all, and I know seeing this is distressing for him.

Jessa was right.

Maxwell had no intention of learning more about Zane.

His love for her crossed all lines and pushed him deep into darkness.

There is no negotiating with madness.

More strikes land across her back as she wails into the room. Her shrill cries will haunt me for the rest of my days. Then Maxwell takes a moment to step back and look at his work, and his chest rises and falls with strained breaths.

She is being punished for all of her choices.

She's being punished for me.

Jessa's back, buttocks, and thighs are covered in welts, and her once pale skin is now bright red, almost purple in some spots and screaming with fury. Draping the belt over the curve of her ass, he bends over and grabs something I strain to see.

He hovers his hand over her back, as though the warmth of her wounds is radiating upward. "This is your lesson, Jessa. You will not search for Jack ever again. He is happy, and he's moved on with his pathetic little life. If I ever find out you even typed his name into your computer, this will feel like a tickle. Do I make myself clear?"

"Yes," she whimpers through trembling lips. The fear sparking off her is like nothing I've seen before. Even before Logan sedated her, her panic was never this intense. This is beyond her fight level, and it's crippling her.

"I don't think you fully understand, Jessa. But you will." Widening his stance, he raises his arm back above his head, and before I can mutter my disgust, he brings it down with force. My stomach turns over at the sound of the switch cutting through the air before it makes contact with her inflamed skin.

White creeps into the corners of my vision as Jessa releases a shrill scream into the room. The localized impact on her already reddened skin would have been like nothing she could have imagined. The searing heat and sharp pain cutting through tender flesh would be unbearable to even the toughest guys here on base.

Maxwell steps back to watch Jessa's body process her new level of pain as she lifts her head weakly off the bench. Her eyes are filled with confusion as she squirms. It's like she's trying to hide from what is coming next. Then, with a heave in her binds, she lets out a desperate gurgle before stretching her neck forward to vomit the food Maxwell overfed her earlier.

Logan bolts up from his seat and takes a quick stride over to the window of his office as the sounds of her retches fill the room.

His hands grip his hips as he looks first to the ceiling, then to the floor before returning and sitting down.

I won't take my eyes off of her. This is my own punishment for not doing enough to protect her.

I failed her over and over again, but I will commit everything to memory so I can be here for her and help her now.

"I'll remind you I gave you a safe word, Jessa."

Dropping her head back in place, she chooses silence, and I understand why.

There is nothing that will stop Maxwell now. He's given her some kind of safe word in the hopes that she'll ask for mercy so he can deny her request, and she knows it.

"Have it your way." The shuffle of Maxwell's body causes Jessa to tense up.

She knows what's coming this time. She just doesn't know where. The switch connects along her lower back, and she sucks hard to suck in air as she coughs out her pain. Her hands remain fisted tight as her head lolls. Her body is still exhausted from the cage, and I silently hope she passes out again from this horror she is barely living through.

My wish is granted on his next swing. Her head snaps back when the switch hits her upper back, then immediately drops limp onto the bench.

Maxwell notices it too.

Pausing only to check her pulse, he smiles at his accomplishment, and I vow to make him feel every single thing he is inflicting on her.

He whips her another ten times as hard as he can while she is unconscious. I couldn't say if it was his intention to continue striking her, because on the tenth hit, the switch snaps in two across her back.

He drops the broken branch to the ground, then steps close, watching.

Slowly, almost one at a time, the strikes that broke her skin swell as blood pours out in trickles.

I glance over to Logan, who is frozen in his seat with his hand covering the look of shock on his face. In the ten years I've known him, he's never inflicted this level of pain on anyone.

This is raw sadism, without control and void of humanity.

The video cuts back to Jessa's body lying limp across the bench, and I'm hoping for the end when a bucket of water is poured over her head. She jolts in her binds, and water spurts from her mouth as she regains consciousness.

The belt has now been fastened around her throat, but she doesn't notice it. Her body trembles as the pain from the beating registers in her brain, and she lets out an exasperated cry.

"IT HURTS. PLEASE."

"Shh. That's all over now, Jessa. I'll have the doctor give you something for the pain. It hurts much worse than it looks." His arrogance knows no bounds. He knows damn well the scars he's inflicted on her.

"Let me go, Maxwell. I'll contact Zane. He'll work something out."

"I'm not ready to let you go, Jessa. Now that you're mine, I think I want to keep you." He reaches his hand slowly between her legs.

He's challenging her to deny she's his, but she doesn't fall for it. Closing her eyes tight, she drops her head back down to the bench, and her upper body heaves as she cries.

"You made a mistake with Jack. You realize that now." He slides deeper into his psychotic break. "It's no matter. You belong to me. Just like it was always supposed to be." Stepping back from her, he continues talking as he unzips his pants. Jessa hears it, and she struggles, pulling against her binds and pleading "no" over and over again. "You still with me, my little crybaby?"

"You don't have to do this."

"No, Jessa. *You* didn't have to do this. It's your choices that brought us here. I wanted your light." Stepping forward, he positions himself behind her, grabbing her hips and jerking her toward him. "Now all I can think about is snuffing out your light and showing you my dark." He snarls as he lunges into her, and she screams a long, painful cry.

Bile rises from my stomach as I bear witness to her forced sodomy. I fail her and close my eyes, knowing if I watch one more second, I will go to a place I will never come back from.

His grunts and her cries fill my head, and I'm moments from spiraling when Jessa screams, "JACK!"

My eyes fly open to find him holding the leash end of his belt with one hand as he fists her hair with the other, wrenching her head back to give her a full view of my fake happily ever after, still plastered on the screen in front of her as he violates her.

Then it comes again.

"JACK! JACK... JAAAAACK!" Her voice is unhinged, and she's shrieking with every last fiber of her being.

That same scream.

The night Logan questioned her comes barreling back at me, and the room sways.

In this moment, I'd give my life to take away her pain.

Her entire body trembles as he pulls his flaccid cock out of her and drops her head on the bench.

There's another transition.

Jessa's listless, naked body is suspended by her wrists, which are tied above her. Only the tips of her big toes touch the floor, and her legs are restrained open. As she shifts her hips, my eyes are drawn to her center.

"What is that?" Logan whispers beside me.

It looks like something is inserted between her legs with two strings running out of it and down to the floor.

An unrecognizable figure stands in the shadows behind her.

Some type of switch is flipped off camera. Then the room is filled with a low hum.

Electricity.

Realization hits Jessa at the same time it hits me.

Those aren't strings.

They're wires.

"Please, don't." Her voice is hoarse from screaming as she jerks against her binds.

"We all make choices, Jessa. You chose wrong. Your life is in my hands. Literally. I can take it away, and I can give it back." Maxwell is past his point of no return. He's allowed his spurned ego to make his decisions, and he's no longer treating her like a human being.

The hum changes in pitch as Jessa's body seizes. He's turned the current on. She spasms as short grunts involuntarily leave her.

As the hum stops, her limp body falls in its binds. Her head drops forward, then she tenses up in one long drawn-out spasm.

The sound of her gasping for breath fills the room, and Logan and I watch the shadowed figure scurry out from the darkness in what looks like a lab coat. He runs to Jessa, checking for a pulse.

"She's going into cardiac arrest!" the anonymous man shouts to Maxwell, who has now moved off-screen.

The video cuts out.

I'm not sure how much time passes after the screen goes dark.

I could have lost her in that moment, and I never even knew she was alive. I worried that knowing what happened to Jessa would break her, but it's broken me instead.

Logan sets his hand on my arm and pushes me out of view of the webcam.

The live feed to Maxwell fills the screen, and everything is different.

I see a monster—one I need to put down. My fury is no longer contained. I'm unhinged.

I must have looked like a madman standing there, baring my teeth at the screen.

Logan moved me aside so I could regain control of myself, and judging by the way Maxwell looks at his monitor, he was hoping to catch my reaction.

"Not so talkative now, are you?" Maxwell's words are for Jessa, but she doesn't respond.

Logan glares at me, and I know that look. He's telling me to get my shit together or leave, and I won't be excluded from this.

I tear myself out of her hell. It happened years ago, I remind myself. Jessa is safe in the common room.

I look for her on the security feed.

Her strength and poise are astounding, and I draw from her example as I school my features, then step back into view.

"Now, where was I? Ah, yes. You will have Jessa contact Zane, and you'll release her back to him. I require their assistance, and they are kind of a package deal." Maxwell continues on as though nothing happened.

Logan huffs at the screen. "And why would we do that? From where I sit, you have nothing to bargain with. Showing us a video from years ago doesn't change anything."

Maxwell goes silent.

He knows he has nothing we want, and we have everything he wants.

As he opens his mouth to speak, an alarm goes off on his end, and he reaches down to punch a button in front of him. Then he continues, "This isn't a negotiation. Release Jessa back to Zane. There will be consequences if you refuse."

Then, shifting his glance to another spot on the screen, he continues, "And, Jessa? I can deliver a repeat performance if you defy me. I'll be in touch with further instructions."

Maxwell disconnects, leaving me in a maelstrom of emotions.

Instinct kicks in, and I'm heading to the door before I register Logan's hand on my arm, trying to stop me.

"I need to find Jessa." I point to the security feed on the wall as I see her turn and run out of the common room.

"Jack, give me a minute. Something's wrong. Maxwell wouldn't contact us without a specific motive. He knows he has nothing to bargain with and his demands won't be met. What just happened here? He didn't just call us up to play that video. We need to figure this out first."

My only thoughts are of Jessa, and before I realize it, my own questions are pouring out of me. "I don't understand. Why didn't she use her safe word? Why didn't she try?"

When I meet Logan's eyes, his expression tells me he's figured out something I haven't.

"Jack, I think she did use her safe word...." Silence lingers as he waits for me to realize it.

The unthinkable enters my head, and my soul fractures as her screams haunt me once again.

"Jack." I say my own name, and Logan nods once in confirmation. "Her safe word was Jack. She knew he wasn't going to stop. He wanted her to call for me to show her I wasn't going to save her."

And I didn't.

He took everything from her, and I didn't protect her.

"I'm so sorry, Jack. While this isn't beyond what we are capable of, this isn't something we would ever choose to inflict on someone."

Logan is right. We could never come close to what Maxwell has allowed himself to become.

"I just don't get it. His whole purpose for the call was to show us the video. He wanted to show me what he did to Jessa. That was all he accomplished."

He had an audience, and he violated her all over again, and for what?

"Was it? What did he say at the end?"

"He told her not to defy him, then he told us he'd be in touch with further instructions." I memorized every second of that video.

"Did he? Or was he telling *her* he'd be in touch with further instructions?" Logan's words stop me still.

How could he reach her with further instructions? He'd have to go through us.

Then, like a slap in the face, everything connects, and it all makes sense. "The mole. Shit. I need to find Jessa."

Stepping back from me, Logan glances at the security feeds on his wall. "By the looks of it, she's heading to the showers."

CHAPTER 23
JESSA

The video call ends abruptly, and I'm thrust back to the room. I hear soft sobs from my left.

Out of the corner of my eye, I see Dana hugged tightly against Grizz's chest. She's crying, while he just stares at me, face drawn and pale.

Now I know.

But I still feel nothing, nothing but sadness. Sorrow for a girl who believed her childhood friend was inherently good.

I've now witnessed my own rape and torture, and I still don't remember it.

My scars still bear no emotional or mental reminder of pain.

There is no recollection, no raw suffering to draw from. And—most importantly—no memories.

I still don't have the piece I need, and I'm suddenly angry. I'm angry at myself because I can't unlock my most important memory from my own head. I can hack my way into any computer on this godforsaken rock, yet I can't access one little memory.

I took a chance at closure, and I failed, and now everyone knows what happened to me.

It's worse than I could have ever imagined.

Tears sting my eyes.

"Jessa?" Dana's broken voice jolts me from my thoughts, and I recoil at her touch.

Startled, she pulls her hand back, and I look around at Hunter and Grizz, who are staring wide-eyed at me, waiting for my next move.

"I want to be alone." I turn toward the door, but Hunter takes a step into my path.

"Orders. I can't leave you."

"Fine. I'm taking a shower—alone."

It breaks my heart to see Dana so distressed, but she has Grizz. I can't be here for her right now.

The walls push in on me. Without waiting for approval, I turn to leave. Hunter follows me out. No doubt he'll tell Jack where I'm headed, but I hope I get a little time to myself before he finds me.

Tears push out of my eyes when I blink as I pick up my pace to the showers.

I know where I'm going, and I want distance from Hunter. If I can just get to the showers, he'll give me the space I need to regroup.

Turning down the last hall, I'm about to reach out for the door when a firm grip on my shoulder pulls me back, and Hunter shoves me against the wall. "Orders. I have a message for you."

His weight pins me, and my brain scrambles to process his words. "What? From Jack?"

"No—Maxwell."

My throat constricts as I struggle to breathe.

I now have one question answered.

I know who the mole is.

Hunter glances up to the ceiling, then slides me a foot to my left like I'm a sack of potatoes before pinning me back against the wall. He's moved me completely out of the cameras' view.

"He's got a job for you and Zane."

"What job?"

"Maxwell wants you to hack the base mainframe and download everything to his team. All clients, bank accounts, snitches, and their internal security access to all the other systems they're connected to."

When I open my mouth to object, he pulls me from the wall just to slam me back against it.

"I don't have time, Jessa. You know if you tell them who I am, another will come for you. Max has a job. Once that's done, we can get out of here—permanently. You know what happens when you disobey him, Jessa."

Hunter is threatening me in error. He thinks I remember every minute of my time there. He thinks I'm afraid.

But I'm at an advantage because I can still think clearly and focus on my plan.

Dropping my calm a few notches, I feign panic to bolster his confidence. "Okay. Just give me some time. I need to figure some things out. I'll get you a list of what I need to do it. Give me a day."

A door opens down another hall, and it snaps Hunter out of his death stare.

When he steps back, I slump onto the weight of my feet and straighten my shirt. Hunter glances over his shoulder, down the empty corridor, then corrals me toward the showers.

"Don't try anything stupid, Jessa. You know what he's capable of."

I shove my weight into the door and stumble into the shower, quickly taking my spot behind the partition to remove my clothes. I have nothing with me. No shampoo, and no towel, but I don't care.

I'm not a possession.

Everyone wants to own me.

They want to tell me what to do and use me up, and I've had enough.

Intimidate the girl and she'll fall in line.

I don't belong to them.

I was never Maxwell's.

The look on his smug face said he believes otherwise, and it took everything I had not to tell him what I had planned for him in the end.

When I'm done with him, he'll be the one on his knees, begging for mercy, and if I'm still standing, I will grant him none.

Then there's Hunter.

I have to admit, I didn't see him coming. Maxwell got as close as he could to Jack and Logan, and they have no idea.

I strip off the last of my clothes and step under the water. I'm so tired of people taking pieces of me I don't want to give. I'm not a commodity to be passed around.

As the water heats up against my skin, I tilt my face into the hot spray to center myself.

Little voices creep in among the droplets hitting my face.

Everyone saw my pain, my torture.

I know Jack saw everything. Of course he did. Maxwell was ready to show that video. Acquiring my release was just a ruse. He wanted Jack to see how broken I am. How used up I've become. And now Maxwell wants me to be the one to destroy Jack. He thinks this is his final step to claiming what is his, but I won't allow it.

Pulling my head back, I suck in a deep breath of air as a sob heaves out of me, and I just can't keep it together any longer. My stomach knots as nausea sets in. Then, all at once, it hits me.

I hate to be cold.

Is that because of my time spent outside, locked in that cage?

As I turn the hot water up, another choked sob bursts from me. My legs turn weak, and I slowly lower myself to the floor. I've held everything in for so long. I run, and I protect, and we stay alive, and I have nothing left to give.

Nothing except my tears, and I let them come.

CHAPTER 24

JACK

"Get out." My demand is delivered on a dangerously low growl as I step into the shower area.

Hunter's face falls as he pushes himself off the wall and straightens in place.

There is no kindness in my voice. He is standing between me and what's mine, and I won't have it.

"Y-you said not to let her out of my sight, boss." Deep down, I feel a momentary stab of regret for treating him so harshly.

He did his job: watching her to make sure she was okay.

He's always been a loyal friend. But I can't manage pleasantries right now. Taking a deep breath, I glance in his direction, and he changes course.

"I-I mean, sure thing." He slips around behind me and disappears.

The creak of the door bleeds into quiet sobs coming from the shower, and I soften. I drop my phone on a dry ledge and step through the water without regard for my shoes.

They aren't important.

There is only one thing that matters right now, and that

one thing is curled up in the fetal position on the tile, naked and sobbing into the drain.

When I step closer, I notice her skin is flushed red as the water washes over her, and the heat from the shower wafts against me.

I reach out to test the water, and it's scalding hot.

"Jessa, you're going to burn yourself," I warn as I turn it down to a comfortable temperature.

Her voice is weak, tired. "I don't like to be cold."

My instincts take over, and I'm suddenly on the ground, scooping her up into my lap. My back and legs warm as the water slowly seeps through my clothes.

The moment she's in my arms, she reaches out to grab the front of my shirt, and she pulls herself as close to me as she can while burying her face in my chest.

There's so much I want to say, but I stay quiet and still and allow her to lead.

The shower rains down around us. I've never paid attention to the sound the droplets make as they hit the tile floor. How could I never have noticed how loud they are?

Jessa ends our few minutes of silence with a shuddering breath.

"Jack, I still don't remember, and I need to remember." Her determination is impressive, but I'm lost as to why she would want to fully understand what happened to her.

"Why? Why put yourself through that? Isn't seeing it enough?"

"You saw how out of it I was. But I still contacted Dana and managed to get myself out of there without leading them to her or Zane. If I could do that, then there's a chance I..." Her words trail off, and I get the impression this is something she is hesitant to share with me.

"What are you talking about? What do you think you did, Jessa?"

Her fingers flex in my shirt as she sits with her thoughts before deciding to share them with me.

"I think I might have been able to hide execution code on his servers. Just a small piece of code, hidden in an old file. All I would need is everyone distracted for a couple of seconds. I know most server vulnerabilities. If I put the code in, I can access almost everything and take control of his programs. Zane and I could hack in, and we'd have everything we need to end him. We have all the programs in place; it would all come together like dominoes, and he wouldn't be able to stop it. But I don't know if I did it, or what the code would be. If we're going to get in, we have one shot. I need to know for sure." Her eyes are both hopeful and hopeless.

Just as I'm about to allow my own hopes to soar, I remind myself that, while this would be amazing news, she still doesn't remember. I'm about to tell her we'll figure it out together when the shower doors creak close.

I shift my body around the stall to find the room empty. No one is with us, so that means someone just left. Someone heard Jessa, and my mind shifts to the mole. If Maxwell's plant overheard what she just said, then they'll attempt to contact Maxwell and warn him. I'll make my way to Logan to check the security feed later. This might be easier than I thought.

But I can't leave Jessa just yet.

She shivers under the heat of the shower, and I realize she's not cold; she's showing the first stages of shock.

"I've got you, Jessa. It's just me." I rock her gently in place as I try to keep her here with me.

Whether she has her memories or not, she still saw most of the time she doesn't remember.

Words fail her as she drops her head and begins to sob into my shirt. Her cries desperately drain out of her in chokes and panicked breaths.

Her anguish is beginning to flow into me, and I need to help her out before she sucks me in. "Talk to me, please. Tell me a thought. Any thought."

"You saw it." She won't lift her head. Her shame weighs it down, and I take a quiet minute to process her words.

I saw it.

I saw a madman consumed by contempt. I saw rage personified. I saw a dead man hurt my treasure. But I also saw her strength, her kindness, and through it all, she never lost that light he spoke about.

Her light can't be beaten out of her.

It is her.

"Yes, I did. I'm sorry, Jessa. He will pay for what he's done. I can't let this go. I will kill him."

"But me. You saw me—" Her voice breaks into sobs, as though the thought is too much for her to say out loud, and I know what's going through her mind.

"You think that makes you damaged?" I ask. Her cries increase as she buries her head in my chest. "You think you're, what? Broken? Worthless, maybe?" My voice is low, and her failure to look me in the eye tells me I'm bang on.

Then, dropping my voice as low as I can manage to show the severity of my next question, I challenge her, "Do you think I won't want you?"

In an instant, her body tenses in my arms. She knows I'm not messing around.

Good.

"I—" Her eyes finally make contact with mine as she searches for validation.

"Jessa. I never stopped wanting you. You gave yourself to me ten years ago, and you gave yourself to me again the other night. You aren't disposable. You aren't something I will let go of."

"But I'm not property." Her body stiffens again in my embrace, and I know in an instant I misread the room.

She isn't looking for validation. She's pushing away. She's trying to build her walls up to protect herself.

Maxwell forced his claim on her seven years ago, and he tried to reinforce it when he made contact today.

Logan and I need her help, and if I'm honest with myself, if I didn't have this connection with Jessa, I would be treating her like a commodity right now too.

But I don't want to use her.

I want to strengthen her.

I want to protect her.

"Jessa, whether you admit it or not, you're hurting. You just saw Maxwell rape and torture you. Even if you can't connect it to your memories, you saw it. You know what he did to you. Everyone knows what he did to you." Her face tilts back to mine, her eyes blinking rapidly as the water splashes near her head. "I know you feel bad inside. And you think this makes you look bad on the outside." My words hit hard, and she coughs out a cry, but I won't back down. She needs to feel this pain. "Being the object of his rage is not a reflection of you. All I saw was your strength. I saw you fighting to stay alive. He put you in a room with no witnesses, and he reduced himself to his basest form while you were bound and helpless. He should be ashamed. He should feel ugly and worthless, and just because he doesn't have the morality in him to feel that, it doesn't mean the responsibility falls to you."

I pause to let my words sink in, and I need a little sign from her to show me where to go next. Thankfully, she offers me a path.

"It hurts, Jack. How could he?" She sucks in an unsteady breath as her hands grip my wet shirt. "And everyone saw it. Dana saw it, Jack. She knows. She'll blame herself. I don't know how to help her." My heart swells knowing how genuine hers is.

Her worry is for her friend.

"He just did that—to me. I said no, and he did that. I feel disgusting." She's grasping at words, and I won't allow her current panic to become future voices in her head.

I correct her.

"Disgusted."

Her thought process breaks. "What?"

"You said you feel disgusting. That is inward. You are not disgusting. You feel disgusted." I need her to process her thoughts differently, and she needs to own her anger.

"Don't tell me what I feel, Jack." Her eyes dart around, searching for her answer.

I have it.

I know what she needs.

She needs to let all of her anger out.

She needs to let go of all of the hurt she's pushed down, and I know exactly who she needs to start with.

"I feel like I'm drowning. I still don't remember, but I—I don't know how to fix this." She meets my eyes in a silent plea, and I lift her off of my chest.

It's time to answer for the part I played in all of this.

CHAPTER 25
JESSA

My reality has become a series of thoughts without tangible emotion.

I know what happened to me. I saw it all. I know why I am terrified to my core of Maxwell now, but I still don't feel the results of his actions. I'm left with only my resolve that I can't let it happen again.

There's a piece missing, and until I find it and put myself back together, I'm useless to everyone I care about.

"I don't know how to fix this," I whisper helplessly.

That's how I feel: helpless.

I've always fixed things. It's what I do. But I can't seem to fix myself, and my confession threatens to swallow me whole.

Jack shifts, moving my body to face his. As my wet skin brushes along his shirt, I realize for the first time since he entered the room that I'm curled up in his lap, on the floor, with a shower raining around us, and I'm naked.

"Jessa. I'm sorry." The sadness written all over his face rattles me.

"What? What are *you* saying sorry for?"

"I'm sorry I never told you who I was all of those years ago. If I had told you, things might have ended differently. I blamed myself for your disappearance for a long time. And if you knew I was undercover, you may have been able to find me—after."

I've spent years drowning in hindsight. I don't want him to succumb to it as well. "I don't blame you for that, Jack. You could never have known what would happen."

"I know you don't blame me for that. *I* blame me. But I know you blame me for something else." His insinuation lingers, unspoken, and I scramble to figure it out on my own.

I have nothing. I never hated him. Not for any of it.

I shake my head to tell him I don't agree, and he continues, "I never came for you, Jessa. Maxwell had you, and I never came for you. I moved on. I got married and had a family."

My chest tightens. "That wasn't true, Jack. He lied about those things," I counter, and he picks up just as quickly.

"Yes, but you didn't know that. You saw my family—my kids. My wife. Until a few days ago, you still believed I had a family, one you were trying to protect by not searching for me. You loved me, and I moved on. You must have hated me for that."

My memories take me back to the cold room where I spent two days recovering after I woke up from Maxwell's torture.

I remember drifting in and out as a result of whatever the doctor kept injecting into my IV. On one occasion, the doctor was sitting in a chair beside my bed. *Maxwell's orders*, he said as he handed me a pile of photographs to look at. *He wants to make sure you get a good look at these before you leave.*

They were photos of Jack's life—his falsified life. His smile was just like I remembered, only it wasn't for me anymore. It was for her. I didn't even know her name or the names he chose for his sons. I remember handing the photos back and waiting for the doctor to leave the room before I cried into the pillow.

But even after that, I still couldn't let him go. I obsessed over him, but Maxwell closed off my outlet. I was too afraid to type his name on my keyboard. I wouldn't let Dana say it out loud for fear that Jack's family would be destroyed.

I was broken, but I couldn't let go of him. Even though I knew he belonged to someone else, I couldn't do it.

And I hated myself for that.

"It wasn't you." I drop my head, and the connection Jack just made for me hits me hard. I'm thankful I'm already on the floor.

"What?"

"I hated myself." My own words hit me like a slap in the face.

I was the one who made the stupid mistake of leading Maxwell's grunts to my door, thinking the Maxwell I knew was still somewhere inside the monster he had become. And when Maxwell showed me those photographs, I was hurt that Jack had moved on, and I hated myself for being so weak that I couldn't do the same.

While I innocently played with my friends, an evil lived all around me, and I had no idea. Everything was a lie. I lived a life that never happened. Nothing was real, except for Dana and my family—and they were taken from me.

And I blamed myself for all of it.

"I looked for you, and you moved on. I was hurt, but at the same time I was happy for you. You weren't living in this hell. You had a family, and you were in love." I can't help the sob that bursts from me at the reminder of how lost I felt when I saw the photos. Quickly composing myself, I continue, "I know that isn't true now, but I lived with that for years. I'm the reason my family is dead. I don't know how to just get past this. I don't know how to forgive myself." I'm momentarily thankful the shower is still on as my tears mix in with the spray all around us.

"I don't think you do, Jessa. I truly don't believe you blame yourself." Jack's arms pull me into him and clamp tight around me, holding me still and forcing me to listen to him. "If you were in a room right now, alone with the one who is truly responsible for all of this, you would place the blame where it is deserved. You don't have a physical target to carry your hate—yet—so you've been punishing yourself in his absence. It was what fueled your will for so long. It kept you focused. But now it's crushing you, and you need to place it back where it belongs, or it will eat you alive."

I blink rapidly up at him while his words sink in.

"I'm going to stop him, Jack." I speak softly, and he attempts to cut me off, but I continue. "He killed my family. I saw it happen. He tortured me, and he—he hurt me. He lied, about everything—about you. He took years of my life away from me. He took my parents away from me. He took you away from me, and I will be the one who kills him for it."

I've gripped his shirt so tight my arms are shaking, and suddenly I feel tired.

Seconds turn into minutes as I exhaust myself into a heap in his arms. As soon as the intensity of my anger leaves me, Jack tilts my chin up to face him. The water is still raining down all around us in a sharp echo off the tiled walls.

Then, slowly, piece by piece, the entire room comes back

into focus as my endorphin high drains away, as if following the water down the drain.

"You're safe, Jessa. I've got you. You—"

As his words float off into the room, my body feels lighter than it has ever been, and darkness creeps in.

Watching Jessa sleep soothes me. Every now and then she takes a deep breath and sighs out a soft whimper, and each time my lips twitch in response.

She's experienced years of pain and loss, but when she sleeps, it leaves her alone. As I sit on her bed, watching her without the demons she fights when she's awake, I can't help but want a future with her. I want to be the man she always needed. I'll shield her from the things that would harm her, and we'll deal with the pain together so she will find her way back to this sweet innocence during her waking hours as well.

Another breath, and she makes a move to roll over, but her exhaustion is too much, and she gives up her attempt and settles back into sleep.

I don't think I could wake her right now even if I tried.

After the shower, she passed out in my arms. The weight of the past few days, a decade of running and the presence of Maxwell in addition to the video she watched, would be enough to deplete anyone.

Opening her wounds and bringing her feelings back to

the surface was necessary for her to start healing. Whether she feels the weight of what she saw in the video or not, she may remember one day, and she needs to be ready to manage her emotions head-on.

Then, just as I was about to tell her how I'll do anything to make up for ten years without her, she passed out in my arms.

As I chuckle under my breath, my phone vibrates beside me on the bed. I'm thankful I remembered to take it out of my pocket before I sat in the shower. Link would be pissed if I broke another phone.

LOGAN

We need to talk. I'm in my office.

His text doesn't offer much, but I know that's his way of making sure I show up.

Logan knows if he gives me too much information, I'd probably just crawl in beside Jessa and fall asleep with her.

Pulling the covers up to her chin, I lean over and ghost my lips over her forehead in a kiss that doesn't wake her.

Then I move into the silent halls toward our offices, with a quick pit stop into my own for a dry change of clothes.

By the time I open the door to Logan's office, the whole day has slipped into night, and everyone is already asleep— well, everyone except for Logan and Link, who is on speaker.

"So it's just Tex and Eagle then?" Logan rolls his eyes in my direction as I enter. Then he continues, "This is moving way too slow for me, Link. Jack is here now." He motions toward the chair in front of his desk, and I pull it out to sit and listen to the rest of the conversation.

"Hi, Jack. Sorry, Logan. Those are the only two I have

been able to clear definitively. We're working around the clock trying to figure this out."

"And what about Maxwell's communication? Can you give us anything on that? A location? Anything?" I know Logan too well. He is frustrated that we aren't ahead of the situation right now.

"Oh, um..." Link shuffles papers on the other end of the line.

His pause isn't from lack of information, although I'm pretty sure he has none. He's uncomfortable.

We're all uncomfortable. Everyone near a screen saw Jessa's hell.

Logan's patience wears thin. "Link, we all saw the video. Set that aside. Was there anything useful?" His tone is controlled and focused, but his jaw is clenched tight.

The video has rattled him too.

"We don't have a location. I'm sorry. His team knew exactly how long to stay connected. We bounced around the whole time, trying to find a destination, and we almost had him."

A piece of our conversation from earlier comes back to me. "The alarm," I offer.

Logan shakes his head, momentarily confused. "What alarm?"

"Maxwell had an alarm that went off when he was talking to us. That must have been his warning to end the call."

"That would probably be it," Link confirms. "As for the old video of, uh..." Link goes silent for a short second. "Jack, I'm so sorry."

As I look up to answer Link, I catch Logan watching me. He's not analyzing though.

His expression is pained. He's sympathizing.

"I know, Link. We all are." I'm comforted to know the guys surrounding me are the best I could ever ask for—all except for one.

Getting back to the issue at hand, Link continues, "I have one team member working on the footage of Jessa's time outside. We're trying to pull anything out of the background that will give us a location. There's nothing helpful inside since there were no windows. I'll let you know what I find out."

"Thanks, Link. I need to let you go. Call me if you find anything else." Logan's words catch me off guard, and I'm sure Link is equally thrown. For the first five years of knowing Logan, I was convinced he never learned proper phone etiquette, because he's only ever ended our communications by hanging up.

This is new.

Before I delve further into his new, courteous direction, I remember the shower.

"Logan. When Jessa and I were in the showers earlier, someone was there for a bit of our conversation. We need to pull up the security tapes from around that time. We might have our mole."

"It was me." Logan's expression remains frozen on his face. "I was concerned—for both of you. I wanted to make sure you were okay, and I wanted to make sure whoever is against us here wasn't listening in."

"Oh."

I'm happy that Jessa isn't in any danger, but at the same time, finding someone hovering around the door would be tough to explain away.

"How is she?" There's no agenda behind his words, and I'm thankful for his support.

"She's sleeping. We—worked through some things."

I'm suddenly aware of my own limitations. Logan knows my priorities are no longer in line with his.

He sighs, then leans back in his seat, taking a moment to read me.

I immediately feel like I'm about to be scolded like an errant child. I don't like it, and he knows I don't like it. We're cut from the same cloth, and this is beginning to irk me.

He ignores my rolling eyes. "Know that my intentions were only for your well-being, but I did overhear Jessa. What's this about hidden code?"

And that's it. Back to business.

I don't fault him. We run a company. We have priorities and goals to achieve, and right now, I'm one step away from being utterly useless.

I know I need to get back on board soon, or I'll be treated as a distraction and dealt with.

"Jessa hoped that seeing the video would prompt her to remember something about her time in captivity. She doesn't remember anything after the first day. She blocked it out, like the night you questioned her. She has no idea how she successfully contacted Dana and Zane without giving them away, but she thinks maybe she subconsciously loaded some type of execution code onto his servers. Like our mole did here. It would have been quick thinking on her part, and she'd need to be completely sure of what and where the code was, because she and Zane would only get one shot at using it."

"Shit. That's brilliant." Logan's impressed with my girl. I knew he would be.

"I know. Except—"

"The video didn't help her remember." Logan finishes my thought, and I nod in confirmation. "So then the question is, what can we do to help her?"

We. I turn territorial at Logan's suggestion. "I will work with her to talk it through. I'll help her remember."

Logan smiles at my sad attempt to retain control, and it grates on my nerves. "Jack, I don't know if simply talking to her"—he pauses long before continuing, and I know we are moving into a more candid discussion as he stares hard at me, and his tone turns challenging—"is going to help her remember."

I know, with enough time, I can help her remember, but I also know time is the one thing we don't have.

Logan waits for me to get back in the game or lose my shit, and right now, I have no idea which road I'm heading down.

"Did you listen to everything in the shower?" is the only thing I can manage to get out. I'm splitting at the seams, and this is only buying me time.

"No, Jack. I didn't. I left after Jessa said she didn't remember. I know you want to help her. I would fight for the same thing if the tables were turned. The difference between you and me is that I understand my limits. I know myself. You assumed all of those years ago that Jessa was dead. You decided that nature took care of itself; therefore, you didn't need to face the demons of your loss. Well, here they are, and you're unprepared." Logan throws his arms up, as if to welcome my demons in for a beer. Leaning over his desk, he places his weight on his forearms, challenging me to deny it.

I can't.

He's right.

When I accepted that Jessa was dead, I couldn't deal with the loss, so I pushed it away. Now here we are, and I have everything I thought I would never have. My feelings for her never left; they just festered, waiting for their chance to crush me.

I know all of this, and I know we are running out of time.

My sense of urgency is finally returning, and I make one last attempt to take care of Jessa myself. "Let me talk to her. We'll figure something out."

Sliding his arms back off the desk, he picks up his phone to check the time.

"Okay. Fine, Jack. We'll do it your way. You have three days." I'm shocked that he's willing to let me try things my way, then he continues, "Just give her a break tomorrow. She needs a day to recover. I'd like to spend some time with her outside all of this. I know we didn't get off to a good start, and I don't want to hinder any progress with you. I'll invite her out for a run in the morning. The fresh air will be good for her, and you're welcome to join us. It'll be an early run though. I have a conference call at eight."

"I, uh—that'd be great, but I'll pass on the run. I need to catch up on some sleep of my own if I'm going to be functional tomorrow, but I'll be by just before eight to take her to breakfast." Logan's support isn't what I expected, but I'm happy to have him around to help her.

"It's getting late, and I'm now getting up early, so I'm going to sleep." Logan stands, and I rise with him.

As we leave the office, my mind works through how I'll possibly begin to help Jessa, and I realize it's going to be an uphill battle.

CHAPTER 27

JESSA

Jack jumps up from the edge of my bed as Logan and I enter my room after our morning run, which turned into a long hike of sorts.

"Where were you guys? I've been here since seven forty-five waiting to take Jessa to breakfast. I tried your phone."

Logan answers as he steps out from behind me. "Sorry, Jack. We were going to do a quick run, then I had the idea to go a little farther up the ridge, to show Jessa the falls. We passed Tex and Eagle, and I asked them to have Link delay my call until ten. I told them to let you know. I guess they couldn't find you. I left my phone on my desk. You know reception on the run is shit."

"It's okay. Really, Jack. I had a great time. It's so beautiful out here." I turn to drop my sweatshirt on the chair beside the door.

After jumping around from location to location the past ten years, I see why the guys love it up here. The fresh air, the stars, and the wilderness that surrounds this place are amazing, and they have it all to themselves.

I was surprised when Logan knocked on my door this

morning, offering me an olive branch in the form of some time together. I jumped at it. It gave me the opportunity to look around their compound while the sun was shining.

I was also feeling a little trapped inside. I want to be back out in the open, even if it is a false sense of freedom.

I don't know if I'll ever truly know what real freedom feels like again.

Running around the camp was helpful. I got an idea of everything they have on base, including their security measures, which will help me access anything I need in a hurry if necessary.

As we passed the farthest point from the building, we ran into two of Logan's teammates, almost literally. The awkward looks on their faces when they initially took me in confirmed that they had either seen or heard about my video, and I momentarily felt ashamed. But then Logan suggested a little excursion outside of the gates.

The hike was a steady uphill climb, but it was worth it when the thundering sound of the falls rumbled through the trees.

Logan was better company than I thought he'd be. Not once did he mention the video or Maxwell. He even left Zane out of the discussion. Despite all of that, our conversation flowed effortlessly and constantly for the entire time we were outside.

"It's almost nine fifty-five. We're going to miss breakfast if we don't get moving. Want to join us, Logan?" Jack asks as he ushers me toward the door.

"I've got my call in five minutes. Thank you again, Jessa." Logan smiles as he leaves us, and I maneuver into the room to quickly change my top and pants.

When we reach the kitchen, we find out Jack was right to

hurry. Breakfast just ended, and most of the food has already been put away.

Jack told me the kitchen is locked down between meals on days when their secondary teams are away, to save manpower, so we have to take what is left over.

As Grey enters the room to take the last of the food away, Jack beats him to the remaining baskets and grabs a muffin and a couple of oranges for us.

"We'll eat a bigger lunch later. Let's go enjoy these outside. It's a nice day."

I walk with Jack to a grassy spot away from the buildings. Once we sit down, he takes charge, peeling the oranges and handing me my half of the muffin.

Our conversation remains light. It's almost a repeat of my prior one with Logan. Jack lets me choose the topics, and I'm thankful, as I'm not yet ready to talk about yesterday. Mostly because there isn't much to say. I know what I saw, but I still don't feel any of it.

While we eat, I wait for him to ask more questions about Maxwell, but they never come.

An unease grows when I realize he's avoiding the elephant in the room. Neither of us are saying anything, but it's there. I see it in everyone's eyes when they look at me.

As we wrap up our breakfast, Jack's phone rings. It's Logan, telling Jack he needs him on the conference call, as their base in Arizona has come across some information on Maxwell's possible location.

It sounds promising, but I learned a long time ago never to get my hopes up. Instead, I focus on my current situation.

This opens up some free time for me, and I decide to rest. I stand to follow Jack inside when Dana comes out, with Grizz trailing behind her.

"We ran into Logan earlier, and he mentioned the falls. We thought you might want to go back up to see them again. Michael says they're beautiful. I grabbed us all some water for the hike." Dana waits for my answer with a hopeful smile on her face. I know she wanted to be there for me yesterday.

As much as I want to close my eyes, the walk up might give me the second wind I need. "Sure. I'd love to."

Her eyes light up at my words. Then, stepping in front of me with a hand on each of my upper arms, her expression turns serious. "Great. I'm going to say this once. We are going to talk about yesterday. But we're going to do it when you're ready." She pinches her lips together in a thin but wide smile, and tears threaten to break free from her eyes.

Since I saved her from her dad, Dana has taken on the role of big sister. It's almost as though she's trying to repay a debt she feels will never be settled.

She's wrong. It's me who owes her the world. She's been my only constant over the last ten years. I'm thankful every day for her sacrifices, and I'll never be able to do enough for her.

Setting aside the consequences of getting up early this morning, I nod. Then I turn to usher Dana toward the overgrown hiking trail, and Grizz follows quietly behind.

The walk up is a little more demanding the second time, but the view is worth it.

I'm reminded that Dana and I would be enjoying our time off right now if things hadn't changed. She would have finally had a vacation.

My guilt seeps into me, and even though I'm tired, I wait for her to decide to head back to camp.

We arrive back on base in the early afternoon, just missing lunch as well. When we enter the cafeteria, there is only a small plate with two bananas and a couple of bars left on the table. It isn't enough for the three of us.

Grizz checks his phone, then tells me Jack texted to say he'll be gone for most of the day, as he and Logan have some business to deal with off base.

I scarf down a banana and leave the rest for Dana and Grizz to share.

As we're making plans to chill out and watch a movie in the common room, Eagle finds us. He asks me if I have some time for a call with Link about systems and procedures.

As much as I want to plant my ass down on the couch and fall asleep beside Dana for two hours, speaking to Link might give me more access and insight into how their systems work, so I send Dana off with Grizz and follow Eagle into the communications area.

While Link made every effort to have most of the computers in the room shut down, I was able to learn a lot about their systems by scanning their equipment.

When I joked around about taking over their compound, I learned they have lockdown procedures in place for every secure room on base, and I made a mental note to check in with Hunter as to what those systems are so I can bypass them.

While I wasn't allowed to sit in the main comms area, I could see it through a window. The glass between the two rooms is thick, I'm assuming bulletproof. This is probably in case of an attack, if they need to secure themselves in the room while they delete files and destroy their equipment.

Their security systems will serve me well, should I need them, and that is the room I will need to gain entry to.

Scanning the control area further, I notice a smaller

room off to the side. It's a keypad entry door, which means I could control both the inside and outside doors.

I'll have to find out what that is as well, because if I do need to get in there, I don't want any surprises jumping out at me.

Most of our conversation is spent with me answering general questions about previous jobs, how Zane and I were able to get around some programs or explaining some of our past hacks for Maxwell.

I like Link. I like him a lot, actually. I share as much as I can without divulging anything important, and I pass on some questions. He never pushes for an answer, and he doesn't bring up my time as Maxwell's prisoner.

Eventually, Link tells me Jack texted to say he and Logan were delayed, but he wanted to have dinner with me, so they called to see if the kitchen would stay open later.

I don't mind a late dinner, but as soon as he mentions food, I become aware of my own hunger. A whole day on little rations has left me with the shakes, and my stomach rumbles.

The lulls in our conversation start to grow. It's like Link is stalling for time, and I'm about to call him on it when Dana stops in to check on me.

"Hey. I thought you'd be done by now. Grizz told me Jack and Logan are running late. Let's grab a shower before dinner. It'll wake you up. You must be exhausted."

With her words, my body feels heavy. This day has been too long. While I'm looking forward to dinner with Jack, I think I'm going to have to turn in after it's done. But for now, a shower sounds like a good idea since my day included a jog and two hikes.

Even though Dana saw the video, I still don't have it in

my heart to show her my scars. I choose the most enclosed shower and make sure to face her when drying off, so my back isn't visible.

As always, she keeps the conversation alive. Talking about the falls and passing comments about Michael make the time fly by.

When I walk into the cafeteria, I'm met with a sight for sore eyes.

Food, finally.

The smell of pasta almost knocks me over, and I head straight for the serving area, leaving my manners far behind me. I haven't had a full meal since dinner the day before yesterday. Everything went south with Maxwell yesterday afternoon, and I missed all of my meals.

But not tonight.

Armed with a heaping serving of two different types of pasta and a couple slices of garlic bread, I turn to find Jack walking into the room, with Logan behind him.

His smile warms my heart. Amusement rises inside me as his eyes drop to my plate of food, then widen at my gluttony.

I meet him at a table off to the side, pull out my seat, place my plate down, and pick up my fork to dig in. "Before you say anything, I missed breakfast and lunch today, and I'm starving."

Jack's face drops, and so does his tone. "Why didn't you eat lunch, Jessa?"

My chest tightens. "Uh—"

"You can blame me for that, Jack. I kept her at the falls a little too long." Dana answers for me as she pulls out a seat, and Grizz takes the one across from her.

Keeping his eyes on me, Jack leans to the side as Logan

passes by. Then he shifts his gaze to his friend. "Want to pull up a seat?" Jack calls, catching Logan's attention.

Logan pauses, looks between us, then back to Jack. "No, I'm going to take this to go. I've got a few things to take care of since we've been gone for most of the day. I'll be back for dessert."

I want to ask if they found out anything about Maxwell, but I keep my questions to myself. I'm enjoying the cease-fire between us, and I'm not ready to rock the boat.

Logan turns his attention to me and smiles. "Jack tells me he remembers cheesecake being your favorite, so I picked some up in town."

I'm momentarily touched by Jack's remembering and Logan's thoughtfulness when Dana snorts, catching everyone's attention.

"And here I thought your favorite was anything with sugar in it."

I return her smirk. She's right. I have a sweet tooth that is out of control. During our spare time, Dana has been perfecting a lot of sweet treats. She's always wanted to open a dessert shop, and we've spent many nights planning our menu and design.

I would be nothing more than her website designer and security manager, and she decided years ago—and I agreed—that I would be paid in pastries, anything with icing on it.

"Yes. Cheesecake is still my favorite. Thank you for picking some up, Logan."

With a quick nod, he leaves the room, and I spend the next twenty minutes eating my heaping plate of pasta.

Jack tells us what he can about his day in town, and Dana recaps our hike to the falls, as well as her review of the movie she watched with Grizz.

It turns out Jack and Logan had a string of meetings to organize their teams for an away mission to one of their other bases. While neither of them mentioned the reason, I have a good feeling it's because they are confident they have something on Maxwell. I can't see anything else that would cause them to lower their numbers here, especially since they have a traitor among them.

As I glance between Jack and Dana, a familiarity I've missed settles in. I almost feel like I'm back in high school again, laughing with my two closest friends.

Relaxed in my memories, my hunger gets the best of me, and I eat a little too quickly. Halfway through my second plate, I realize how full I am, and I forgot about dessert. At least until Logan pops his head back into the cafeteria with the cheesecake he bought in hand.

"Everyone ready for dessert?" He smiles toward our table.

"You okay, Jessa? You look like you're going to explode," Dana observes, and Logan pauses to look at me with a sudden sad look that only I catch.

I don't have it in me to turn down a piece of my favorite dessert, especially when he went out of his way to pick it up, and I push my plate in his direction as his smile creeps back across his face.

"Just one piece, then I think I need to turn in. It's been a long day." I look up to find Jack watching me closely.

Logan cuts me a large piece, and I'm not sure I'll finish it, but I'll try since he went to the effort.

As I eat, I listen to Jack and Logan talk about the bakery in town, and Dana perks up, asking questions every few minutes until I am done eating. Finishing up my last bite, I push myself back from the table to stand, and the weight of the food hits me as I let out a soft sigh. Jack stands to join me as I say good night.

"Jack, remember I need you to help Hunter and Tex out back. I know it's going to be a late night, but we need those trucks ready to roll out in the morning. Grizz, can you lend a hand as well? I have a few things to take care of inside." Logan looks between the guys, and I sense Jack's hesitation over leaving me, but Dana takes his choice away from him.

Standing, she moves to hook her arm with mine. "It's okay. I'm heading back to my room as well. I'll walk with Jessa."

Before anyone can argue, she's already pulling me to the door, muttering something about how tired I look. I take one last look over my shoulder at Jack, who's watching silently as I'm led away from him.

Entering my room after the fastest good night to Dana, I head straight for the bed and take my pants off. There is nowhere in the world I want to be right now except for in my own dreams, and I shuffle under the covers to find the perfect position to drift off in.

A few minutes later and my limbs relax as sleep quickly approaches.

A soft knock at the door has me wondering if I should just pretend I'm asleep, but I think better of it.

"Come in."

It's Logan.

"Hey, Jessa. Link found something in the video from yesterday, and Jack and I wanted to check it out with you quickly before you fall asleep. He's just setting it up. It'll take less than a minute." Logan peeks into the dark room and waits for my response.

His voice is quiet, so as not to disturb Dana across the hall, and I step out of bed and grab the robe draped over the back of my chair. I want nothing more than to sleep and digest my dinner, but my curiosity is now getting the better of me.

If there's a chance I can find out where Maxwell is, I have to take it.

Tying the robe at my waist, I follow Logan down the dark halls.

As we near their operational area, his voice grows from a whisper, and I'm busy listening to him describe all of the other desserts in the shop from earlier when he opens a door and ushers me through.

Confusion sets in as my eyes adjust to the dark and quiet room.

Where's Jack?

Logan steps in behind me, and the door closing is the only thing I hear as the remaining light is snuffed out.

"Logan?" All familiarity drains from my voice.

My stomach is uncomfortably full, and an anxious feeling creeps into my veins. I'm tired, exhausted, actually, and the room is cold—noticeably cold.

The quick click of a switch behind me floods light into all corners of the room, and I realize instantly we are in one of the interrogation rooms. But this isn't like the other one I was in. There's no table and no chairs.

My eyes focus on the only piece of furniture in the room, and my heart sinks.

As if the bench has a life of its own, it calls out to me, mocking me, and I tremble from the inside out.

I can't help myself.

It's a simple thing, really. Nothing more than a cold

metal bench, except this one comes complete with restraints tied at the base. Just like one I've seen before.

My body viscerally reacts to everything around me. I'm trembling from the inside out, and I can't run away.

I can't hide.

Memories of my first day in Maxwell's custody hit me all at once, and there's something just out of reach: emotions. Fear, maybe.

Logan stands between me and my only exit, and I take a cautious step into the room, to buy myself a little space and time to think.

Slowly, I turn to find Logan watching me.

I thought he dropped his guard today.

He didn't.

He put it up.

He played a part.

The personable guy I went jogging with is gone.

The friend who picked up my favorite dessert is gone.

Like a whisper in my ears, my own voice chastises me.

I've just made a horrible mistake.

I followed the lion right into his own den.

Jekyll is back, and I'm on my own.

I don't know where Jack is.

Just like last time.

I twitch as something snaps into place.

This has happened before.

I feel almost as though I'm watching everything unfold from a different room. I'm protected, distant, but I'm still controlling my actions.

"You d-don't need to d-do this." I don't know what I'm referring to. Part of me feels like I'm moving automatically as I scramble to figure out my next move.

Logan reaches across his torso to roll up the sleeve on his opposite arm while keeping his eyes trained on me.

His face is cold.

Distant.

Then I notice he isn't armed. There are no knives, and unless he has his piece in the back of his pants, he doesn't have a gun either.

As he reaches over to roll up the sleeve on his other arm, I glance quickly around the room.

There's nothing else here.

"Yes, Jessa. I do." His voice is low and calm.

I can't stop my heart from pounding out of my chest as my need to curl up in the fetal position builds.

But I can't lie down.

I can't allow myself to lose any ground.

I already know by the confidence in his movements that he is stronger and faster than I am.

This is another fight I'm going to lose.

CHAPTER 28
LOGAN

The instant Jack challenged me in my office, I knew I would have to deceive my closest friend by tearing down the love of his life.

I didn't come to this decision lightly. Hell, I was up half the night trying to come up with another solution. But there is no time for drawn-out strategies.

Three days. I can't give Jack three days with Jessa. He knows Maxwell moves faster than that.

If Maxwell is ever in my hands, I will kill him for what he's done to Jessa—and for what I now have to do to help her remember.

I've been involved in my fair share of torture situations, always involving men who deserved it, in search of information that, very literally, saved lives.

The depths that Maxwell sank to in the name of unrequited love is something I will never be able to fathom.

I could never reduce myself to my absolute base and take advantage of a truly helpless and innocent person.

We've followed Matteo and Maxwell for over ten years,

and we've seen the destruction he is capable of, but this is beyond anything I've witnessed.

His evil exists on another level. The damage he's done to Jessa is deep, and it's hidden.

My next move needs to be precise.

I know exactly how much time I've got alone with Jessa before Jack finds out what I'm up to and comes barging through that door.

I've planned out this whole day.

From getting her up early, to exhausting her body by taking her on a hike, to making sure she missed her first meal. Her second meal was a gamble. I wasn't sure they would definitely miss lunch, but ordering Grizz not to mention the time until it was too late was a good idea.

Hooking her up with Link was a last-minute thought. I knew he would jump at the chance to talk to one of the two people who can out-hack his entire team. I also knew she wouldn't pass up the chance to get a glimpse of our comms room.

Dinner was my last piece. If I was going to get as close as possible to the same conditions I saw on that video, I needed her starving by dinnertime. The fact that she had a relatively easy day, and that I showed her a more passive side of me, lowered her guard. Her anxiety dropped, and as a result her hunger came raging back at the worst time for her: when she hadn't had the chance to eat all day.

I ate dinner in my office and watched them through the security cameras as their conversation became relaxed and she ate her second helping.

Then I waited until she showed signs of slowing down.

There's a genuine kindness in Jessa when she isn't trying to protect herself or those around her. I knew that playing the guilt card would force her to eat that dessert for her *new friend*. Then her exhaustion would take over in the form of a final sugar crash, and I would have her right where I wanted her.

And here we are.

Reaching down deep, I allow my dominance to rise to the surface. As if awakening from a long slumber, my demons stretch out, shaking off the dust and decay as I step into the room behind Jessa and close the door, welcoming us into the dark.

She says my name so softly, it's almost a whisper, but I can't allow her to reach me. I can't acknowledge my own culpability right now.

I have one chance to help her pull her memories out, and if I give her any slack, this will fall apart.

The click of the light switch echoes into the cold room. I've purposefully lowered the temperature to make this as uncomfortable as possible. I know being warm is important to her. She's mentioned more than once how much she hates to be cold.

Only the back of her head is visible to me right now, and I take this chance to let my expression drop. My anger at the situation is palpable. The situation Maxwell has forced on Jessa.

Her whole body deflates in realization as she turns to look at the bench, and my stomach knots at the thought of what's coming next.

Knowing people is what I do.

Knowing their thought processes, what they need, and what they are about to do is my job, and I already know what she's going to do before she does.

I can already tell she's going to fight, and I'm proud of her courage.

She must be scared. But not scared enough. Yet.

Taking a step into the room, she places some distance between us. It's a superficial move. It will only buy her a false sense of protection.

Then she turns to face me, and I paste my indifference back across my face.

"You d-don't need to d-do this," she stutters, and I notice a small change in her. She's ever so slowly closing herself off. This is the look I should have noticed on the first night in the interrogation room.

If I knew then what I know now, this could have been over days ago. I never would have sedated her, sending her and her possible memories off to sleep.

Her gaze jumps around the room as I roll up my sleeves. She's doing exactly what I would do in this situation. She's scanning for weapons or an escape route—or both.

It's self-preservation at its finest, and it's instinctual in her.

There's a reason I came in here unarmed. I want her to fight hard for the escape I won't grant her. The truth is, I'm prepared for her this time. She'll put up a good fight.

In the end, I know I can subdue her in less than a minute, but she's building up some adrenaline, and I need her to burn through all of it before I begin.

"Yes, Jessa. I do." At the finality in my words, she pales. It won't just be my actions that bring her to where I need her, so I start to paint a picture with my words. "Let me tell you a story about my arm." I lift my arm to show her which one I'm talking about as I roll up my sleeve. Her eyes follow my movement. "When I was a kid, I rode my bike down a hill near my house. It was a dare, and you know boys. We don't back down from a good dare."

I finish rolling up my sleeves and square myself on her as she takes another half step away from me and into the room.

"Long story short, I broke my arm. My mother cried, and my father yelled. My family lived paycheck to paycheck, and there was no money to deal with the actions of their foolish boy. But my uncle was a veterinarian, so he cast my arm the best he could and sent me on my way. Three weeks later, when the cast was removed, my arm was bent, and I still had a lot of pain in my fingers." I pause for a long minute, waiting for Jessa to grow curious, and she doesn't disappoint me.

"Wh-what happened?"

As I continue my story, I take cautious steps toward her, ever so slowly. I don't think she's registered that I'm approaching her, but she instinctively steps back until she is a foot away from the wall.

I pause two feet from her, my eyes locked on hers as I continue, speaking softly so I don't alert her defenses.

"Well, my mom had a small savings stashed away, and she hauled my sorry ass into the doctor's office. It turns out my broken bone didn't heal right. So the doctor had to rebreak my arm, then set it properly in a cast. And now I think you'll agree it works just fine."

Jessa's eyes widen as I close the remaining two steps between us and wrap my fingers around her throat, demanding all of her attention for my next words.

She struggles to free herself, but my grip is firm.

Bracing her upper body with my forearm, I pin her to the wall and continue, keeping my voice as detached and cold as Maxwell's was in the video.

"You see, Jessa, you're like my arm. You were broken,

and you didn't heal right. And the trouble with things that don't heal properly is they need to be broken again so they can be set correctly."

Her face crumples a split second before she strikes, and I'm ready for her.

Pushing my hand down between us, I deflect the knee that was heading straight for my groin and spin her around. Then I push her up against the wall and drop my weight against her.

"STOP! HELP ME!" She's louder than I thought she would be, but it's no use. This room is different from the others. It's been soundproofed for our more *difficult* interrogations, and unless you are right outside, you won't hear a thing.

Reaching in front of her, I tug at the cloth belt around her little robe and pull it loose. Then I step back and yank the neck of her robe down, ripping it off her and pulling her arms back, tangling them in her sleeves, leaving her in her shirt and underwear.

I pause for a moment to see if she's run out of steam so soon, and she takes the break to step into me as she lifts her foot up to the wall in front of her for leverage.

She kicks off the wall hard, and we tumble backward into the room. I lose my footing, as I half expected her to jerk to the side.

When we fall to the floor, her weight hits me, and I grunt as the air is knocked out of me.

Jack's girl is a feisty, unpredictable one.

Judging by her slow reaction, she didn't expect her move to work either, and I take the opportunity to begin pushing her into the headspace she would have been in with Maxwell.

"Remember, Jessa. You brought this on yourself." I choose my words carefully. I know she's processing everything around her, and I'm hoping to match it up to some of her forgotten memories.

A sharp pain hits just below my rib cage on my left side. She rolls off me and pulls one hand free, but I'm back to standing as quick as she is—just in time to dodge a right hook wrapped in a robe.

Spinning on her feet, she realizes she is the closest one to the door now, and she runs, reaching out for the handle with her free hand. But I grab the cloth wrapped around her other hand and whip her back into the room.

I'm not gentle.

I can't give her any indication that I'm on her side, or this won't work.

She needs to completely understand that my priority is getting what I want—just like Maxwell's was.

Tripping over her bare feet, she skids to a stop. The sound of her raw skin squeaking against the ground cuts into my head, but she doesn't stay down. She stands up and spins to keep me in sight as she pulls the robe off and holds it out as a shield in front of her.

"You will give me what I want, Jessa." My words are an order.

I take another step toward her. Her entire body is shutting down. Her exhaustion must be overwhelming. As her adrenaline drains out, so does her strength, and I'm almost ready to begin.

Raising my hands unnecessarily high, I show her my belt again. She instinctively removed it last time, and I'm betting, if I give her enough space, she'll do it again.

My confidence in my assumption soars as she glances down to my midsection then meets my eyes.

She attempts a distraction by tossing her robe at my face. I lift my hands to remove it, and she takes the opportunity to loosen my buckle. She's faster than before, and she has it off and in her hands, sparking a fire in my bones.

My arrogance is at an all-time high. I'm barely controlling myself, but she needs to see this side of me, or I'll never be able to grant her the peace I want for her.

Taunting her, I step dangerously close, daring her to attack.

"Tsk, tsk, tsk," I chide. "You should know you need to ask permission before you play with someone else's things. You will pay for the choices you've made, Jessa."

Tears well in her eyes as she releases a sorrowful groan.

I have her now.

She's in that same headspace of panic and helplessness, and if her memories are going to come back, they are going to come back now.

She raises a fist, but the instructions from her brain aren't reaching her extremities, and her swing is weak and off target. Grabbing the belt, I step out of her way, and as she lunges past me, I push her facedown on the ground and hold her in place with my knee in the middle of her back.

Her fear has taken over, paralyzing her. I roll her slightly to the side as I grab both wrists and wrap them together in front of her with the tie from her robe, which is now on the floor beside her. Then, pulling them close to her throat, I wrap the cloth belt around the back of her neck, securing her wrists close to her as I tie it tight to itself. I lift her deadweight with one arm around her waist as I pick up my belt with my free hand.

Her sobs flow freely, and her body shakes as I lower her onto the bench—which I know she wanted to avoid more than anything.

Stepping behind her, I kick her legs open and bind them quickly to their restraints, holding her upper body in my hand with the robe tie.

Behind me, the door rattles on its hinges. I know Jack is outside, testing the lock.

I've got seconds, maybe a minute left.

I'm running out of time, and I need to hear her break before he gets in.

Lying on the bench in just her shirt and underwear, her body trembles uncontrollably.

"Please, you don't need to do this." Her words are eerily similar to those in the video, and I pull her toward the painful break I know is coming.

"No, Jessa. You didn't have to do this. It's your choices that brought us here. I'll remind you, you have a safe word." I'm copying Maxwell's words, and she doesn't challenge me.

She's no longer here in the room with me.

She's somewhere else.

Stepping behind her, I take a deep breath.

I am not a man who prays, and so I hope instead that I'll be forgiven for what I'm about to do.

Pulling the cloth tie hard, I lift her head back off the table. I fist the fabric of her underwear with my free hand and tear them down and off her, letting the cold air flow over her.

The two-way mirror vibrates, and I know someone has opened the door to the viewing room.

I'm only going to get a couple of strikes in before it's over.

She inhales sharply, and her upper body goes limp. This is the moment. I've either helped her, or I've lost her.

Raising the folded belt, I go in for the kill.

Any remaining hope that I'm bluffing drains from her as the belt hits her bottom, and she screams into the room as the mirror vibrates once more.

Jack's coming.

"You still with me, my little crybaby?" I recite more of Maxwell's words. I don't give her a chance to answer as I bring the belt down a second time, hard, across the fleshiest section of her ass.

She fills her lungs, then tenses, and I loosen my hold on the cloth belt of her robe just enough for her to—

"JACK!...JAAAAACK!" She screams the safe word just like she did on the video. Just like the first night in my interrogation room.

She's there in the moment, and she's broken.

An echoing crack sends the door flying open. Splinters from the frame spray into the room, and the man who enters is not the friend I know.

Jack's entire being is threatening to explode away from himself.

His face is stained red with rage as he barrels across the room, pain and anger etched into every part of his being.

I drop the belt and stand back from Jessa's trembling, half-naked body.

I entirely hate myself for what I had to do to Jessa. For what I did to both of them.

I raise my hands to show I'm not a challenge, but I know what's about to happen, and I deserve every ounce of retribution that's coming.

CHAPTER 29

JACK

The slam of the last truck door brings a groan from my left as Hunter stretches out his back and grabs his pack from the ground.

"Thanks, man," Grizz calls. Hunter grunts, spins on his heels, and waves his good night over his shoulder.

After making my own excuses, I head back inside, but it's not my own bed I want to sleep in.

Today was long—too long—and now that Jessa's back in my life, I don't want to be away from her. I also don't want her to be alone after everything that happened yesterday.

Making plans to quietly slide into bed beside her and wrap myself around her body, I open the door and walk down the corridor leading to her quarters. My boots echo all of the way until I reach her door.

Frantic footsteps sound from behind Dana's door, and when I hear a knock from the inside, I unlock it.

"How did it go?" Dana looks a little too interested in my night, but I set it aside for now.

"It went well. The guys are all ready for tomorrow." I attempt to make small talk, but there's something about the look on her face that tells me it isn't the answer she is looking for.

Nervously looking down the empty hall, she steps out to make sure she sees the entire space, as if she's looking for someone. Then it hits me.

"Are you waiting for Grizz? I think he went to sleep." I keep my voice low. Jessa's had a busy day, and I don't want to be the reason she wakes up.

"What? No. I'm waiting for you to bring Jessa back. Was she able to help you guys?"

Blood drains from my head into my feet in confusion. A sick feeling twists into the pit of my stomach.

"What are you talking about?"

"Logan came by earlier. I heard him through the door. He said something about the video. You guys needed her help. He was taking her to—you." Dana's features pinch in worry as she says the last word.

I see it written all over her face.

She knows her friend is in trouble.

As I scramble to think of something to say to diffuse the storm that I see coming, I try the knob to Jessa's room. It isn't locked. I'm no longer quiet. A small, nagging voice inside me is screaming that she's not there.

She's not safe.

How could I not see this coming?

I should have known Logan would attempt to pull the information out of her. It's what I would have done.

Heat rises up from my stomach. I want to tell Dana to stay in her room, that I'll handle it, but I know Jessa's friend. As soon as I confirm Jessa is in trouble, this timid little woodland creature will morph into a screaming banshee, and this whole compound will be burned to the ground.

Damage control it is.

I glance quickly at the chair by the door. A small pile of clothes sits folded, and I put on my calmest smile.

"Oh, right, sorry. I left them about five minutes ago. They're wrapping up. Jessa just asked for her sweater. It's cold in the room." I punctuate my quick response by grabbing her black turtleneck off the chair and showing it to Dana. "She's fine, but she is tired. We all are. Do you want me to tell her to check in when we're back? I was hoping to take her to my room to sleep. I'm in the other direction."

A deep sigh of relief leaves her, and a small, hesitant smile creeps across her face. "No, that's okay. I'm tired too." Dana pauses to look at me. My heart knots because I know, right now, I don't deserve any kindness. "Thank you, Jack. For—well, good night."

I nod and secure her in her room, then turn to move down the hall. As soon as I reach the next door, my walk turns into a run as I mentally list the places Logan might have Jessa.

There are only two that make sense to me. The first is the communications room, but she would only be there if she already remembered what Logan needs. That leaves the one room where he can be alone with her—isolated and confined. The soundproof interrogation room.

Bursting through the doors into the compound, I run at my top speed.

My rage is the only thing keeping her sweater in my grasp as my fist clenches tight around the fabric.

The room is closer if I go through the buildings, but I can reach it faster outside, without barriers or the possibility that some of the doors may be locked.

My heart pumps at a furious pace as images of what I

could do to pull such information from someone flash in front of my eyes, fueling my panic and driving me faster as I hit the doors to the secluded area.

Inside, the halls are quiet. But some lights are on, confirming I've made the right assumption. Someone is here who shouldn't be.

I won't waste time. I know which room he'll be in. I rush past the first two, square myself against the third, and try the handle.

Locked.

Raising my hand, I'm about to knock, but a fleeting thought pushes me into clarity. What if he has been able to help her? What if he was able to do what I couldn't? What if she's about to remember, and I take that from her?

Moving quickly down the hall, I open the room to the viewing area and step in to see Jessa's nightmare being played out in the other room.

My sanity abandons me.

Blood drains from my body and is slowly replaced by liquid fire as I see Jessa tied to a bench. She's at the mercy of my closest friend as he raises his belt above his head.

Everything slows as the sounds from the room echo into me. It's as though they've been muted to a whispered scream.

But the moment the belt hits Jessa, the volume jumps to a deafening pitch. Her scream rattles off the walls, piercing into me.

Madness takes control, and I push through the door and race back down the hall.

Logan knows I'm coming for him.

My rage is too much for me. I know where Logan is coming from. It's what I would have suggested myself if...

If I didn't love her.

My realization sears through me. I do love her. I always have. She belongs to me, and protecting her is the only mission I know.

My body trembles with the need to wrap myself around her and destroy anything that comes between us. And right now, that includes Logan.

As I reach the door, I hear it. Her scream is muffled, but even the soundproofing can't hold back her cries.

Adrenaline surges through me as she screams my name over and over.

She's trying to use her safe word.

He's done it.

She's broken, and she's back where Maxwell put her all those years ago.

My world turns black. As I kick through the door, all I see in my tunnel vision is them.

Instantly, Logan drops the belt and steps back, leaving Jessa tied down on the bench with two bright red welts forming across her bare ass.

Rushing Logan, I don't give him a chance to explain.

I fear myself right now, and I know, without doubt, if he says the wrong thing, I will kill him.

Pulling my arm back, I let loose on him with all the anger I wish I could aim at Maxwell, and Logan goes flying back against the wall.

The sound of Jessa retching her dinner onto the floor ends me. As she sobs in her binds, I take one last glance at Logan to make sure he isn't moving.

I growl at him through clenched teeth. "Stay down."

If he understands me so well, he'll know how I feel, and he won't move.

He doesn't.

The color has drained from his face, and I know this is something that will haunt him for the rest of his days.

Without another word, I move to the table to put a hand on Jessa's back. She jerks in her restraints as she yells out, "DON'T—"

But I won't let her finish.

I won't let her stay in her hell.

"Jessa, it's me. Jack. Jessa, I'm here. You're safe. You're on the compound. I'm going to untie you."

Her limbs pull taut against her restraints as she processes my words. Then she coughs and offers me a small nod.

I move quickly to her ankles, releasing her legs. Then I free her arms and neck from their binds.

She shivers, and I look to my hands for her sweater, but I don't have it. I must have dropped it in my haze.

I scan the area for something to cover her with. Her robe sits crumpled on the floor, and I grab it, wrap it around her lower half, then scoop her into my arms.

Her breathing is deep and labored, and she is trembling uncontrollably in shock.

"If you remember, hold on to it, Jessa." Logan speaks but keeps his head down, indicating he is no longer a threat. I don't respond.

I look down at Jessa's splotchy face. Her eyes are wide.

"You came for me, Jack. You saved me." She's looking at me in wonder, and it punches into my heart.

In this instant, I know. I know she remembers her pain now.

Clutching my shirt and shoving her face into my chest, she releases a guttural sob as I turn and carry her toward my room.

I'll deal with Logan and our business another time.

Jessa is lost. Part of her is still back in that dark dungeon Maxwell had her in. Her body heaves with her silent cries as I carry her across the compound.

Every few seconds, she pushes her face further into my chest, wiping her tears on my shirt. I stay silent, allowing her the space to process that she's safe.

At my quarters, I slowly drop her bare feet to the ground. My keys are in my pocket, and I can't reach them with her in my arms. I'm also done kicking in doors for the night.

Opening the door to my room, I step through and lead Jessa in by her arm as her free hand holds her robe around her waist. A slight pull tells me she's beginning to shut herself off, and I can't let her retreat from me.

I push down my anger at the situation and speak calmly. "Jessa, this is my room. We're going to sleep here for the night. We're only going to sleep. I'll stay with you."

I'm not sure if my tone hides my concern for her anymore.

"I don't want to be touched." She's still swimming in her shock, but I'm happy she's choosing to tell me how she feels.

"I won't touch you. I won't sleep in the bed if you don't want me to. I'll sleep on the floor, or by the door. Just tell me where you feel safest."

"I feel safest in your arms. But I don't want to be touched. That doesn't make sense." She pushes her fingers into her hair, fisting, then tugging on her strands as she looks to her feet in confusion.

I have an idea.

"Jessa, come with me. You need to sleep, and I want to try something. Do you trust me?"

She nods, first once to confirm, then a few more times.

She watches as I walk to the thermostat on the wall and

raise the temperature. I don't want her to feel cold. I also decide to leave the light on, but I dim it. Jessa has enough darkness around her tonight.

Turning to face her, I pull off my shirt but leave my pants on, and her eyes follow my every move.

"Wait here," I command in the most soothing voice I can manage. I step to my closet and retrieve two of my business ties. When I turn to face her, her eyes go wide at the thought she might be bound for a second time tonight, and I shut her down before she lets her fear take over.

"They're not for you," I say calmly and wait for her reaction.

"What?" Her eyes move up from the ties to meet mine.

I'm hesitant about this plan, but she needs to get to a point of security, so she can sleep. "They're for me."

Jessa's mouth drops open, then closes.

I kneel on the bed. Then I reach behind me and bind my ankles together with the first necktie. I hold the second one out for her to take.

"I—I don't understand."

"You want me close, but you don't want to feel vulnerable. Bind my wrists, and we'll go to sleep. You're in charge."

Jessa's brows knit together as she processes my words. Then I watch as she slowly raises her hand to take the tie from me. As soon as I release it to her, I look ahead and clasp my hands behind me.

Her soft fingers send shivers up my spine as she works the fabric around my wrists. Every fourth breath of hers is still a sniffle as she works to fasten my arms together.

I close my eyes to the sound of her breath and the touch

of her cool skin on my arms. I want more than anything to talk to her. I want to ask what she remembers.

But this isn't about me. The control can't come from me tonight. She needs to know that she has control over the room and herself right now.

Lost in my thoughts, I fail to notice she finished tying my wrists, and the sound of her gingerly clearing her throat brings me back to the room. I open my eyes and focus on her standing in front of me, wearing the shorts I left on my bed this morning.

My eyes drift down, and I notice the size difference between us as she barely manages to keep them on her hips.

"Um, I didn't have anything else...." Her voice trails off when she shrugs.

She knows I don't mind. I offer a smile, and for the first time since dinner, she returns it.

I take the cue to lie down on the bed, staying to one side so I don't crowd her. She'll have plenty of room to sleep on her own. Resting my head on my pillow, I watch as she slowly climbs onto her side and gets comfortable beside me. Then, turning on her side, she looks at me for a long, muted minute.

"I'm happy you found me, Jack."

"Jessa, I don't think Logan would have hurt you. He was trying to get you to remember. He—"

"I'm not talking about that. I want you to know I'm happy I saw you again. I'm happy you found me before it was too late."

She smiles at me with watery eyes. Pools of her tears threaten to run onto the pillow, and the sight of her vulnerability drains the last bit of fight from me for the night.

When she closes her eyes, tears soak into her pillow, and

she takes a deep breath. Her eyes don't open again, and her breathing becomes deeply rhythmic as she drifts off.

Just as I close my eyes, the bed shifts, and her warm arms wrap around my torso as she slides her body close to mine.

I strain to kiss the top of her head. Then I close my eyes and welcome the exhaustion that has been waiting to take over.

CHAPTER 30

JESSA

Jack's breathing evens out. He's drifted off.

I should be asleep as well. Everything about today should have me comatose, but I can't let go.

Willing my body to calm itself and give the impression I've fallen asleep is one of the hardest things I've ever done, but I take strength from Jack and relax myself convincingly enough.

Feeling his firm lips on the top of my head almost makes me jump up and start kissing him, but I can't allow myself to become complacent again.

Maxwell is right. I have a job to do, and I need to focus all of my energy on completing my task.

If you remember, hold on to it.

Logan's words rattle around in my head—along with a few other new memories.

In that interrogation room, I remembered feelings. Fear and pain filled everything. As if I were back in Maxwell's custody, I was hopeless and helpless to save myself.

Then he was there. Jack rewrote the ending of my story and set everything in motion.

Back then, I knew Jack was never going to save me. I knew he didn't even know I was in trouble. He was married with a family. But it was all a lie.

I felt myself beginning to slip. His name echoed in my head as though I wasn't the one screaming out for him. I was about to go to the place I forget.

But I didn't.

All of a sudden, he was there, and I anchored myself to him when he released me from my hell.

Then I remembered.

Not everything at first.

Just bits and pieces.

But as I tried to grab at those memories instead of letting them go, they materialized. Then they led to another memory, and everything connected.

I remember Maxwell's words. I remember the stale smell in the room and how my skin burned like acid had been poured on it after he beat me. I remember my sadness at seeing Jack's happy face staring back at me as Maxwell hurt me. I remember replacing my childhood memories of Maxwell with his disgusting grunts. I remember the second I realized I couldn't stop what was happening.

I remember every moment until Maxwell hoisted me up to the ceiling and flipped the switch on his contraption.

But most important of all, I remember everything from the moment I woke up—the *real* first time my eyes opened.

After I came to, one of Maxwell's men handled me. I did see Maxwell again the day after, but he kept his distance. He was detached; everything about him had changed. I remember being told to make the call to Zane, and I knew what I had to do.

When he had me in captivity, Maxwell never knew the

full extent to which I worked with Zane. He considered me an assistant at best, but he underestimated my abilities.

I'm always being underestimated. Maybe it's my size, my gender. Or maybe that day it was because I'd just had the shit kicked out of me and I looked like I was at death's door, but I was underestimated again, and that was my in.

I remember it clearly now. Maxwell stood by the door. He kept his distance from me. It was almost like he was trying to hold himself back, and I was thankful for the space. Two men sat on either side of me as I logged on to their server and accessed the websites and chat rooms that would take me to Dana.

A third man sat quietly at a desk behind me, no doubt trying to gain access to the connections I was making. I could tell by the nervous shuffle from either side that the men knew nothing about computers. Their confused glances as I accessed site after site gave them away.

Maxwell was all about power and muscle. So I figured there was possibly a team in another room watching me, but I'd know as soon as I was in the chats.

Once I made the connection with Dana, I sent out red herrings in a few different directions. Only one tracker started the chase, so I knew right away the men in the room were all I had to deal with.

Greed is the driving factor in everything Maxwell does, so the chance he could find out anything about Zane was the carrot I dangled. His donkey took off after it, leaving their own server exposed.

And that was my in. The two goons beside me had no idea what they were looking at, and I was able to jump into a hidden file on the server and code in everything I would need to open access while they watched me contact Dana to coordinate my release.

The code itself is short. It's the program I will use to run it that took forever to create, and it didn't need to be done on his servers.

In the minute we waited for Dana to connect, I had put my own little Trojan horse to sleep.

And now I know what I need.

Jack's chest rises and falls in a steady rhythm. He's deep asleep, and he's going to be stiff in the morning.

Binding his own body to give me security gave me some of my power back. He gave me the sense of control I needed to heal and make myself stronger.

I know I'm a mess, but I can't begin to sort through all my new feelings now.

Jack saved me twice.

He saved me when he found us at the farmhouse, and he saved me tonight. He won't stop trying to save me until Maxwell is dead and everything that threatens me is gone.

But that day will never come.

As long as I'm alive, there will be someone out there trying to get to Zane. Jack will eventually die trying to protect me, and I won't let that happen.

I take a deep breath to push down the tears as I work on my final plan to end this the only way it can be ended.

With everyone walking away free.

Well, almost everyone.

The weight of the day lifts off me as I wrap my arm around Jack's still body. Dots connect, and my plan takes shape as I surrender myself to the only thing I have left tonight—sleep.

The next time I open my eyes, it's morning. The room is bright, and the first thing that comes into focus is Jack, staring back at me with a relaxed smile ghosting his lips.

"Good morning."

It's the simplest of things, saying good morning, yet it's foreign. Something so natural is completely unnatural, and a lump forms in my throat, causing Jack's eyebrows to pinch together in concern.

I shake my head, hoping to jar loose the anxiety building inside of me.

I want nothing more than to wake up like this every day for the rest of my life. Except for the part where he's tied up —although I do see the appeal in it.

I slide off the mattress and circle the bed to kneel on the floor behind Jack. He lifts his head and strains to watch as I loosen the ties around his ankles.

When I free his legs, he rolls over and tries to sit up, slipping one foot over the edge of the bed.

He stills when I place my hand on his chest.

"I—um—I—" I lower my eyes as I flex my fingers against his chest, then nibble at my lower lip when I fail to find the words.

Jack scans my face as I shift my gaze to his eyes, then drop them away again. "It's okay, Jessa. Anything you need."

I inhale, then speak in a whisper. "I need you."

He doesn't answer me. He just sits still until I look him in the eyes, and when I do, he nods, urging me to move at my own pace.

I glide my fingers over his skin, and his composure cracks

when I reach the base of his neck and thread my fingers into his hair.

This time, when I lean in to kiss him, he moves slow. His soft lips open for me, and he yields, allowing me access.

When I move to untie his arms from behind his back, he tugs at his hands a couple of times and releases himself. He was always able to get out, yet he stayed bound for me.

He rests his hands on the bed as I create space between us so I can unfasten his pants. He stays focused on me as I pull them down and off, freeing him, then remove the shorts he let me wear.

My shirt still covers me, and I know I could stay like this, but I pull it over my head and drop it to the floor. I want him to see all of me.

My chest tightens as his gaze roams over my body, and I close the distance between us, returning my palm to his chest and pushing him back onto the bed as I climb up and straddle his hips.

"I love you, Jack."

The corners of my eyes sting as they fill with tears.

Then one falls, breaking our moment.

Jack sits up to meet me. He wraps his arms around my back and covers my scars as he pulls me into him, claiming me in a kiss that he deepens until his teeth grind into my own.

"I love you, Jessa."

I don't know why hearing that makes me sad, and more tears roll over my cheeks.

I adjust my hips, desperate to have him inside of me. When I wrap my fingers around his length and angle him toward me, he slides his fingers into my hair at the base of my skull and waits for me to relax. Then he tightens his grip, and my body goes slack for him as he slides me over him.

We move together, much slower than the last time, as though we're committing every single nuance to memory, and I never want to be anywhere else.

Slipping his hand between us, he glides his fingers through my folds, drawing a moan from me as my spine straightens and I tip my head back.

"That's it, Jessa. I'm here."

He rubs his hands over my back, and for the first time, I don't flinch when it becomes obvious he's found the slight ridges of scar tissue. Instead, I roll my hips and lean into him. Our lips crash into each other again, and our movements become frantic as my orgasm approaches.

Jack follows my lead. He pushes me over the edge when he pinches my clit and rubs, sending me soaring. When I tip my head back to come, he tightens his hold, angling my face to his, and he watches me as I break apart for him.

Then he rolls us over until he's on top and pushes into me at a deeper angle. When I recover and look into his eyes, I find hesitation. He's still worried he's going to hurt me.

"Please. I need you."

Jack's dominance returns, and he slides all of the way in. I dig my fingertips into his back as he builds to a punishing pace, hurtling me toward a second orgasm.

Mine hits me at the same time Jack's hits him, and we writhe against each other in a desperate attempt to crash into oblivion as one. The orgasm obliterates me. It tears me apart and puts me back together in the same breath.

It isn't until Jack kisses my cheek that I realize I'm crying.

"I'll never let you go, Jessa."

I don't know what to say to that, and I cry some more because in the end, I think he's going to have to do exactly that.

CHAPTER 31
JACK

Being tied up for the night had some unexpected results.

Last night, when Logan stood over Jessa, I saw red. I wanted to kill and protect and tear everything apart.

I had the power to do it. I had the strength and the freedom.

But spending eight hours with my arms and legs bound together, I had no choice but to accept everything as it was. I had no other option but to lie beside Jessa's still body, helpless to offer the comfort I wanted to, and all I could do was process and think. And when she woke up in the morning and freed me, I was calm and more rational than I've ever been in my entire life.

Logan has this turn of events to thank for saving his life.

As I walk into his office, he stands cautiously, drops his pen onto his desk, and keeps his hands ready by his sides.

I know what he expects.

If it were me in his situation, I'd expect to be eating out of a tube for the foreseeable future.

"Jack..." Logan lets my name linger, and I'm not sure if it

is a greeting or a question as I take a long, hard pause to look at my closest friend.

Logan has been there for me every step of the way since the night Jessa disappeared.

He would give his life for mine without hesitation, and he wouldn't have done what he did without considering the consequences.

"Logan." I move across the room to pull out a chair.

The truth is, I'm drained.

Being without control has enlightened me to the aftereffects, and I'm filled with an odd sense of peace I haven't felt in a long time.

Then it hits me.

I haven't been in control for a long time.

I've been tempered.

I've been getting by.

Logan was right.

I never dealt with my unresolved feelings over Jessa's loss.

Waking up two hours before Jessa this morning, and being forced to lie still as she slept with her arms draped over my torso, allowed me time to surrender to the pain I should have faced long ago.

My mind wandered to memories of her in high school. Her first time, and the last time I thought I would ever see her. I replayed the video in my mind and went over every single expression and word she spoke last night. Then I thought about Logan. How quickly he backed off, his intentions, and what I would do to him the next time I saw him.

As the first hour passed, my fury subsided into anger, then disappointment. Then, listening to the soft sound of

Jessa's breathing as she slept, I let go of my demons altogether as I remembered her words when she thanked me for saving her.

She's with me now, and I'll do everything I can to keep it that way.

I'll find Maxwell and kill him with my bare hands if it means keeping her safe.

I buried the hatchet with my demons, and I understand Logan's intentions.

There was no other way for Jessa, and he saved me from having to be the one who took her there. She needed me to be the one who saved her.

I would never have been able to bring myself to do what Logan did, and he'll carry his own guilt for a long time.

Watching me take a seat, Logan slowly lowers back into his own.

"We good?" I point to the black eye I left him with last night. It's all I'll offer him.

"We're good," he answers as he reaches across his desk for a pen. He writes something down before discarding it onto his desk and leaning back. "And Jessa? Is she—good?"

I know he's testing the water for sharks.

"She struggled last night. We got through it." I'm careful with my words. Our friendship is still here. It's still strong. We just need to ease back into everything.

"Look, Jack—"

"Save it. I've had some time to think. About a lot of things. It was your only option. I spoke to her about it this morning. She understands as much as she's going to." Logan's eyes widen at my words. I know he was expecting me to come in here with guns blazing, and he's surprised by my reaction.

"And her memory? Does she remember?" He's slipping back into business mode, and I couldn't be happier to move past this for now.

"She remembers her fear, and she remembers what happened until the end of the video. She said pieces are slowly coming back to her. She doesn't remember anything she needs yet. We talked this morning, and I just left her with Dana. She's asked that Dana not find out what happened last night. It stays between us. I think, for your own personal safety where *that one* is concerned, you'll agree."

Logan chuckles, and our tension eases as he updates me.

"I think it's for the best that we keep all of it between us. We still don't have our mole narrowed down. Link called this morning. He hasn't been able to completely clear anyone else yet. In our core group, only Grey, Eagle, and Tex are clean." He pauses, then looks at me, back in tactical mode. "Has she mentioned if anyone has spoken to her yet?"

"I haven't asked. I was focused on the video and—last night."

"Fair enough. We should find out. Some of our team are heading off base on their mission, and I want to make sure, whoever the mole is, that he stays close to us until we can deal with him. This leaves Grizz, Waldo, and Hunter. Grey has the least experience leading a team, so I'm holding him back. Tex and Eagle can each take a group. We'll update them with the real reason they are heading out to Arizona. Until we clear more, everyone else stays in the dark."

"I agree, then we—"

A shuffle in the hall stops my train of thought, and both of us turn our attention to the closed door.

262 CODE NAME: PHOENIX

"Come in," Logan hollers, and the commotion outside stops.

The door opens to reveal Jessa's wide eyes as she steps into the room, with Hunter trailing behind her.

"Jessa?" Logan's voice is regretful, and I know instantly he wishes he could take everything back.

"Yeah, hi. Um..." She gathers her thoughts along with a deep breath, which makes me notice I haven't taken a breath of my own since the door opened. "I want to speak with you, Logan. Your guy..." She motions to Hunter, who is standing by the door, looking nervous. "Uh, he said you were busy, but I'd like to talk to you."

"Sure, come in. It's okay, Hunter. We've got it from here." Logan and I stand, and I move to grab a second chair as Hunter takes a step back toward the door.

"Um." She's frozen in place as she smiles at me warmly. "I mean alone, Jack. I'd like to speak with Logan alone."

"Oh." I don't recover well enough to hide my shock, and now both sets of eyes are on me as I nod with a smile, then excuse myself and follow Hunter out. "I'll wait outside. We still need to discuss the team's departure."

"I won't be long. Thank you, Jack." Logan offers me a warm smile, as if trying to say he has no intentions of a repeat of last night, and I agree with a curt nod in return.

I reach out and graze Jessa's hand as I pass her.

When I reach the door, I turn to see Jessa taking my seat in front of Logan. Then I leave and exhale yet another breath I'd been holding.

CHAPTER 32

JESSA

"You okay?" Dana's words pull me out of my daze.

"Hm?" My plate of barely touched breakfast sitting across from the crumbs left on hers tells me I've been lost in my head for a while.

"You've hardly said anything all morning. It was just me singing in the showers, and you know I hate singing alone." She grins. She's trying to get me to open up, so I smile back. My reassurance sets her at ease, and she leans in as though we're sharing secrets, then whispers, "So, what's the plan?"

"What plan?" I try my best to paste on my poker face, hoping she can't read me that well.

"The plan to escape, of course. You always get that look before you and Zane work on something big. It's like you're running code through your brain or something." She snorts to herself and reaches across the table to grab a strip of bacon off my plate.

"Ah. No plan yet, but you'll be the first to know." I grab my fork and shovel some cold scrambled eggs in my mouth, cutting off my need to fill the silence with more words.

"Okay. Oh, I forgot to tell you. Hunter was looking for

you earlier. I think it's his turn to watch us soon." She picks up her yogurt, and I stiffen.

Dana tilts her head, silently sizing me up. She has no idea what is happening, and I'm going to keep her out of it. I slowly tilt my head to the side to stretch out some of the tension building in my neck.

"Oh, I was working on something for Link. Some additional security suggestions. Hunter probably wants to get the information to him. Give me a second to add to it, then I need to go find him."

Pulling my scrap of paper out of my pocket, I review my writing to make sure I have everything I'll need written down.

It's a short list, but with Jack and Logan looking for their mole, it won't be easy to get without raising suspicion. Then I have a list of questions that need answers before I can get into base servers and move forward.

My eggs sit heavy in my stomach as it twists.

Jack and Logan are not bad people. No one here is—with the exception of Hunter.

They've become trusting, and Jack has put himself on the line to vouch for me. Tomorrow, I'll be destroying all of that goodwill, piece by piece.

I read the last line, positive I listed everything I'll need.

"I can come with you. Then maybe we can walk up to the falls again," Dana offers, but as much as I would love to spend time with her, I need to temporarily ditch her and complete this first step on my own.

The perfect distraction walks in, and I take full advantage. "I see Grizz is here for breakfast. Logan mentioned some of the guys are heading out on a mission today. Is he going with them?"

"I don't think he knows yet." Her coy glance over her shoulder is a dead giveaway.

"Hm. You know what? I'll be quick. Why don't you spend some time with him in case he's going? You never know if we'll be released, so..." I leave my suggestion open, and she takes it as her cue to go over and say hi, leaving me to make a hasty retreat before Tex notices I'm gone.

Moving quickly down the halls, I pass the door to the comms room and the common area, and I almost give up on finding Hunter when I run into him down the hall from Logan's office.

He glances past me for stragglers, and there is no time for small talk. "I heard from Maxwell this morning. He wants to move this along."

Every fiber of my being wants to scream at him.

I want to drag his ass into Logan's office and tell them everything, then let Jack and Logan take care of him.

But I can't.

In the grand scheme of things, Hunter is no more than an errand boy. Maxwell wouldn't miss him, and my deception would cost me dearly.

Hunter is just a replaceable cog in the wheel of Maxwell's organization. He means more to Jack and Logan than he ever would to Maxwell, and his misplaced loyalties will just get him buried in an unmarked grave at the end of the day.

Pasting on a compliant mask, I play my part. "Here's a list of what I need. It's specific. I need exactly those things." Then, looking at him to show my urgency, I continue. "I need *my* phone. Not *a* phone. *My* phone, and I need Dana's phone too. If they aren't ours, then nothing will work. I need two laptops, and they must already have complete access to the servers on base. I need any usernames and passwords necessary to access the mainframe. Tape them to the top corner of the screen."

Reality sets in, and Hunter pales. He's been with these guys for years. Once this begins, they will know exactly who the mole is, and I need him to focus. I need him to think it's him and me on our own team now.

"Once I start this, they'll know it was you, but I've planned it out for both of us. You will be with me in the comms room. I can lock it down, but I need every single one of these questions answered completely to do this." I tap the piece of paper he's holding in his hand.

"But if we're locked in the comms room, how do we get away once it's done?" His question is legitimate.

Hunter is in self-preservation mode now.

I look over my shoulder to make sure no one is coming, then jab my finger at the piece of paper again. "Have these answers to me by tonight. Once I connect to Maxwell's team and Zane, it'll alert everyone left on base. From what I've heard, most of the guys are leaving on some mission today. Everyone left will pile into the observation area to take us out once I'm done. Link mentioned something the other day about gas deployment as part of your defense procedures. It's on this list. I think I can lock them in, reroute the gas meant for the comms room into the observation room, and knock everyone out. Once I'm finished, we'll just walk out of here, but only on one condition." I stop to lead Hunter along, and he follows like I knew he would.

"What's that?"

"I want Maxwell's word that he'll release us. Zane, me, and Dana. We're done after this. There are no more

JESSA   267

contracts. Nothing. And he promises never to go after Jack again."

"I—I'll tell him." The apprehension in his voice tells me he doesn't believe I'll get what I'm asking for.

I already know I won't.

Maxwell won't let me go. He won't let Zane go free, and he definitely won't stop until Jack is dead, but I need him to believe that I think he will.

I need him to think I'm still that naive girl who went into his dog cage, but I'm not. Now, I'm the fighter who came out of it, and when he underestimates me this time, I'll see to it that it's the last thing he ever does.

"Good. Get that information to me tonight. Once those questions are answered, I'll tell you when we'll contact Maxwell. Now I need to talk to Logan."

I turn away from Hunter, closing the distance to Logan's closed office door.

As I reach out to knock, Hunter grabs my arm, spinning me in place, and I bump into the door.

"Why?" His defenses go up. I'm not surprised.

Everything is rushing to the end for him, and I understand the pressure he's under.

"We had words last night. I'd like to smooth over any tension, to keep him off my back, and I need some information from him to be able to work for Maxwell tomorrow."

As Hunter opens his mouth to object, Logan's muffled voice calls out from behind the door. Hunter freezes in place, panic clearly plastered across his face.

In his surprise, he loosens his grip on my arm, and I use the limited freedom to spin around and open the door, exposing both of us to the two men in the room.

Jack looks surprised to see me, but not half as surprised as Logan sounds. "Jessa?"

"Yeah, hi. Um..." Then I realize I really don't know what I wanted to lead with, so I buy myself some time by taking a step into the office, and Hunter watches me from the door. "I want to speak with you, Logan. Your guy, he said you were busy, but I'd like to talk to you."

I turn to Hunter, who relaxes his nerves but stays still near his only point of exit.

"Sure, come in. It's okay, Hunter. We've got it from here." Both Logan and Jack stand to welcome me, and Jack goes for a second chair as Hunter cautiously steps back to the door.

The worry that Hunter could listen from outside the door hits me. I'm going to need Jack to leave in order to make sure Hunter isn't eavesdropping.

"I mean alone, Jack. I'd like to speak with Logan alone."

Jack's expression falls at my request.

I know he wants to be here for me, and he doesn't realize that right now, I need him to be out there, in the hall, for me.

"I'll wait outside. We still need to discuss the team's departure." He finishes with Logan as he recovers and replaces his shock with a smile. Moving past me, he gently offers his support. As he touches my hand, goosebumps run up my arm.

I reassure him that it won't take long, then I turn to take a seat across from Logan.

A negative silence fills the room.

If there is something more quiet than quiet, this is it. Logan is still. Only his eyes move as he studies my face, and I decide to jump right in so I don't give anything away.

"I want you to know I understand why you did what you

did." He moves to speak, but I'm not done. Raising my hand gently, I ask for his attention, and, closing his mouth and leaning back in his chair, he grants it. "This doesn't mean I accept it, but after talking to Jack about it this morning, I understand your intention, and I know you were not planning to follow through?"

I allow my voice to end in a partial question, and he responds.

"You're correct. Jessa, I am sorry. There was no other way."

I raise my hand again to ask for more time, and once again he complies.

I realize I'm treading on thin ice. I won't be able to control this conversation much longer.

"I need time to work through a lot of things, Logan."

"I understand." There is a hint of remorse in his tone.

I know he is nothing like Maxwell.

I nod in acceptance and continue, "I need time to forgive, and a lot of that has to do with me separating my experience last night from the one I am beginning to remember with—him."

Logan's expression changes. I'm no longer leading the conversation.

"Jack mentioned you are remembering parts of your time with—him." He takes my cue and decides on a softer approach, and I'm grateful he hasn't gone into interrogation mode.

"Yes. I remember everything from the video. Almost to the end." As the final image flashes into my memory, I break eye contact with Logan. Humiliation washes over me as I lower my gaze to the desk and attempt to steady my breathing.

"I am truly sorry, Jessa. For your experience, and for my part in bringing those memories back. I know Jack and Dana are here for you, and I want you to know that I am as well, if you'd like to talk to me, considering..."

I chance a glance back up at him. I know he is dealing with his own fallout over what happened between us.

"I'd like that—in the future. I think that would be good for us."

"I can also get access to a counselor, someone with no personal attachment. Whatever you need."

I know deep down what I need. I need to see Maxwell dead. I need this to end. I need all of this destruction, a decade of pain, to wash away.

"Hey, you okay?" Logan's concern shakes me out of my thoughts.

In my haze, he's leaned forward in his chair. He seems to be monitoring me for signs of breakage.

The truth is, I don't have time to break.

Just like Logan had no other choice, neither do I.

There is only one way out of this, and it is a road that no one will let me go down.

So I'll be traveling it alone.

I'm about to burn everything to the ground, and I'm not entirely certain who'll still be standing when the smoke clears. As soon as I get access to both sets of servers and connect them to Zane, all hell will break loose, and I'll be the one ripping everything and everyone apart.

"Yeah. I'm good. Just tired." I flash a small smile, just enough to register as authentic on Logan's bullshit radar.

A look of relief tells me he's buying my response for now.

"Have you remembered anything else yet?" He tries to

make it sound inconsequential, but I know he wants into Maxwell's whole operation almost as badly as I do.

"I haven't yet. I'm sorry, Logan."

"Look, I know your entire history with the Sparr family. Most of our team has a personal score to settle with someone in that family. I know it feels lonely, but you aren't alone, Jessa."

Logan's words carry an air of understanding. We may be more alike than I thought.

I know Jack's history with Maxwell, but I always assumed it was just another day in the office for everyone else.

"Do you have a personal score to settle?"

My question causes Logan's left eye to twitch. "That's a story for another time." Abruptly switching gears, he gets back to his task at hand. "Has anyone approached you since we arrived on base? Anyone who might be working with Maxwell?"

Judging by his question, they haven't narrowed down the traitor yet, and this will work in my favor.

"No, but I've almost always been with someone. You don't know who it could be?" I'm no longer interested in this conversation. I already know more than they do.

"Right now, we only know who it isn't, and it's not a long enough list to keep you safe."

"You mentioned a mission today. Is Jack going?" I hope he'll think I'm asking for my own sense of security.

"No, he'll be staying back here." He takes a long pause, staring me down. My first instinct is to fill the silence, but I wait a little longer. Logan's jaw clenches before he inhales deeply. "Listen, some intel has come in on Maxwell's location. It's nothing exact." His soft chuckle to himself carries no humor. "We think he's somewhere in the lower half of California. Not a lot to go on, but it's enough that we're sending a couple of teams out to our base in Arizona. We've arranged for backup to take their place here. They should be arriving tomorrow evening."

For a moment, I'm surprised Logan offered me the additional information. After last night, we've crossed a line. Either he feels guilty about what happened and this is an olive branch, or he's decided that this will open communication between us.

Once again, I'm reminded of how often I'm underestimated.

My job will have to happen before their team returns, to limit the number of bodies on base, but knowing they have a base in Arizona may prove useful.

I decide not to push my luck with further questions.

Logan and Jack are smart. They won't let anyone out on that mission if they haven't cleared them, so I know Hunter will be kept behind, along with any others still left on their list.

After the team departs, I'll get a better idea of who I have left to work with.

A smile effortlessly tugs at my cheeks as Jessa laughs with Dana while they work in the kitchen.

After Jessa walked out of the office, with Logan behind her, my day became a series of nonstop tasks and checklists.

With the majority of our tactical team on the way to their assignment, we were short-staffed on base. Between all of the guys we held back, three of them had moments when they were either temporarily missing or not where they should have been, which has Logan distracted and my stress level at an all-time high.

Only Grey stayed with us the entire time.

Both Hunter and Waldo disappeared at awkward times with no real excuse as to why they were gone. Grizz showed up to prep late without even offering an excuse. I'm going to assume it was because of Dana, as this is out of character for him.

Link was with us through comms the whole time, and his team ran simulations and tests as we packed.

Jessa and Dana stayed out of our way, for the most part.

Jessa dropped by to ask if she could grab us any supplies from the kitchen, but Logan politely dismissed her.

We need to keep in mind that, until we find a way to take care of Maxwell, no one is to be fully trusted, and he's granted a lot of leniency where Jessa is concerned.

As Tex and Eagle drive our two units off base, a low growl in my stomach reminds me we missed lunch. Not only that, but with most of our team deployed, we forgot to schedule kitchen staff for supper. So when the women ask if they can make us dinner, everyone left on base jumps at the chance for a decent meal.

I can't help but feel smug watching my girl work happily in the kitchen.

Logan was on edge because we needed all hands on deck today, but his concerns weren't necessary.

He checked with Link earlier and confirmed neither of the women went anywhere near the comms area, and Jessa made no attempts to access anything other than the microwave when they heated up some leftovers for their lunch earlier.

"How many of you are left?" Dana's head pops up from the cutting table as she continues to chop. "We need to know how many plates to set."

"Oh, uh..." Quickly doing the math in my head, I count the six of us and add the two women. "Eight in total, including you two."

She nods, then immediately shouts over her shoulder to Jessa, "Eight plates, Jay."

There's a faint reply from the pantry.

This is a welcome change from my every day. It has always been just the guys on base, and none of us have exemplary culinary skills. Hearing their laughter brings a sense of home to our compound. It's a familiarity I didn't know I missed until now.

"Something smells good." Grey catches my attention as he saunters into the cafeteria, with Grizz following behind.

"Perfect timing. Grizz, can you help Dana in the kitchen? And I need your help grabbing the cups for everyone." Jessa smiles, all business, as she enters the room with an armful of plates, and the men jump into action.

"I thought you guys were on first duty." Logan speaks to Grey and Grizz as he enters.

Grey smiles. "Word travels fast that we're getting a real meal. Hunter and Waldo are out there until six, so we're going to eat fast then relieve them and send them in for theirs. We'll take 1800 hours until 0300 hours. Then they'll do 0300 until the late morning shift arrives. Then we all get to eat."

"Sounds good to me. As long as we're covered on the grounds. We should have more bodies on base by midmorning. Jack and I will be around for backup overnight as well." Logan talks as he walks over to me, but I don't look at him.

I can't take my eyes off Jessa. She looks so comfortable here, chatting with the guys and carrying bowls of food to the table.

"How is she?" Logan asks. Neither of us looks at the other.

"She seems good. I think some time with Dana today helped. I don't know if she's remembered anything else. But she knows we need to know, so I think she'd tell us if she did. I'll talk to her about it in the morning."

"Okay. Listen, I was thinking maybe we should set up a meeting with her tomorrow." Logan eases into his suggestion, and my back goes straight. He continues before I have a chance to reject his idea. "Not an interrogation, Jack. A meeting. A real sit-down meeting with her. I'd like to start bringing her in on some of the things we know about Maxwell. We need to work together on this. I know you feel the same way. Maybe we could talk with her for a bit after breakfast. Our away teams don't need us on comms until noon, and our backup team isn't scheduled to arrive until later in the day, so we'll be free."

I pause to consider his words.

It's a start. I want nothing more than to work with her. It's the only way I can fully protect her.

"I think that's a good idea. I'll mention it to her in the morning," I say as I watch everyone walk out of the kitchen with their arms full of food.

"Soup's on!" Dana exclaims as bowls are placed around the tables, which have been pushed together to create one large eating area.

"Wow, ladies. This smells amazing. You know you didn't have to go through this much trouble. Most of us would probably be happy with a box of mac and cheese that's cooked properly." I pull out a chair for Jessa and watch as Grizz does the same for Dana.

Grey feels the need to explain himself. "That was one time! It was my first time cooking for you guys, and I was nervous, and..." The rest of his sentence is drowned out with laughter as chairs slide along the floor.

"Interesting story. That's how Grey got his nickname. Isn't that right, Trent?" I use Grey's real name, and he shoots me a glare.

"Hey. I was so focused on making a good impression that my mind was elsewhere. I wasn't paying attention."

"You made an impression all right," Grizz cuts in.

"Anyway, long story short, it didn't quite turn out." Grey pauses, and Logan steals his thunder.

"Let's just say I never knew macaroni and cheese could be that color: grey," Logan finishes, and both women try to contain their laughter.

"And what's worse is, you all told me I got my nickname because the greyhound is the fastest dog in the world. I ate that bull up for months before I found out. Now I like the name, and that's just not right," Grey retorts, drawing *awwws* of sympathy from the ladies.

As the giggles die down, Dana jumps in. "It was Jessa's idea. I miss cooking and baking. I always do the cooking for the two of us." Dana glances quickly to Jessa.

"She does. And she is a great cook. She could be one of those amazing chefs from TV if, you know, we weren't running from—everyone." Jessa defers to me to gauge how inappropriate her comment might be.

I smile, and Logan surprisingly jumps in.

"I can see how that would be a problem." He smiles at both of the women and reaches across the table for a bun, breaking the tension as everyone relaxes.

Jessa returns his smile. "Anyway, dinner will be delicious, but my favorite is Dana's baking. She made a chocolate cake with the most delicious chocolate icing."

"Are you telling me we have the ingredients to make that? Like, here, in this kitchen?" Grey asks in absolute shock.

"You don't need much. You have enough here for a lot of things. It's actually a chocolate ganache. I'm thinking of making cupcakes next time." Dana beams back at her best friend, then looks around the table. "What are you waiting for?"

Grey and Grizz take a quick glance at each other and dig in, leaving their formalities at the door. They only have ten minutes before Waldo and Hunter come walking through those doors.

Cutlery clinks against plates, and the conversation falls off as everyone eats. As I look from Jessa to Dana, then around the table, I notice a stark difference.

Sipping their soup quietly, they share a smile as they watch the guys shovel their meals into their mouths with nothing more than grunts and deep breaths, so as not to pass out from lack of oxygen while chewing.

The sound of Logan clearing his throat alerts everyone to our collective lack of manners, and the men still, then sit up straighter in their seats.

"You boys still have time to be courteous." Then, shifting his attention to the ladies, Logan continues, "Dana, Jessa, this is delicious. Thank you."

The women exchange a pleased smile as the rest of us echo our thanks, and the clanking of utensils against plates evens out as our dinner becomes a bit more formal than it was before.

"How did you get your code name, Jack? Was there an incident in Arizona?" Dana asks.

Grizz and Grey look at me with smirks spreading across their faces.

"That's a story for another—"

Logan's bark of laughter surprises me. "Now that's an interesting story. It had nothing to do with the state we were in. It was more the state of mind Jack was in." Logan has both girls' attention. As our team continues to eat, they listen to the story they've heard before.

"We were executing a takedown mission on a drug ring operating in a little town outside of Chicago. It wasn't your average bust though. These guys were into the heaviest of drugs, and they'd started to experiment with cutting in some hardcore agents. They were responsible for spreading those drugs among wealthy kids at parties. A few of those kids ended up dead, and others are still in the hospital with brain damage. We had secured the area, or so we thought..." Logan rolls his eyes at me. It was my job to secure the room, but I missed a hidden closet.

"Jack opens a door to a little cabinet, and out jumps a scrawny kid. He blows an unknown powder into Jack's face to try to buy some time to get away. Long story short, it was hallucinogenic. The rest of us were all outside, securing the drugs and packing up the trucks, and Jack jumps out a window, naked, and starts running around the area, flapping his arms and yelling, 'It's so hot in here.... I'm a Phoenix! I'm rising from the ashes.... I can fly! Why is it so fucking hot?'" Logan ends his story abruptly, waiting for the reaction, and both Jessa and Dana are sitting with their mouths open in disbelief.

Slowly, Jessa meets my gaze, and both of them let out a laugh I'm sure they tried hard to contain.

"I'm sorry. I shouldn't laugh." Jessa takes a deep breath, and Dana wipes a tear from her eye. "You could have been seriously hurt. You jumped out a window?" she asks.

"He was on the first floor. The only thing he hurt was his ego when we showed him the video we took," Logan answers, and now Grey and Grizz are chuckling too.

"Wait. There's video of this?" Dana's eyes are wide, and

she sounds a little too excited to witness the most embarrassing moment of my career.

"Another time. So, tell me more about these cupcakes. When will you be making those?" I cut in, and Logan sits smugly back in his seat, grabbing a glass of water and taking a drink. I can clearly tell the fucker has amused himself.

"Oh. I just meant that I'll modify them and add them to my list." She opens her mouth to continue, but then she looks over at Jessa and pauses.

Our eyes follow Dana's to Jessa, who finishes her soup and smiles. Then she shrugs, as though the glance wasn't important.

"It's okay, Dee." She starts looking around the table. "I said you could tell them anything you knew."

"Okay." With a little wiggle in her seat, she begins. "I've been making a long list of items I want to sell in my bakery when Zane releases us. I can't decide if I want to have a coffee shop that serves desserts, or a bakery that serves coffee, though—" She tries to continue with her grand plans, but Logan already has some questions.

"What do you mean when Zane releases you? I thought you were working with him willingly."

Dana looks over to Jessa, who offers another shrug for her to continue, and she does. "Oh, we are. I mean when our work is done and there is no longer a threat to us. Zane set up nest eggs for some of the people who work under him. We'll get a notification on our phones with everything we need to start over. New names, bankroll, properties, and IDs. It's our cue to disappear if it ever happens."

"Interesting." Logan looks to Jessa, who merely smiles. Then he shifts his attention back to Dana, and I notice Grizz has started to pay extra attention as well. "And you are going to run a bakery?"

"I'd like to. Hopefully somewhere remote, with no internet access. I could bake all day in peace."

"And what about you, Jessa? What would you like to do with your payout and new identity?" My question flows a little too eagerly, and she looks between me and Logan.

"I don't know." Then, looking at her friend, she says, "We just always said that I would meet up with Dana. It would be nice to not be—hunted."

Logan goes quiet beside me, and, for once, I can't tell what he's thinking.

My mind is blank too.

"Time's up, boys." Waldo walks into the dining room, followed by Hunter. Grizz and Grey both stand and move to the table with the cake.

"I don't mean to be rude, but can we grab a piece to go?" Grizz looks at Dana, and she shifts her hair over her face to cover her shy smile.

"Yeah. Sure. I'll cut you each a piece." She stands and turns to the men in the doorway. "There are plates on the counter, just help yourselves."

Grabbing plates and cutlery, Hunter and Waldo take the newly vacant seats at the table and begin serving themselves.

As Dana returns to finish her dinner, Logan drops his fork onto his cleared plate beside me and reaches for his water.

"We should discuss a couple of things." Both ladies look up from the meal hesitantly as Logan continues, "Just housekeeping items. We're short on manpower until late tomorrow morning at the earliest, so some of our normal routines need to change." He nods in my direction, looking for backup, and I step in.

"What he's trying to say is, we won't be able to always have one man on you, but you will be locked in your room for most of the night. Grizz and Grey are out on duty until early morning, then Hunter and Waldo will relieve them. We need them sleeping when they aren't on duty. Logan and I will be working with Link across both their shifts as well, and we have some tactical simulations we're running tonight with our teams in the field. You two will stay together until the morning. Someone will drop by to escort you both to the bathrooms at lights out."

Hunter quickly swallows his bite. "I'll do it, boss."

I nod to confirm, then split my attention between the women. "We'd like both of you to sleep in Dana's room tonight. We—I would feel better if I knew you were together and safe."

I won't be able to watch Jessa, and the four men left on base with us haven't been cleared yet, so I don't want anyone making contact with her in the night while I'm busy.

"That's fine, Jack." Jessa smiles and nods at Dana. "We appreciate you all thinking about our safety."

Logan relaxes beside me. I realize that Hunter and Waldo are close to finishing their meals, and we're ready for dessert.

"Great. Thanks for your understanding. Now, let's see what's so great about this dessert." Logan stands to clear his plate, and Jessa stops him.

"I'll take that for you." Then, looking around the table, she continues, "I'll clear all your plates, and Dana will help serve the cake."

She reaches out to grab Hunter's first. Then she

continues around the table as Dana sets the cake in the middle. The strong scent of cocoa wafts on the air, and I'm momentarily distracted by the icing. As my piece is served, I look up as Jessa heads into the kitchen with our plates stacked in her hands.

Deciding to help, I slide my seat back to stand, but Hunter catches my attention. "Excuse my manners, but holy shit, this is amazing. Boss, you need to try this cake. Who made this?" he asks me.

Looking back at my piece, then around to see the satisfied smiles, I decide to sit back down and clear my plate. "This was all Dana."

"Delicious, ma'am." Waldo speaks for the first time since entering the room, and everyone murmurs their agreement.

Thoughts of assisting Jessa in the kitchen fade with my first bite into the pure chocolate delight. Hunter is right: it is amazing.

As I take my last bite, Jessa is back out and sitting down to eat her dessert. "I just put on some decaf. I know you guys need to sleep tonight."

Moving through the halls at five o'clock in the morning is more sobering than any other time I've walked down them—though I think my feelings of foreboding have more to do with the situation than the time.

Scenarios and outcomes race through my mind as I make my way to the comms room. Butterflies are angrily fluttering around in my gut, grating against my nerves.

According to the paper Hunter slipped me as I cleared the plates last night, the only ones awake on base now are Hunter and Waldo. Jack and Logan finished running their tests with Link and their away team an hour ago, and they are taking advantage of the downtime to sleep before morning.

I took a chance that Link's attention would be elsewhere and the cameras would not be closely monitored with everything else going on. I also know that Link runs system reports and diagnostics at five because it's their most quiet time. Security goes down around the same time, to clear its data and reboot, so the cameras will be off for the next fifteen minutes. This will make it easy to gain access to a computer that's already running and not actively guarded.

As I enter the hallway outside the comms room, my nerve endings tingle in anxious anticipation.

I had half a day to organize this.

My final move.

All of my information came in at once last night when Hunter slipped me his note, and I had minutes to forge my plan and put the pieces in motion. The planning and execution of ops has always been a process of weighing risk and reward, but this was different.

I pulled out a pen and a piece of paper and quickly scrawled out some instructions for Hunter. I told him to leave our door unlocked after he returned us from the bathrooms just before lights out and I would meet him outside of the comms area at five. The good thing about locking doors with keys instead of cards is that when the door opens, it doesn't alert anyone.

I only have one shot. Then this game turns into a whole new one, and I'm not prepared for any other version to play out.

It has to end like this.

Footsteps fall behind me, and panic forces my heart into my throat. I glance over my shoulder. Hunter follows me silently down the hall, raising one finger to his lips.

Opening the first set of doors, Hunter walks across to the observation window, looking into the comms area where I'll be sitting. He drops a duffel bag on the counter in front of the window, unzips it, then steps back and turns to me.

"Everything you asked for is in there."

I pull the bag open, grab my phone, turn it on, and

unlock it. All of my apps are still in place, and I slide it into my front pocket, then continue digging.

Dana's phone is the next item I pull out. Turning it on, I punch in her lock code to check that it is also still intact, and it is.

I place her phone down on the shelf beside the bag. I only hope she finds it and she's able to make it out of here with everything on it.

I take a deep, cleansing breath. Everything from now on will fall as it may.

Digging around in the bag, I find the two laptops I requested.

Hunter is watching me uneasily.

"Where's Waldo? Aren't you two supposed to be on duty now?" I ask, trying to distract him.

He's all business. "I asked him to double-check the fence along the south side forty minutes ago. It's the farthest side. He should be far away for another five minutes or so. Is that enough time to get secure?"

"Yes. I only need about five minutes in there." Grabbing the bag with the laptops, I move around Hunter, through the door, and into the comms area to set up. "Do whatever you need to do out there. I'll be locking us in this room in three minutes. That will set off the first alarm. They should be here within ten minutes."

I move to the main table and pull out the two laptops. Hunter wastes no time in stepping into the comms room, where he stands back against the wall to let me finish my work.

I power up the first computer. This is the one I'll use to take over the servers on base. Once I grant myself access, I'll override Link's authorities, lock us in, and take control of all of their systems and programs.

As the first screen comes to life, I open the second laptop. I'll use this one to connect to Maxwell and run the communications, which reminds me: "Is Maxwell standing by?"

"Yes. I told him to be ready at five and we would come online a little after that. Here is his number and information." Stepping toward me, he places a folded piece of paper beside me on the table. I open it, then slide it under the corner of the laptop. Then I shift to remove my phone and access the screen, placing it off to the side of my work area.

The first laptop finishes its startup. When the security screen pops up, I enter the login information that is taped to the corner of the screen. The computer pauses for one long moment to verify the information. Then my heart both leaps and sinks simultaneously.

I'm in.

"Wake up, Jack. We've been breached."

I instinctively jolt out of bed and grab my clothes as I move across the dark room toward Logan, who is yelling at me through my door.

I feel like my head just hit the pillow minutes ago, and confusion sets in. We knew we were sitting ducks. We're low on manpower, and only Hunter and Waldo are on the grounds. A breach could happen at almost any point around our perimeter.

I glimpse at my clock on the shelf.

5:08 a.m.

As I open the door, Logan is already turning to run, and I fall in on his six and catch up to be briefed. Grizz and Grey join up with Logan in the middle of the compound, and there are no pleasantries.

"Grey, get a vehicle supplied and ready to go in case we need it. Then take the bike and circle the perimeter. Eyes open for Hunter and Waldo. Base comms are down, and no one is checking in. If you come across them, send them to the control center."

Grey nods, then runs past me toward the garage. I turn my attention back to my team, trying to piece together our situation.

Logan squares his attention on Grizz. "Get Dana. Bring her to the comms room now."

Grizz spins on his heels and runs toward the girls' room as Logan yells out to him, "I don't have time for her shit. Get her there."

Then, without looking me in the eyes, he continues running in the direction of our control center.

"What's going on? Why Dana and not Jessa?" My heart rate is higher than it should be, and dread hits me as a thought I don't want to entertain enters my head.

"Our servers have been infiltrated. Link was able to get a short message out before all communications were cut. We've got headsets to an old communication system, and I need to get to them. Both Hunter and Waldo are MIA. Our computers and all systems are shutting down. Jack, I need you to prepare yourself."

Jessa.

My thoughts run wild as we reach the main building.

As we rush down the hall, I notice our camera lights are out. Our compound security system is offline.

Logan stops outside the control center, removes his gun from its holster, and opens the door. Inside, the first room is quiet. The lock on the inner room is engaged. Someone's made it through and locked themselves inside.

Logan drops his gun on the table. We both know that room is completely bulletproof. It's everything-proof.

Walking to the side of the room, he opens up a cabinet and rifles through boxes. Then he pulls out the headsets we need to speak with Link on backup.

My world spins, then breaks apart as I move to the window to see Jessa in the other room, sitting at the table with two laptops. Oblivious to her surroundings, she's shifting her attention between both computers and a phone on the table.

I know that look now.

She's on autopilot.

Anger rises inside me, and I lunge at the window, banging my fists against the bulletproof glass, jarring her out of her concentration.

She jumps in her seat, and her eyes meet mine. Her fingers stop typing for a few seconds as a look of remorse replaces her shock, and nausea surges at the uncertainty of what she's about to do.

Then she drops her eyes back down, and her fingers pick up where they left off. She's back in her head.

"Link, speak." Logan steps to the window beside me, handing me a headset. I put it on, keeping my eyes on the situation in front of me.

"Waldo and Hunter haven't checked in since 0400. The servers were accessed at 5:02 a.m. She had a username and password, so she was able to gain access and move around the system for three minutes virtually undetected—she accessed our mainframe and began to shut everything down at 5:05 a.m. The username and password she used belong to—"

"Hunter." Logan's response snaps my attention to him, and I follow his line of sight into the room, looking just past my Jessa.

Stepping out of a room behind her and looking at the two of us is the shell of the teammate we've known for almost ten years.

Hunter is our mole.

Except it doesn't look like him. With his gloves off and nothing to lose, there's no love lost in his eyes.

Without giving Logan or I the respect that our time together warrants, he lowers his eyes to the ground and moves to Jessa, handing her a pen and paper. Then, backing up against the wall, he watches as she continues to do her thing.

"She's turned off communication into the room and deactivated our cell tower. She can't hear you, but you can hear them." Link's talking fast, and there's no mistaking the defeat in his voice. "Logan, I'm a sitting duck here. My team is trying to get back in, but right now I can only watch her take over. She's fast. Faster than I ever thought she'd be. Wait. She's linking off-site. Shit, I can't even run a trace."

The first video screen on the wall flashes to life, and Hunter stands up straight as Maxwell's face fills the screen. My heart breaks as pure rage fills my head and rings into my ears.

After everything she saw, everything she remembers, how can she work with him?

The severity of our situation sinks deep into me as I realize she not only has control of everything we have, but she can connect to Maxwell now and hand everything over.

"What's going on?" Dana's voice is shaky as she enters the room. "That's my phone."

She walks toward us and stands beside me. Grizz follows behind her as she processes everything we've just taken in. Then, seeing Maxwell on the video screen, she puts her hands against the glass.

"Jessa?" Dana's first instinct is fear for her friend. She thinks Jessa is trapped in there.

"She can't hear you. She's turned off communication. If you know anything, now is the time, Dee." Logan wastes no time, but Dana isn't having any of it.

"I don't know anything. What's happening?"

"I'm bringing Zane online in one minute." Jessa's voice flows through the comms link in our room, and everyone momentarily freezes.

The second video screen powers up, and the entire room goes silent.

This is it.

Zane's identity, everything, will be put out there, and we have absolutely no control on our end to stop what's about to happen.

If Jessa can do this kind of damage on her own, I can't fathom the destruction that will come once she accesses Zane.

"Hunter tells me I have your word, Maxwell. We do this, and we're out. All three of us." She makes eye contact with Dana and flashes a regretful smile.

"No, Jessa. Don't do this." Dana bangs on the glass.

"You have my word," Maxwell bites out through gritted teeth.

His words are hollow. He has no intention of ever letting her go.

Dana looks at both of us. "I don't understand. It's a safety thing. She shouldn't be able to connect to Zane without me."

"Need-to-know, Dee." Logan's words sober me, and my heart sinks to think she's played everyone, including her best friend.

Tapping at the keypad, Jessa turns her head, and all of us follow her eyes up to the video screen as it flashes to life and Zane's real identity fills the screen.

CHAPTER 36

JESSA

I can't go back now.

Even if I could, I'm not sure I could have done anything differently. Looking up and seeing my closest friend stare at me in confusion is too much to bear, and I know this needs to end.

Typing in my final bit of code, I check my phone one last time to make sure I have what I need. Then, taking a deep breath, I connect to Zane.

As he fills the screen, my heart swells.

The man I did all of this for smiles back at me as my brother's image joins our meeting.

"Travis?" Maxwell's surprised voice stabs into me, and I need a second deep breath just to maintain my composure a little longer.

I need everything to hold together for a few more minutes, then I will tell them all the truth and face my fate as I burn everything down.

I turn back to my computer and begin linking my server to Zane as I listen to the conversation for response cues.

A quick glance to Logan and Jack confirms that my

distraction is working. Now that Zane is online, I'm secondary once again, and I'm more than happy to use this to my advantage. All eyes, including Dana's, are on the image of my brother on the screen until...

"Zane, I'm in. System is open for your access." I speak into the room.

Turning off the video connection to Zane, I enter the codes I need to run all the programs that have been set up over the years.

With Zane offline, all eyes are back on me. I can only assume Link is filling Logan and Jack in on my progress through the headsets they are wearing. Then, with two final keystrokes, I'm done, and I need to make my next step believable.

"Zane has everything he needs, Maxwell. Have your team accept our access request, and we'll begin by transferring their financials. Then we'll move to their security and systems access; he's still working on those." I glance as calmly as I can over my shoulder and confirm Maxwell's greed has overridden his common sense once again.

"We're ready for you." Maxwell nods to someone off-screen as a disgusting sneer spreads across his face.

My stomach is ready to jump out of my throat at the thought that I'm only seconds away from having everything I need. I stop typing and stare at my screen, waiting for the authorization I need to continue.

Seconds feel like hours as my heart beats hard into my ears, and my mouth goes dry as my blinking cursor turns into an acceptance code. And just like that, I'm in again.

Everything outside of my immediate surroundings fades away.

This is it.

A quick search of his server shows me Maxwell's team put up their own protections against an outside attack. This would have stopped me had I not remembered what I needed.

Maxwell's team is decent, but compared to me they are entry level.

Maxwell is arrogant, and his amateur IT team is no different. They never thought to protect themselves from the inside out, and I access the hidden file I need and let it go to work from behind their firewall.

It'll run for a minute before it is detected, and by then, it'll be too late.

I access the first piece of information I need in seconds: Maxwell's current location. He's in a remote area southeast of San Diego near the California–Arizona border.

Switching my attention back to Cypher's servers, I search for a way into their entire network.

On my own, I've never been strong enough to take out Maxwell, but Cypher has something I don't: a connection to much bigger guns to bring to this knife fight.

I had no idea of Cypher's reach until Logan told me about their base in Arizona. Now that I know I'm searching for more, I'll be able to access their entire operation. If I do this right, Arizona won't even know I've taken over until everything is done, as the orders to proceed will be coming from Link himself.

My heart skips a beat when I find what I'm looking for, and I send my first transmission out to their away teams to be ready to deploy.

I only have one more hurdle. I need Hunter out of the

way, and I need to type in the codes to finish the program. And they both need to be done at the same time.

"Hunter. There should be a cable attached to the back of the computer in the side room. It's blue. Disconnect it and bring it to me." I hold my gaze on the screen.

He pushes off the wall and walks into the smaller room. I glance through the door to see him wedging himself between the wall and the desk. I have seconds to make my move.

I key in my last piece of code to gain control of Maxwell's servers, then I hit the lock button on the side room door. As it clicks, I jump up and lunge across the room as Hunter tries to disentangle himself and get back to the door from his side.

My pulse racing, I beat him by a fraction of a second and close the door before he can wrench it out of my hands. Then, stepping back with my arms raised, I look around the room and see all eyes on me, mouths open.

Time stands still, and everything freezes in complete silence.

No one knows what the hell I'm doing.

I'm not even sure if I know.

But whatever it is, I'm now in complete control, and it's time to begin what I always set out to do.

Hunter pulls hard on the door handle, but it won't open. It's sealed as tightly as his own fate.

I turn to the desk and take a seat.

Then I go to work hacking the rest of the way into my only way out.

For a brief moment, my conscience makes an appearance. I feel guilty for what I'm about to do. I want Jack to see the good in my intentions, but that is exactly what the road to hell is paved with. It's fitting—since I'm going after the devil.

I tap a key, cutting off all outside communication and pulling up their away team's details. They are already heading toward Maxwell, and I zero in on one unit.

It turns out their Arizona base has two Black Hawk helicopters, and one of them has not yet been deweaponized. They are both in the air and heading to the general location I transmitted, along with three teams on the ground.

I choose the one that has active ammunition on board, scan their call sign information, clear my throat, and open up a direct line to the pilot.

"Ranger Three, this is TacCon. Come in, Ranger Three. Do you copy?"

My heart hammers into my throat, and I second-guess using the call sign for Link's tactical control. One wrong step, and I might be questioned.

I meet Logan's gaze as I wait for a response. He's gone pale, and his eyes are wide as realization dawns on him.

I'm taking control of their mission.

"Loud and clear, TacCon. This is Ranger Three. We thought we lost you for a moment. Over."

"Just double-checking some intel. Ranger Three, your strike package has been updated. Maxwell Sparr is confirmed on site. You have new mission parameters. Engage at these coordinates." I hit enter, sending Maxwell's location through, along with an order to launch the aircraft's air-to-surface missiles when ready. "Stand by for authorization." I open the updated clearance files, then relay the code I need. "Ranger Three, you are a go. Authorization: November—Alpha—Two—Two—Eight—Lima—Delta. Over."

There are a few seconds while the pilot checks the code

before he returns. "Roger that. We're on our way. Time on target is eight mikes. Out."

I glance at the clock to note the time. I need to hold it together for eight more minutes.

Punching some keys, I open the communication line to the outside room. Everyone is silent as they watch me carefully.

There really isn't anything they can do now, and they know it.

Logan looks like he's trying to formulate his best course of action. Jack is angry. But more than that, he looks devastated, and it crushes me to know I've let him down. I only hope in the end, he understands I had no choice.

Before I'm able to speak to either of them, I'm pulled away by the one voice I can't wait to stop hearing.

"Jessa, what's going on? Get Zane—Travis back on the screen right now," Maxwell barks without a clue about what's heading his way.

I punch a couple of keys, and the video comes back on. My brother's image waits for Maxwell to speak, and I'm surprised no one has noticed yet.

"What's going on, Travis? As soon as we accepted the transfer of the financial information, our systems began to shut down."

No one has noticed how still my brother sits, how his expression hasn't changed since the last time he was on the screen.

He doesn't look real.

And that's because he isn't.

Turning to my laptop, I type out one more set of instructions. Then I hit enter, and my brother's voice answers Maxwell's question.

"I don't think I'm the best person to answer that. You killed me. Remember?" Travis's image responds without emotion.

Maxwell's face pales at the accusation.

My programs are now eating through everything Maxwell has online and on his servers, and his team is about to tell him there is nothing he can do to stop it.

It's time to answer everything.

"You'll pay for this, Jessa. You and Travis," Maxwell threatens, and now I'm done.

"NO! YOU DON'T SAY HIS NAME." Spinning in my seat, I stand and clench my hands into fists at my sides as I continue, raising my voice with each word. "YOU KILLED MY BROTHER! YOU DON'T GET TO SAY HIS NAME."

As I barely hold back my tears, the last ten years come flooding back.

I had planned on a different course of action at this moment. But those plans were made when I was thinking without feeling, and I failed to consider everything that could have possibly happened over the last week.

So now I don't even know where I'm going with this, but, looking up at the combined shock and rage on Maxwell's face, I know the only thing I have left is the truth.

"I've waited for years. Ten years. I watched you kill my family."

"That was my dad, Jessa. I—" The first sign of panic cracks through Maxwell's lies.

"Don't. Don't lie to me. I know you were carrying out your father's orders. I saw your bright yellow Jeep parked on the bridge as their car went over the side. I saw it all. My brother never made it out. I hacked in and picked up the report of a body being found downstream a week after they died. I changed the age and gender in the report right away, so it would be overlooked, and then I had Travis's remains transferred out of state for burial."

I turn to the devastated looks on Jack and Dana's faces, and my heart is almost too heavy to continue.

Tears flow freely down my best friend's cheeks.

She deserves better.

We all do.

It's time to let everyone go.

Moving back to the computer, I sit down to key in the code that will release everyone.

Dana's eyes leave mine and move to her phone.

Through sniffles, she's reading the message, and her eyes slowly move back up to meet mine.

I know by the relief in her smile she doesn't yet realize what is happening.

"Jessa, we're out. This is it. I got our release information." Innocent glee fills her face as she presses her phone to the window, and I take a moment to memorize her smile as I smile back.

I'll take this memory with me.

As she looks into the room at my phone on the table beside me, her expression falls into concern. "Where is your message, Jessa? You said Zane would let us go together or not at all. That was the deal. We did it, right?"

"Dana, I'm so sorry," I manage through a weak tone as I tap a couple of keys.

An alarm starts wailing outside the comms room doors.

Jack and Logan's expressions tell me Link has just notified them that I've taken access of their base shutdown procedures, and I'm filtering the gases into the rooms that Hunter and I occupy.

It's unavoidable. The only way to stop the gas is to cut all power, and I need to remain online for final strike confirmation or this is all for nothing. I won't risk sending the gas anywhere else without knowing the positions of everyone outside of this room.

"Jessa?" Jack slams his fists against the glass, and the pain on his face crushes me. "Don't do this. You don't need to end it like this. Don't leave me again."

Tears run down my face as I continue to type. Dana screams my name, and I assume it's because one of them must've filled her in on what's happening.

I glance over my shoulder. Maxwell is barking orders at his people off-screen and watching everything unfold. The image of my brother is still on the screen. Another set of taps closes my connection to Travis's image as the air pressure around me changes.

"Who's Zane? I don't understand," Maxwell, still unaware that gases are being rerouted to my room, asks incredulously. A sardonic laugh escapes me.

"There is no Zane. There never was."

"I don't under—"

"I'm Zane." I look around the silent room. No one is moving now. " I created Zane in high school to use as an alternate identity if I ever needed one for hacking. I coded a system that could follow my cues and work with me. After you killed my family, Zane became my lead. *He* could never be found. *He* could never be caught, and *he* would never be yours, just like I was never yours, Maxwell."

"Jessa, you don't have to do this. The gases you are filtering in are deadly. It's cyanide." Link's concerned voice comes through the speaker on my laptop, and now everyone knows what is happening.

At Link's words, Hunter bangs violently against the door he's locked behind as he realizes his end will be the same as my own.

"This is how it has to end. I'm Zane, and I'm taking everything with me. My programs are all set to destroy themselves once I've pulled everything I need and decimated Maxwell's servers. It's the only way to free you as well." I look up to Jack, who is in full panic mode.

Behind me, Hunter is still banging on the door, and Dana is screaming for all of this to stop.

I can't take the sight of her pain any longer.

"Dana, I love you. Thank you for always being with me. You never let me down. I won't let you down—" I try to continue, but her anger cuts me off.

"You're letting me down now, Jessa. STOP IT. STOP THE GAS. PLEASE." Her voice is broken, and she's outright begging now.

Swallowing the lump in my throat, I look at Grizz standing behind her, and I push him to take control. Leaning over the laptop once more, I tap in a new command, then look up at the group again.

"Grizz. That outside door is locking in twenty seconds. She shouldn't see this."

At my suggestion and without a second thought, Grizz steps forward to Dana. Lifting her around the waist, he pulls her out of the room, kicking and screaming, until the door closes behind them and locks.

"Jessa, I'm sorry. Take deep breaths. The first gas coming in is meant to disable you, then you won't feel anything. It'll knock you out before the cyanide releases. You can still stop it. Just kill everything." Link's voice echoes in the room, but there's no going back.

Feed from my speaker cuts into the room, and I hit the mute button once more to block Maxwell out while I speak with the pilot, who should be approaching Maxwell's location. I don't want to give him the chance to get away now.

"TacCon, this is Ranger Three. We are locked on target. Awaiting strike confirmation sequence. Over."

A few more keystrokes, and I've cracked the final code I need. "Ranger Three, this is TacCon. Confirmation sequence: Tango—Alpha—Kilo—Four—Six—Echo—Echo—Foxtrot. You are cleared to engage. I repeat, you are clear to engage. Over."

The pilot rattles off a combined sequence of his own in acceptance before ending with "out," and the line goes dead.

I turn on all speakers, and my body shudders on my next exhale as the weight of all my choices hits me.

I have one thing left to do, and I have seconds of consciousness left.

"Jack," I choke out. My fear is taking over now, and I can't control my panic as the realization of my mortality hits me. "I love you. I wish there was another way. I'm glad I got to see you again. I—" My body sways to the side as Maxwell cuts me off.

"JESSA!" Anger carries his words into the room, and I spin to look him in the eyes one last time.

"NO," I command. "You don't get to order me around. It ends now. Your servers are dumping everything into Logan and Jack's servers. Link, you'll be back online in fifteen minutes."

There's a thud behind the door as Hunter's body falls to

the floor in the smaller room. Following Link's advice, I take deep breaths to avoid feeling the pain of what's to come as I look up at Maxwell.

"We all make choices, Maxwell. You chose wrong." I repeat the words he said to me when he held me captive as I raise my hand to offer him my middle finger.

The expression on his face morphs into pure hatred. It's a look I've only seen once before, but it is short lived. There's a piercing wail through the speaker. Then the room around Maxwell goes blindingly bright before everything goes dark, and I lose my connection to him.

My arm drops quickly back to my side as I turn and see Jack. He's frantically attempting to find a way into the room, and my body floats out from under me.

I'm not scared anymore.

"I'm sorry, Jack. I love—"

CHAPTER 37

JACK

"How does she sound like me?" Link yells at his team. He's silent for a minute before he comes back to us. "Jekyll, I—Zane has accessed our previous mission tapes and pulled my voice and all call signs. Our teams in Arizona think they are taking orders from me. They're executing their *mission*." There is no mistaking the shudder in his voice when he says, "The Night Stalker is in the air."

One of our newest acquisitions is a fully operational and highly weaponized helicopter. We purchased it from the government under the condition that we decommission it from warfare use—except we haven't yet.

Logan reflects my shock when we exchange a glance.

"Shit." It's not the first time in the last five minutes Link has used this word, but something in the severity of his tone tells me this is different.

"Link?" Logan's low tone tells me he's bracing for a blow as I watch Jessa type.

"Dammit, Jack. I'm sorry." Link breaks off as he yells some unintelligible orders at his team then returns to us. "I—Jessa's takeover has activated our defense systems. They are

306 CODE NAME: PHOENIX

on a fail-safe. The only way to stop it is to cut everything. Jessa is rerouting the gases away from our locked rooms and into the area she and Hunter are in, including the cyanide. Jack, once it starts, they'll be dead within minutes."

Dead.

Link's words burn deep into my bones. She has chosen this path. She's made the stupid decision to sacrifice herself to protect us.

I waited ten years. All of that time, living a half-life without her, only to have her back to be taken away again.

In a moment of panic, I hurl the weight of my body against the glass. I see red, and every fiber of my being wants to break through the window and drag her sorry ass out of there.

"JESSA!" My body moves on its own as I growl her name in the form of an order. "Don't do this. You don't need to end it like this. Don't leave me again." I no longer care about maintaining the composed façade I wore for everyone standing around me.

Behind me, Logan relays Link's information to Dana, and I glance over my shoulder to see her face pale.

Within a minute, she went from utter relief at being released from Zane to realizing the depths of hell we are all descending into, and she shrieks her friend's name.

I look back at Jessa, and her expression has changed. The weight of her world is crushing her, and I can't help her. I'm forced to watch as she slowly crumbles underneath the storm she has created, and my rage turns to agony.

She's giving her life to save ours.

Travis's image is removed from the screen behind her, prompting Maxwell to speak.

I want to tear him apart for what he's made Jessa do.

That piece of shit doesn't even know what she's done yet.

I've missed part of their conversation but Jessa's pained laugh cuts through my anger as her beautiful voice, now laced with a rage of her own, begins to speak.

"I'm Zane. I created Zane in high school to use as an alternate identity if I ever needed one for hacking. I coded a system that could follow my cues and work with me. After you killed my family, Zane became my lead. *He* could never be found. *He* could never be caught, and *he* would never be yours, just like I was never yours, Maxwell."

She's Zane. All of this. The planning, the hacking, and the hiding was all her. She fought to keep herself and Dana out of Maxwell's grasp.

Maxwell has turned his attention to someone off-screen, no doubt trying to buy some time. The realization that he's been played is hitting him, and he's trying to stay afloat while his team works to protect themselves against Jessa's hack.

But he'll fall just as easily as we did, because he underestimated her. Just like we did.

We all had our eyes on a prize that didn't exist.

Glancing at Logan, I see it written all over his face.

We are not in charge.

Maxwell is not in charge.

Jessa is running the show now, and there is nothing that will change the course she's set for us.

"Jessa, you don't have to do this. The gases you are filtering in are deadly. It's cyanide." Link's voice rings into my ear, and it's only now I realize she's turned communication back on.

The door rattles behind her as Hunter hears Link's words at the same time I do, and Dana sobs beside me, paralyzed with panic for her only friend.

"This is how it has to end..." I don't hear the rest of Jessa's response as my body becomes both heavy and lighter than air at the same time.

Dana's cries turn to anger as she yells again for everything to stop. In her haze, Jessa's eyes return to her friend, and her face softens for a moment before tears flow down her face. "Dana, I love you. Thank you for always being with me. You never let me down. I won't let you down —" She opens her mouth to say something else, but Dana isn't having any of it.

"You're letting me down now, Jessa! Stop it! Stop the gas! Please!" She blinks hard to clear her eyes of her tears. Then everything becomes blurry, and I realize it's my own tears that are blocking my vision.

"Grizz. That outside door is locking in twenty seconds. She shouldn't see this." Jessa speaks to my teammate, and he jumps into action, lifting Dana almost effortlessly. She fights against him to stay until the end.

As the door shuts behind them, the click of the lock echoes into the room, and Logan and I take one last glance at each other.

Logan's face, now void of expression, takes me back to the first day I met him. He knew then Jessa was gone, just like he knows now what will happen once she gets enough of the gas into her lungs.

"Jessa, I'm sorry. Take deep breaths. The first gas coming in is meant to disable you, then you won't feel anything. It'll knock you out before the cyanide releases. You can still stop it. Just kill everything." My anger flares at Link for telling my Jessa how to kill herself, but I know deep down he's trying to spare her—and me—the experience of a painful death.

The speaker crackles, prompting Jessa to turn her attention to the laptop in front of her and tap a key.

"TacCon, this is Ranger Three. We are locked on target. Awaiting strike confirmation sequence."

Link mutters a long string of profanities that I feel in my bones. I can tell he is equally impressed and terrified of Jessa right now—we all are.

As their conversation goes on, I realize she must have muted her line to Maxwell, because the guy is sitting there completely unaware that she's just managed to call in an air strike on his location.

"Jack." Jessa's sad voice shatters my soul, and I know in my heart I will never get over this. "I love you. I wish there was another way. I'm glad I got to see you again. I—"

Maxwell cuts off whatever else she was going to say, and she takes an unsteady step to the side.

The gas is doing its thing.

"JESSA!" At the sound of Maxwell's voice, a second wind fills her, and she spins to stop him from speaking again.

"NO. You don't get to order me around. It ends now. Your servers are dumping everything into Logan and Jack's servers. Link, you'll be back online in fifteen minutes."

"Thank fuck." Link's relief is obvious.

Jessa's chest rises and falls more deeply, and I'm thankful she's taking Link's advice. The gas is disorienting her, and she's become unfocused.

My reality sinks in as she slowly sways from side to side.

She doesn't feel anything anymore.

She'll pass out shortly, and once she hits the ground, she'll be dead within a couple of minutes. We didn't fuck around when we chose to use cyanide.

There has to be something. Not again. Thoughts rage

through me as I move to test the door, then try twice to push it open. It's futile, I know this, but there has to be something.

I catch her expression. For a brief moment, I wonder if the gas is working as clarity crosses her face and she lifts her head toward the screen on the wall.

"We all make choices, Maxwell. You chose wrong." Lifting her arm, Jessa gives Maxwell the finger in a final go-fuck-yourself.

Maxwell bares his teeth, then opens his mouth to respond, but everything abruptly goes dark. The strike was successful.

I want to be relieved, but instead, despair rages through me when Jessa turns on her shaky legs to look at me, dropping her arm back to her side.

There are no tears running down her face now. Her pain is dulled by the gas.

It's her time.

"I'm sorry, Jack. I love—"

Her beautiful life leaves her. Her body sways, then succumbs to its end as my entire body goes limp. But the floor doesn't greet me as it does her.

Logan grabs each arm and holds me up.

A ghostly silence fills the room as we stare at Jessa's lifeless body. I want to hold her, but we still have too many minutes before Link will regain control of our servers.

Until then, she's by herself.

She'll be gone before we can get to her.

"Link, priority is on shutting off the gas and opening this door. There's an antidote kit on the wall in this room, and we can still it use on her, but time is running out." Logan is all business. He knows one word of sympathy in my direction will cause a breakdown, and I don't want him to sedate me again like he had to ten years ago.

"Where's the kit?"

I follow his line of sight to where our emergency pack has sat attached to the wall for the last six years. But I only find the faint outline of where it should be.

"Logan. My system shows the gas is currently being flushed from the room on its own. We're working to cut the delay down, but it still won't be enough to get to her in time. I'm so sorry, Jack."

My world crumbles all over again as my life slips away from me, and Logan stands still beside me as we wait to hear Link confirm he has access.

Seconds feel like an eternity as we stand in limbo.

Breaking the silence, Logan sighs beside me. "Jack, I—"

But he's cut short.

Out of nowhere, a loud beeping echoes hard into the room, and I look at Logan, who reflects my confusion.

We turn our attention into the room. It seems to be coming from the computer Jessa was working on, and almost instantly, a cabinet to the side of Jessa jerks to life.

The doors on the cabinet bang once, then burst open from the inside.

First a duffel bag is thrown into the room, quickly followed by someone in a gas mask. They're crawling out of the cabinet and across the room to Jessa's lifeless body.

They unzip the bag, and the emergency kit that should have been on our wall is removed. Then the person pulls out an air tester, holding it in front of their mask as both Logan and I watch, dumbfounded.

They must have gotten a clear read, because they waste

no time dropping it and tearing off their mask. It's Waldo, and he digs into the emergency kit.

I brace my palms against the glass. "Waldo? What the fu—?"

"Sorry, boss. Can't talk," he stammers as his focus turns to Jessa and he slides in beside her still body.

"Jack, let him work. He still has time. Not much, but hopefully it's enough." Logan watches patiently beside me as we witness our teammate go to work on the only thing I want in this life.

As I watch, confusion sets in.

What was Waldo doing in the room to begin with?

Placing an oxygen mask over her face, Waldo turns back to the kit and quickly removes syringes and vials. Then he starts to fill one and injects the contents into a vein in her arm.

As I watch him work, moving around her body, hope returns. Hope is all I have left until I have her back, and I take a deep breath to clear my head.

"I have a pulse. It's faint. She's breathing. I'm starting the amyl nitrate." Waldo updates us without looking up.

In all truth, I have no idea what he's talking about. I never thought in my lifetime we would use the cyanide. And even if we did, it never occurred to me that we'd need to bring someone back from it.

"We're coming back online in one minute." Link's voice is confident, and my attention shifts between Jessa and the door as I watch Waldo's final attempt.

With ten seconds to go, everything slows around me, and as the time reaches zero, there's a deep gasp for breath from inside the comms room.

Click.

I'm through the doors and at her other side as she struggles for air, and her eyes shoot open and land on mine. Before I can say anything, her body jerks in shock, and I reach across her from my side as Waldo holds her steady.

"You have an oxygen mask on. Stay still. We're going to— Jessa?" Dread creeps into my relief as her eyes slowly close on me.

"She's okay, Jack. Her vitals are better now, but her body is tired. I need to keep her out of shock. Let her rest." Waldo continues to work around her.

Grizz joins us in the room. When he moves to take my place at her side, I hesitate. I don't want to let her go. Life is coming back into her fragile body, and I don't want her to be without me. I don't want to be without her.

"Jack, let Grizz take over. Link's called back all teams. We need to debrief. Jessa needs you to keep working right now." Logan grounds me with her name.

He's right. Our team is the best there is. I can't do any more for her than Grizz and Waldo can, but I can get to work on damage control.

A nod to Logan, and I'm up and ready to work with renewed fervor.

"Link, status," I bark into my headset while the men work away on securing Jessa to a stretcher to move her to our sick bay.

"She did it. We have everything, and our servers are intact for the time being. Our team is running diagnostics and closing any gaps, but we are secure."

"Define 'everything.'" I need this to be over. For Jessa's sake, she can't continue like this. This was the final hand she could have played, and I need it to be a game ender.

"Boss, it's everything, and stuff is still coming in. All of his financials have either been dumped into our accounts or are frozen until we can get to them. Hold; one moment." The frenzy of fingers tapping on a keyboard replaces his voice as we wait for more information. Then he returns, and his voice has picked up in speed and pitch. "Shit, she's brilliant. I can't believe this, Jack. If Maxwell made it out, he's as good as done. Jessa's files are detailed. She has everything on him. Compromising video, records of blackmail. There are a few solid instances of treason in here. With the records she has on him and his father, they won't see a court of law. Someone will just do away with them. Top-level, secret-clearance shit." The excitement in his voice tells me she really did do it, and a surge of pride bursts out of me before I hear Link's next question: "Do you want me to call an ambulance?"

Logan nods at me, and I know his answer. It's the same as mine. "No, Link."

Waldo and Grizz look up for a moment in confusion, and I continue, "We'll need to get her mobile here and transfer her over to your area for recovery. The conversation with Maxwell was broadcast out. The authorities and anyone who would want to use Jessa or Zane for their benefit heard her confession; they saw her die. She needs to remain dead, Link. Do you understand?" I wait for his response as Grizz turns his focus back to Jessa, with Waldo following his lead.

They are on board.

"Affirmative, boss. I will begin procedures for handling our two DOAs. Neither have any family to claim them, so they will be cremated and buried in unmarked graves at your approval."

"Approved." As I answer Link, I stand to move across the

room, opening the door to the small area that held Hunter until his final breath.

The door pushes against his leg, then opens reluctantly to Hunter's lifeless body facedown on the floor.

Disappointment sets in as a decade of memories turn into lies.

I'll never know why our friend, one of the longest-serving members of our team, did this.

"She's almost ready for transport to sick bay." Waldo's voice reminds me I have some questions for him.

Before I open my mouth to ask, Logan takes over. It's like we share the same brain. "Waldo, what the fuck were you doing in that cabinet with a gas mask on?"

Grizz smirks to himself as he continues to work, thankful he's not in our line of fire as Waldo stands up.

"Well. Okay." Raising his arms in a plea to hear him out, Waldo continues, "Look, there wasn't any time. There I was, sound asleep, when your girl wakes me up. She scared the shit out of me. She said that something was going down, and I was the only one here who could help." My back goes straight at his suggestion that she didn't consider me trustworthy.

Before I can defend myself, he cuts me off. "She said she had a chance to take down Maxwell's organization. All of it. But she needed to do it her way. She needed you both to be present, and she needed Maxwell to see your real reactions. She said she was only going to route the harmless gas into the room to knock her out. I didn't know until I heard Link say the cyanide came in along with it. By then it was too late to stop it. I knew I had the antidote kit though."

"And you trusted her? Just like that?" Logan is a little

unhinged. The events of the last half hour have us all operating on adrenaline.

"Well, now that you're saying it like that, I—shit, boss, it was a rush decision. I didn't take a side to deceive you. I took the side I thought was going to help us. I've been with you guys for a long time—eight years. Maxwell has been our target for all of that time. This was our chance, and whether I told you or not, something was going to happen. I didn't want it to be another eight years." He's looking between us.

If I'm being honest with myself, he made the right decision. I wouldn't be thinking this if Jessa wasn't breathing right now, or if our servers weren't back online. But once the dust settles, we may be in the clear because of both Jessa and Waldo.

Fucking Waldo. Of all people.

"Look, I made the choice to trust her. She left me with my gun, she told me to grab a gas mask, and she told me where to be and what to do. After Hunter ordered me to check the perimeter, I doubled back and got into place. She told me, no matter what was said or done, to not come out until the beeping alarm went off. The only thing she didn't divulge was that the gas was deadly. By the time I heard Link, it was too late. I was locked in the room, and it was coming in no matter what. I had to stay the course." Then turning to me to plead for support, he continues. "Jack, I—"

"It's okay, Waldo." I hold my hand up to stop him as panic inches across his face. Logan shoots me a surprised glance. "It worked out. I need to process this. Thank you for having her back. She wouldn't have asked for help if she wasn't desperate. Thank you for not letting her down, and for protecting the unit."

My words catch Waldo by surprise, and he stammers, "I —thanks, Jack."

I point to Jessa, and he steps back from us, then turns to help Grizz pack up the emergency kit.

There's still a bit to sort through, and we'll properly debrief him later.

Right now, our priorities are shutting down communication and containing the information we now possess.

"Uh, boss?" I crane my neck up to Grey standing at the door, taking in everything around us, and his eyes are wide.

"No time to explain," Logan starts as he formulates our next steps. "I need you to bring Dana back to her room. We'll need to—"

Before he can finish, Grey sheepishly cuts him off. "Boss. That's why I'm here. She's gone."

"WHAT?" Grizz jumps to his feet, startling everyone in the room, and I'm momentarily comforted by the fact that I'm not the only one who has lost their shit over a woman today.

Standing back with his hands raised, Grey attempts to calm his friend. "I circled the perimeter. When I came back, the Jeep was gone. Dust was kicking up down the road about a mile out. The security cameras just came back online. She can't be more than ten minutes out. What do you want me to do?" Both Grey and Grizz are frozen, waiting for further orders.

"Nothing," Logan starts. Then, looking at Grizz, he explains. "It's just us, and we're already down one with Hunter dead." Grey startles at his words, and I realize this is his first time hearing the news. "It's your call, Grizz. We can't leave our team and the base vulnerable. The vehicle has

GPS, and our first team is coming back on the chopper. They'll be here in about forty-five minutes. Then you and Grey can pick up her trail."

I've never seen Grizz so fortified in all my life.

The amount of energy radiating off the guy is sucking the air out of the room. I don't even want to be here right now, and the love of my life is lying helpless on the floor.

As if he's settled his demons and come to a conclusion, he huffs and turns to help lift Jessa, muttering under his breath, "Damn woman. When I get my hands on her, I'm gonna..." The rest of his sentence is one long run-on I can't quite make out as he leans down to help Waldo lift Jessa's stretcher.

I gather Jessa's laptops and phone. Then I follow everyone out of the room.

Jessa has a lot to answer for, but until she wakes up again, I'll live, sleep, eat, and work by her side.

"Okay, Jessa. This is it. It's been three weeks, but I finally get to say it: You're cleared. You're the healthiest deceased person I have ever had the opportunity to care for." Waldo smiles as he closes my patient chart.

"Thank you, um—Waldo." My mind is fuzzy, and this feels like déjà vu.

"It's okay. Remember, my name is Samuel. Waldo is just my call sign." As he steps aside, Jack and Logan come into view. They're sitting at the foot of my bed, listening intently. "Last time, you just called me Doc when you got confused."

Turning to the men, he continues, "So, she's okay to leave. Her short-term memory is fine. She's just been on some painkillers, and her brain is catching up to her body."

Pausing to look between Jack and me, he hesitates, and Logan spurs him to continue. "For fuck's sake, Waldo. Spit it out."

"Well, it's just that—okay, I'm just going to say it: no strenuous activity for a while." He flinches as his words register with Jack, and I pinch my lips together to hold back a smile. Then Samuel backs up a step, taking another approach. "I mean, like running—or *something*."

Jack sits still, shifting his eyes between Samuel and me, and I get the feeling he wants to question his expert opinion.

But Logan backs him up. "We get it. Jack, no *or something* until you get the green light. Understand? We have other things to talk about. Thank you, Waldo. You can leave us now."

Logan tilts his head toward the door, and Samuel takes his cue, offering me a quick smile before leaving.

"Wait!" I call to Samuel, and everyone looks at me. "Thank you for helping me. I mean, with my recovery, and for showing up that morning. I wasn't sure if you were in the cabinet."

Samuel looks between Jack and Logan before replying, "You're welcome, Jessa. I have to be honest, I was going to give it five minutes, then jump out and end everything if I thought you were playing them. But once I heard Hunter in the room with you, I knew I had to stay the course."

We share forced smiles as he brings the sting of Hunter's betrayal back to the surface.

I change the topic. "I'm sorry I dropped an elephant statue on your head when I first saw you."

"Apology accepted. I was lucky; it just missed my melon." He smiles, tapping the top of his head.

Logan nods once more toward the door, and Samuel makes his way into the hall outside.

Taking the space Samuel left, Jack slides his chair beside my bed and reaches across to take my hand. His fingers are warm against my cool skin, and I hold on to him as tight as I can.

Since waking up a day ago, it has been nothing but a

steady stream of tests and recovery. No one has said a thing to me about what happened. All I've been told is I've been out for almost three weeks, and I'm now on a different compound. No one has asked any questions, and I'm hoping this release means I finally get some visitors.

"Does this mean I can see Dana now?"

Jack's hand tightens around my fingers, drawing my glance from his hand to his face. His jaw is clenched, and his eyes are sad.

Logan clears his throat. "We wanted to wait until you were recovered to tell you this. Jessa, Dana has disappeared."

"I don't understand." Tilting my head, I whisper to Jack.

He takes a deep breath. "After you told Grizz to remove her from the room, he put her outside in a safe area and came back to see what he could do to help. They both thought you died—you did. You gave her the payout she needed, and she took one of our vehicles and ran. We haven't been able to track her down. She dumped the truck, and her trail went cold within two hours. We scoured through all of your data looking for a lead, but..."

"But my server was programmed to destroy everyone's new identities as soon as they were assigned." I finish his sentence, and he stops to watch me process everything.

My best friend is in the wind.

Whatever identity I gave her was only meant to be temporary. I taught her how to dump it for a permanent one that only she would know, and I'm slowly regretting giving her those tools.

I've taught her how to elude me.

"That's not everything we need to talk about, Jessa." Logan rises and stands at the foot of my bed. "It's Maxwell.

We were able to identify most of the remains from the air strike. He was among the deceased."

For the first time in a long time, I feel like I can breathe, but it's fleeting. "I thought I would have closure, but someone else will just come after me in his place."

Logan's voice stops my downward spiral. "Jessa, as far as anyone outside this base knows, you are dead. Two bodies were cremated and buried. Jack and I arranged your service and put you to rest ourselves. You are no longer on anyone's radar. After Waldo brought you back, you were stabilized, and he and Jack transferred you here before our team returned. It's a smaller area, but it's better protected than our own base. This is where Link's team operates. Jack and Waldo have been with you ever since."

Picking up the chart Samuel left at the foot of my bed, Logan flips through a few pages before continuing, "Out of everyone you could have asked for help that morning, I don't think you realize you made the best choice possible. Waldo —*Samuel* is also our resident doctor. Medically trained and all. Regardless, you broadcast everything out, and our system analytics show that multiple connections saw your big finale. According to the world outside this base, you are at peace and resting beside your parents and your brother now. No one is actively searching for you or Zane."

"Travis? But how did you find him?"

Jack shifts beside me as he picks up the conversation. "When Link's team was sifting through the mountain of information you dumped into our servers, they found a personal folder of yours with the location and name that you buried him under. We had his remains exhumed and transported back to join your family. Jessa, why did you hide Travis in the first place?"

"At first, I didn't want to accept that he was gone. He died with my parents because they came looking for me. I wasn't thinking straight. When I found his body, I hid him. I wanted to give him the escape he should have had. I didn't want Maxwell to know he had won. Then he became my safety blanket. There was always the chance he was hiding out under this secret identity, and I used that to keep me and Dana alive."

For the first time since I opened my eyes yesterday, tears flow down my face. I've only wanted Travis to be at peace, and they did that for him.

My whimper turns into a sob as Jack covers his body over mine to comfort me. He knows how important Travis was to me. He was the one I looked up to growing up, and finally placing him with our parents is more than I had ever hoped for.

"Okay. I need you two to take it easy before this turns into an *or something* situation and I have Waldo all up in my grill for not following his orders," Logan says. Then, muttering under his breath, he speaks to himself. "Dammit, Waldo. Of all people."

I smile at Logan's words as Jack releases me and sits back down.

It seems Samuel and I have something in common around here: we were both underestimated and overlooked.

"Jessa, why did you do it?" My smile fades at Jack's question.

Without looking at him, I can tell he is still sorting through his experience, and his question requires a serious answer.

All eyes are on me, waiting for the answer that will justify my actions, but I'm not sure there is such an answer.

"It may be too hard to explain now, but I really believed there was no other way, Jack. Before you found us, I'd been hovering and waiting for my in. I compiled a lot of information, but it wasn't enough for someone like him, not with the connections he has. Until he became more of a liability than an asset, his business partners and everyone he was blackmailing would support him. The jobs he had Za—me do for him never gave me access to his internal servers. I needed something that would dig deep into his greed. When you came along, I was thinking about telling you everything, but when Maxwell came through with that video, I realized there was a chance, and I needed to take it. There was no other scenario in which he would just let me waltz in through the front doors of his digital house." I shift up the bed to make myself comfortable, and Jack asks another question.

"But the cyanide. Shit, Jessa."

He's hurt.

His eyes are glassy, and I imagine he's replaying my final moments, which, thankfully, are a bit of a blur for me.

"That was a risk. I knew there was cyanide, but Hunter didn't know enough about the security procedures to tell me how the gas was distributed. I took a chance based on the assumption the gases could be controlled, but your setup pushes them all in one after the other during a breach. I couldn't stop it because I needed to stay online to give the final strike codes. I gave Waldo the gas mask just in case. Regardless, Jack, I wouldn't change my decision. It was my only shot."

Jack opens his mouth to speak, but I'm not done. Raising my hand, I ask for more time, and he allows me to continue. "After I woke up, when Maxwell told me he would kill your family if I ever looked for you, he said something else. He told me that some things in life are just taken. He said I was his, and once he had his hands on Zane, he would come for me. He'd destroy everything I loved, and he would take me back. He was unhinged. I was so scared, I couldn't speak. I remember all of it. I had my chance, Jack. I needed to end it before I slipped up. I'm sorry I put you through that."

Jack leans back, processing everything I've said.

Logan has been sitting quietly, watching us talk, and regret settles into me.

I probably could have done a lot differently.

I've hurt Jack, and Dana is missing.

She thinks I'm dead.

"I think that's enough debriefing for one sitting. Don't you, Jack?" Logan clears his throat and stands to control the conversation. "Jessa, your actions, although excessive at times, did something we've never been able to do. In short, Maxwell is gone, and you are free from all of it. If you wish to be." Logan stops talking, and his lingering last words hit me.

"If I wish to be? Are you saying—what are you saying?" My heart leaps in my chest as I wait for him to clarify.

I worked for Maxwell for almost ten years. In some ways, I'm as guilty as he is. I should be spending my life behind bars.

Logan speaks slowly as he lays out what this means for me. "There are only a handful of us who know you're alive. You've done more to Maxwell than any of us could, and we are offering you freedom. You are not a prisoner, nor anyone's puppet, no matter which choice you make. Your first option, once Waldo gives you a clean bill of health, is to disappear. We'll grant you access to a new identity and enough of Maxwell's money to live out your life away from everything. Our only requirement is no hacking once you're out. You are completely off the grid. I mean not even an email address, and no connection to Cypher."

Logan pauses to watch me. I shift my eyes to Jack, my gleeful smile meets his frown, and the kicker hits me. "But you? And Dana?"

"There's the rub. You would lose contact with both. You would be free, but alone."

Pausing to let the severity of the situation sink in, Logan takes a long look at me before continuing. "I'll be honest. The second option is the one, I think, we all hope you'll choose. We'd like you to work here, with us." I lean back and cross my arms at the thought of being used again, and Logan keeps talking. "You'd be a full team member. You would have access to everything. Link's specialty is in tactical and operations control. He doesn't have time to manage most of our clients' digital requests on his own. His team is good, but they aren't at your level. You could still choose the first option at any time—no strings attached. Link has asked me to stress that he really wants you. He's been working with his team to learn from your breach. They've already put new procedures into place because of you. He keeps running around saying 'WWJD.'"

"What would Jesus do?"

"What would Jessa do." Logan chuckles. "The guy is your biggest supporter. I've told him he's not allowed to fangirl you until you've made your decision, but he asked me to tell you he already has a"—he holds his fingers up in air quotes—"*badass* code name for you if you're interested."

Jack and Logan settle into silence while I consider what lies in front of me. Both options offer me the kind of freedom

I never thought I would have. I have no need to keep my guard up anymore. I have no plans to put into action and nothing more to run from. As I let the depth of my possibilities sink in, Logan pulls me out of my thoughts.

"Look, we're offering you a new identity, a paying job, and a new family: us. This compound is a one-hour drive from our base. As an added incentive, you'd have all of our systems at your disposal to begin looking for Dana in your downtime. I know a certain someone who is hoping you'll stay and help him find her." At the reminder of Dana's connection to Grizz, I smile. "Jessa, I'll leave you two alone to talk your options over. I just want to add—"

"Option two," I blurt.

"What?" Jack perks up beside me.

I don't think he was ready for such a quick response.

"Being without you and Dana is no freedom." As I look at Jack, I see it written all over his face: relief. "I'll go wherever you are, if you'll still have me."

"Are you kidding me? Of course I'll have you. I want to *or something* you so much right now!" Jack bursts out of his chair and slides onto the hospital bed beside me, prompting Logan to prepare to make his exit.

"I'm happy to hear this, Jessa. Jack, you have ten minutes alone before I tell Waldo you aren't following his orders. Starting now."

CHAPTER 39
JACK
(ALMOST ONE YEAR LATER)

At some point, I died.

That's the only explanation I have for the bliss that hits me every morning when I open my eyes against the bright morning sun to find Jessa curled against me. My arms and legs wrap around her, cocooning her close.

With one hand, I carefully reach over to the nightstand for the remote. Pointing it at the coffeepot near the door that leads to an outside sitting area, I press the power button, and the little green light comes on.

The sun shines in through the floor-to-ceiling window facing the water. The previous owners of this property paid great attention to detail.

Our new and very private home is situated on a small cape that juts out into a lake at the foot of a mountain. It's only accessible by floatplane. We wake up to our own sunrise every morning and eat dinner on the other side of our cabin with a new sunset every evening.

It is important to me that Jessa has as much freedom as she can without making herself a target. While she wouldn't be able to live in a bustling metropolis, she had her pick of many destinations.

When we came across this listing, her choice was made.

In the end, Jessa and I chose a hybrid arrangement with Cypher. During the colder months, Jessa works with Link's team on his secure base. I split my time between Logan's compound and hers.

When the snow melts, we will work remotely from our new cabin.

I chuckle every time I say that because everyone knows we're pretty much going to take four months off together each year.

They know how to reach us if it's important.

While we don't plan on doing much work while we're out here, we've been vigilant about making sure we are online right now. Jessa is still searching for Dana, and Grizz has been sending her any small lead he finds. We're coming up on the one-year anniversary of her disappearance, and so far everything has been a dead end.

I spend much of the time we get together now reintroducing myself to Jessa. When we met in high school, she knew one version of me. Most of what I showed her back then was who I was, but there were details I had to change to protect my cover.

I told her about my parents' accident and what I remember of my family. She knows my experience with high school—the first time I went through it wasn't as wonderful as the time I went through it with her. I skated through, barely passing and keeping my grades high enough to keep my teachers off my back. I shared the anger I felt at being left on my own. I grew up fast, and I lashed out by hiding myself away. As soon as I could, I joined the military.

Then I told her all about how it felt to know her. How I knew in my bones I was the luckiest man when she smiled at me. I never thought it was possible to love her more deeply than I already did, but we've been surprising each other a lot this past year.

A soft sigh against my chest draws my attention as Jessa stretches without untangling herself from my hold.

I kiss the top of her head. "Good morning."

"Mmmorning." She groggily draws out the word as she flexes her slender fingers around me.

I tilt my head to capture her gaze. "You're sleeping better."

She sits with my observation for a moment before she smiles and wriggles her midsection against mine.

We've been fully moved into our new place for a few weeks now. Jessa mentioned she doesn't sleep well when we are on base, but she has been improving over time. Training her mind to accept she is safe is easier said than done, but I've noticed a change in the last week.

She's slept through the last two nights, and she woke up after me for the first time this morning.

"Let's grab a coffee and wake up on the patio. I have a couple of things to talk to you about."

She leans her head away from me, looking down the length of our entwined bodies and past the foot of our bed at the coffee maker and chuckles.

I built a coffee corner in our bedroom after our first week here. I hated crossing the place in the cool mornings to turn the coffee on. The pot sits on top of a cabinet with a mini plug-in cooler that holds our creamer and the powdered cocoa and caramel I know Jessa loves.

I swing my legs off the bed and begrudgingly leave the

warmth of her touch to cross the room in my underwear. She rolls over to hang off the bed and reaches for the T-shirt I tossed on the floor in our haste to enjoy each other last night.

I love it when she wears my things.

"I thought we'd try the paddleboards today if the water is calm." I pour coffee into each of our mugs, smiling as I always do when I fill hers.

Link gave her this mug shortly after she recovered, and Jessa laughed her ass off when she saw it. The mug is black, but once it is filled with hot liquid, a hidden image appears, and they both got a kick out of it. Everyone else just stared at them. Then Jessa said it was computer code, and Link added that it was JavaScript for her cup of java. Then they laughed until Jessa's eyes glossed over with tears.

I still don't get the joke, but I smile because that was the moment the girl I lost returned to me.

"Oh, that's a great idea. Just don't be surprised if you spend the day pulling my soggy ass out of the lake." She laughs as she opens the dresser, pulls out a pair of panties, and slips them on.

That's pointless, I think to myself, because I'll just be tugging them off her shortly.

I meet her at the sliding door and hand her coffee mug over, then grab a knit blanket out of the basket we keep by the door.

Jessa follows me out, shutting the door behind us and joining me under the blanket on the couch on the deck.

She slips into thought, her eyes skimming over the lake in front of us and drifting away with the gentle waves.

I don't like to leave her in her head too long. "We'll find her."

The corner of her mouth twitches, and she lifts the

coffee to her nose and inhales, closing her eyes. When she opens them, she looks down at her drink. "Sometimes I wonder if she is better off—wherever she is."

I know Jessa carries a lot of guilt because of Dana's loyalty.

"We talked about this," I remind her. "If you find her and she is happy, you can make the decision then."

She nods, her voice the ghost of a whisper. "I hope she is."

I don't tell her that there is someone back on base who may not be so willing to leave her be. Grizz has immersed himself in finding Dana, but he won't share his reasons why with any of us.

"You wanted to talk to me." Jessa changes the subject, and I let it go for now.

"I was thinking about Travis and your parents. I know you mentioned visiting them a few times." She pinches her lips together in a thin line. It's a sore subject. She's never been able to pay her respects, and Logan listed their cemetery among the places she can never return to in order to remain hidden. "I thought we might talk about bringing their ashes here."

"What?" Her eyes quickly fill with tears, and at first I wonder if I've stepped out of line before she adds, "You would do that for me?"

I puff an incredulous breath through my lips. "It's like you don't know who you're talking to. I would do anything for you." When she doesn't continue the conversation, I fill it with what I was thinking about when I woke up this morning. "I wasn't sure if your parents had specific wishes about resting there."

She shakes her head. "No. They had no remaining

family. Their lawyer picked that place." Her eyes flit between mine. "Can you really do that?"

I shrug. "We'll keep their plot where it is to keep up appearances. It will just be empty. I can put a couple of the guys on it." I point over to the new apple saplings we planted near the water when we first arrived. "I thought you might like to work with me on a sanctuary in their memory."

She glances at where I'm pointing. It's only when she clears her throat that I realize she averted her gaze to hide her tears. "It's coming up on the anniversary of my death. I'd like to bring them here—I mean *home*." She chokes on the word.

Family meant everything to Jessa. I know it still does.

I stretch my arm around her and pull her into me.

We sit like that, nestled in silence and enjoying our coffee for a while.

I'm right where I want to be, and I'm in no hurry.

I suffered ten years without her. I want the rest of our time together to go by as slowly as possible.

With a deep sigh, Jessa leans forward and sets her empty mug on the table in front of us. Then she lifts the blanket and slides her leg over mine, straddling my lap and wrapping the knit blanket around us.

I set my mug on the side table and shift in my seat, grinding my hips into her as I adjust my position. Her mouth opens on a silent *oh*, and she combs her fingers up the back of my neck before scratching her nails into my hair and along my scalp.

My eyes roll up at her gentle touch, and I groan. "You know, we can always go paddleboarding tomorrow."

Her breath is warm against my face as she leans forward, licking along my lower lip.

She knows she's on borrowed time when she teases me like this.

Slipping my hands under the blanket, I tense my abdomen to lift us off the couch, and she groans against my mouth. "I want to stay out here."

When I relax into the seat, she reaches between us, rubbing the length of my erection over my shorts before hooking her fingers into the waistband and freeing me. I lift my hips to help her out, but I refuse to stand and break our contact, so my underwear rests tight around my upper thighs.

The sun is warm on my face, and I tug the blanket off, dropping it onto the deck. "We'll stay out here, but you're not in charge of how this is going to go."

The slight tick at the corner of her mouth tells me she likes the thought of that.

Reaching between us, I drag my knuckles over her panties, pausing when I'm met with her wet warmth. My eyes flash to hers, and her cheeks flush.

She knows I know she's ready for me.

I tip my head back, watching her intimately as she hovers above me. "Kiss me."

She bites her bottom lip, then licks along the plump flesh to moisten her mouth for me before leaning in.

As she presses her mouth against mine, I reach behind her, drawing my fingers along her ass, then between her legs to pull her panties to the side.

We groan in stereo as I line her up against my length and grip her hips, sliding her all of the way down.

"Jack." She whispers my name on a desperate breath as she looks deep into my eyes.

I sometimes wonder if the realization is hitting her all

over again. We are here, she is safe, and we are together. It's how I always feel in this moment.

We are the sum of two souls that have been shattered, only to find our way back to each other.

"I'm here." I slip a hand under my shirt she's wearing, cupping her breast as she lifts her hips to ride me at an achingly slow pace.

Tilting her head back, she rocks her hips and loosens her grip, letting go and relinquishing herself to me. I lean forward, catching her in my arms and holding her against me as we move in unison.

Her nipple pebbles under my palm as her body tenses, and she moans, her pace erratically picking up.

"Jessa, you keep doing that and I'm gonna—" I clench my mouth shut tight to will what's barreling toward me to hold off a little longer.

I woke up ready for her. At two separate times, while she slept soundly in my arms, I had to force my dick to stand down, so there is a one hundred percent chance that I'm going to go off if she so much as makes a peep.

All bets are off when she pulls her shirt off over her head. I zero in on my fingers pinched around her nipple as goosebumps swell across her chest as she rides me to our oblivion.

"J-Jack. I'm going to—"

I don't have to tell her to open her eyes or look at me when she comes, because every damn time we've made love, her gaze bores deep into my soul as we break apart together.

She is mine. But when she looks at me like she is right now, like she'd go through everything all over again for a chance at this happiness, I understand the real meaning between this connection: I am hers.

I've always belonged to her.

"I've got you."

Her forehead wrinkles as her lips part, and she comes, calling my name and mending my soul all over again. The intensity of her gripping my cock pulls me over the edge with her, and I hold her tight against me as though I will never let her go again.

I never will.

When her crest drains her, she rests against my chest, where she rises and falls with my deep breaths as I float back to earth and join her.

Jessa makes a move to lift herself off of me, but I tighten my grip. "Just for another minute."

I swear, without looking at her, I'm sure she's rolling her eyes and smiling, but she allows me this one thing I often ask for.

We've talked about having kids. It's been confirmed that she most likely won't be able to conceive, but if we ever did, there isn't any indication it would be anything other than a regular pregnancy.

I know the chances of growing our family are low, but we've both overcome worse odds. Whether we are successful or not, everything after this moment is gravy, because I have more than I ever thought possible.

And, in the end, it is one more thing we will face together.

CYPHER WILL CONTINUE...

Want to discuss the Cypher Black Ops Security series with the rest of our book club or be the first to know when there's another book in the series?

JOIN THE CYPHER BLACK OPS SECURITY GROUP ON FACEBOOK

The stories within the Cypher Black Ops Security series are interconnected standalones, meaning they can be read on their own if you wish, however, main characters appearing in later books will usually be introduced in earlier titles.

ACKNOWLEDGMENTS

I first want to thank my family. Their support and love knows no bounds. My father passed when I first started writing this book and small pieces of him are weaved into the story.

Thank you, Mom, for encouraging me to follow my heart.

Thank you to my beta readers and everyone who supported me during the writing and rewriting of this story for your time and for providing such valuable feedback.

I also want to acknowledge and thank everyone who gave their time and talent to this book:

Cover design: Kirsty Still (Pretty Little Design Co.)
Editor: Caroline Knecht
Photographer: Wander Aguiar
Cover model: Vinicious

Until next time...

ABOUT LUNA

Luna Kayne is a multi-genre romance author located in Canada. She writes intense, explicit, suspenseful romance with a hint of humor and angst. Her men are dominant and often stubborn, and her women are usually underestimated. As for tropes and sub-genres, nothing is off the table.

In 2021, she won an IPPY (Independent Publisher Book Awards) award with her novel, *Step Darkly* which earned a bronze medal.

You can learn more at LunaKayne.com

BB bookbub.com/profile/luna-kayne
f facebook.com/lunakayne
o instagram.com/lunakayne

Ingram Content Group UK Ltd.
Milton Keynes UK
UKHW010059100623
423095UK00016B/72